Foreword by *New York Times* bestselling author Debbie Macomber

Happy birthday, Harlequin Superromance, and congratulations on twenty-five groundbreaking years!

I was a struggling young writer when this romance series was introduced back in 1980. It was a wonderful opportunity for new writers, especially women. Many of us excitedly submitted our books, and over the years, Harlequin Superromance has launched many careers. In the early years I cherished books written by LaVyrle Spencer, Margaret Chittenden and many other authors. Their stories touched my heart.

Through these twenty-five years, Harlequin Superromance evolved, along with its writers. (And I'm proud to say I'm one of them, with a novella in the twentieth anniversary anthology, *Born in a Small Town,* and a Christmas story, *Those Christmas Angels,* in 2003.)

This twenty-fifth anniversary anthology, which you hold in your hands, features stories by three talented writers: Tara Taylor Quinn, Margot Early and Janice Macdonald. These writers are following the traditions created through the years by those who came before them. Traditions of love, courage, honor and dignity that remain the very heart of the romance genre. Because a Harlequin Superromance novel is a longer, richer story, it can offer more depth and range than other romances. There's an emotional maturity, an added quality to these wonderful books.

Congratulations, Superromance! At twenty-five, you're in your prime—and you just seem to get better and better.

Debbie Macomber

ABOUT THE AUTHORS

With thirty-seven novels, published in more than twenty languages, Tara Taylor Quinn is a *USA TODAY* bestselling author, with over four million copies of her books in print. She is a three-time finalist for the Romance Writers of America's RITA® Award, a multiple finalist for the National Readers' Choice Award and the Booksellers' Best Award. Tara is the president of RWA, a 9200-member international organization. When she's not writing or fulfilling speaking engagements, she enjoys traveling and spending time with family and friends.

Margot Early is the award-winning author of eleven novels and three novellas. She lives high in the San Juan Mountains of Colorado with two German shepherds and twenty tarantulas. When she's not writing, she's outdoors in all seasons, often training her dogs in obedience.

Born in Lancashire, England, Janice Macdonald came to the United States as a teenager—just a few short years ago. How she got old enough to have grown children and a granddaughter she has no idea, but the mirror offers the ruthless truth. Janice divides her time between Port Angeles, Washington, and Vista, California, where she lives with her husband, Joe. One of her biggest fans is her ninety-three-year-old mother, Dorothy, who lives in Seal Beach, California, is still active in community theater and grumbles if Janice writes too graphically about sex. Janice has written six previous books for Harlequin Superromance and is also a freelance writer specializing in travel and health care.

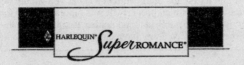

HARLEQUIN *Super*ROMANCE

Celebrates

25

years

with three incredible new stories by
TARA TAYLOR QUINN
MARGOT EARLY
JANICE MACDONALD

Foreword by
DEBBIE MACOMBER

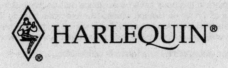

HARLEQUIN®

TORONTO • NEW YORK • LONDON
AMSTERDAM • PARIS • SYDNEY • HAMBURG
STOCKHOLM • ATHENS • TOKYO • MILAN • MADRID
PRAGUE • WARSAW • BUDAPEST • AUCKLAND

ISBN 0-373-71297-9

25 YEARS
Copyright © 2005 by Harlequin Books S.A.

The publisher acknowledges the copyright holders of the individual works as follows:

BEST FRIENDS
Copyright © 2005 by Tara Taylor Quinn.

WADE IN THE WATER
Copyright © 2005 by Margot Early.

A VISIT FROM EILEEN
Copyright © 2005 by Janice Macdonald.

TABLE OF CONTENTS

For Jeanine. All my life you were the wind beneath my wings. Now you are my wings. I hope and pray you were as blessed by our friendship as I have been....

BEST FRIENDS

Tara Taylor Quinn

Dear Reader,

This story is unlike any other I've written. It is deeply personal in a way even I didn't understand until I had difficulty quieting my mind enough to hear the voices and allow the words to flow. And while the characters and plot are fiction, the story I'm telling here—the story of a lifelong friendship that surpasses every earthly distance—is completely true.

I was lucky enough to be blessed with such a friendship. Though neither of us could ever remember not knowing each other, I first met Jeanine Hall when she was four and I was five. From that moment on, I never took a breath in this world without feeling her love and support. Our families vacationed together—and then moved states apart, and still the friendship endured. And I will never take a breath again without knowing that such a special love is possible. Tragically, Jeanine was killed in a car accident a few years ago, but the love and support and belief she instilled within me are very much alive and thriving. She still helps me through all my difficult moments and is included in all my joyous ones. She's here now as I write to you, smiling at me through her tears.

I'm very honored to have been asked to bring our relationship to you. I hope I have given you a story that you can make personal. I wish each and every one of you the presence of someone in your life who believes in you just because you're *you*, who accepts you as you are, who loves you in spite of knowing everything about you, who celebrates the day you were born.

Tara Taylor Quinn

P.S. I love to hear from readers. You can reach me at P.O. Box 13584, Mesa, AZ 85216, or visit me at www.tarataylorquinn.com.

CHAPTER ONE

"DID YOU JUST SAY you want a divorce?"

Jolene Hamilton Chambers shoved a couple of bras into the duffel open on the bed she'd shared with her husband for the past seven years. And nodded.

Not the best way to start a week.

The bras covered a corner of the eight-inch blue rectangular box poking out from the pajamas she'd already packed on top of it. Except for a brief glimpse to ensure that she'd grabbed the right package from the back of the bottom shelf in her linen closet, Jolene hadn't looked at that box for months. Not since she'd purchased it and then unexpectedly not needed it. She didn't need it now—but she was waiting until she was with Tina, until she was stronger, before she tackled that one.

Steve, standing with his arms crossed on the opposite side of the bed, watched her silently. He was still wearing the dress shirt and tie he'd worn to a new teachers' July orientation meeting at the school earlier that morning. He'd been an elementary school principal when they'd married. His eyes had been softer then.

Now, seven years later, he was principal of Boulder's Valleyview High School and his gaze could intimidate even the most pierced, purple-haired, grunge-wearing students under his authority.

Jolene wasn't intimidated. She knew the tender-hearted man beneath the "Dr. Chambers" look. Adored him.

"Talk to me, Jo."

His tone pleaded with her. She turned her back, scooped a handful of socks out of the open underwear drawer. So what if they didn't match? She was only going to the cabin. That drawer shut, she yanked on the larger one below it. Three pairs of jeans, faded to varying degrees, followed the socks into the suitcase. And sweaters, she'd need sweaters. Didn't matter that they were in the middle of Colorado's hottest summer in years, the state's northern woods still got chilly at night.

"You want a divorce." His voice was deadpan. A complete antithesis of the emotional tug-and-pull twisting her insides.

Not trusting herself to speak, or to look at him, she meticulously refolded a couple of perfectly well-folded sweaters, and nodded again. The sweaters fit on top of the jeans with room to spare.

"Jo." The back of Steve's hand appeared in her line of vision. It rested on hers. She needed to slide her fingers from beneath his, to decide which blouses to take. Tina's plane from Roanoke was landing just after two. That only gave her an hour and a half to load the car with the groceries and cooler and linens she'd packed that morning and get to the airport early enough to meet her best friend of twenty-five years.

His hand was warm, thrilling and comforting at the same time. "I...mean it, Steve." While her words were barely above a whisper, her voice didn't waver. And neither did her intent.

He released her hand. "Why?" Thrusting his own hands in the pockets of his dark brown dress slacks, he paced to the end of the bed. "Is there someone else?"

She couldn't blame him for sounding incredulous. How could she possibly be hungry for another man when she was so easily aroused by the man she was leaving—as their usual Sunday morning in bed had shown him quite clearly the day before.

"Of course not."

"Then…why?"

She walked to the closet, her legs shaking as she pulled open the folding door. "Because I love you so much it's killing me."

Hand trembling, Jolene reached for a group of hangers and dropped the whole pile on the sweaters in her suitcase. She went into the adjoining bathroom, carried out her bag of toiletries, plopped it on top of the rest. And couldn't avoid her husband's gaze any longer.

He hadn't moved. His face, normally so expressive, was stiff, his eyes glassy with shock as he stared at her. Jolene stared back. She didn't know what else to do. She was so close to falling apart she didn't trust herself.

She'd made the right decision. There was such absolute certainty about that she knew she'd be able to go through with it. But she felt no clarity about anything else. How did one go about divorcing the love of one's life? And what would come afterward?

"Could you explain that?"

Jolene jumped. Had he read her mind?

Then she understood.

He'd been responding, about five minutes late, to the reason she'd given him for the divorce.

"I can't do it anymore, Steve." Emotion suffocated her, making it nearly impossible to speak. Yet in spite of the trembling of her lips, the tears pushing against the back of her throat, she was resolute.

"Do what?"

"You, me, us. Our need to be parents. No baby. I can't get over the guilt."

He moved so quickly around the bed, he had her by the shoulders before she could shift to avoid him. "*That's* what this is about?" he asked, his voice almost light, as though at any moment laughter would burst forth. "This is just another bout of pretest jitters?"

His grasp, as he pulled her against him, was fierce, almost crushing. She could feel the shaking in his arms, hear the pounding of his heart. "Thank God," he murmured raggedly. "We'll get through this, babe, we always do. No matter what we find out, we'll go forward just like we have every other time."

Drawing back, he held her arms, staring at her, moisture glistening in his eyes. "You have no idea how scared I was, Jo, thinking I was the only one here who's still so much in love I can't see straight. I couldn't figure out how your feelings had changed without my knowing. I'm so damned relieved, I'm babbling like an idiot…."

His grin scorched her from the inside out. If she could have, she would've grinned back. If it had been a year ago, or the year before that. If she hadn't already gone through the crushing disappointment so many times, she might've had the capacity to handle more, might've had shoulders strong enough to take on his disappointment as well as her own.

But it wasn't last year. Or any other time. It was now.

She was thirty years old and couldn't spend the next seven years wasting her energy on something that would never happen. She couldn't spend another year living with the shadows in her husband's eyes whenever they went out to eat and were seated near a couple with a small child, or went to the grocery and passed a toddler sitting in the store cart, or went to church or to the movies or shopping, or stopped at a light next to a van with a car seat. She was through with this—had to be. The pressure was too much.

"I've lost ten pounds, Steve."

"You've had a rough couple of months at work—"

She shook her head, effectively cutting him off. Yes, her position as social worker at the local crisis nursery was stressful. Yes, it had been particularly bad this spring and into the summer as her files filled with more children than there were acceptable foster homes to accommodate them.

"My inability to conceive is destroying me."

"So we'll adopt—"

"Steve!" She was as shocked by her scream as he was.

Lowering her head, Jolene zipped her bag and pulled it off the bed. "I'm sorry," she said, extending the handle as the suitcase landed at her feet. "But this is exactly what I mean. The guilt, the disappointment, the pressure—it's just too much for me. I can't even maintain control of my emotions." She looked at him because she couldn't *not* look at him. "I know how much you need children of your own—not someone else's children to care for. You do that all day long, and so do I. You need children who are a continuation of you, of your father…."

Steve's father, a policeman, had been gunned down

by a desperate homeless teenager trying to break into a pay phone. Steve was ten. His mother had died shortly after he was born from a blood clot following simple outpatient surgery to fix a prolapsed bladder resulting from his birth.

She yanked on the suitcase handle and headed out to the hall, the bag feeling like a mass of hundred-pound rocks moving slowly at her heels.

"Sure I want kids." Steve was right behind her. "But not more than I want you. You're my life, Jo…."

And she'd had ovarian cysts that, once removed, had left scar tissue making it unlikely she'd conceive. Unlikely that she'd ever give Steve—her healthy and perfectly fertile husband—the one thing he wanted most out of life. A child of his own.

The last time they'd spent the thousands of dollars necessary for the medical procedure that had a twenty percent chance of impregnating her, she'd started her period almost immediately. That night, he'd thought she was asleep when he crept quietly from their bed. She'd been lying quietly beside him, trying to regulate her breathing, but she'd been far from asleep. She'd crawled out of bed, too, thinking they'd share a late-night drink as they had after a couple of the other disappointments. He hadn't heard her. And he hadn't gone for a drink. Instead, she'd seen him in his office, staring at a photo book she'd never seen before, but one she'd perused several times since. It was filled with pictures of him and his dad.

And that night, while she watched from the doorway, her husband of more than five years, the man who'd never shed a tear in her presence, had wept like a baby….

"I have to go…."

Opening the door off the kitchen leading to the garage and her year-old Ford Explorer, Jolene fled.
And didn't look back.

CHAPTER TWO

THE CABIN HADN'T AGED a bit, or so it seemed to Tina Randolph as she peered through the Colorado spruce and aspen trees for her first glimpse of the place. Certainly the road in—two tire tracks in the dirt—hadn't changed much in the twenty-five years she'd been coming here. Taller trees maybe. She was taller, too, but they still seemed to tower as they had when she was a child.

There was a certain comfort in the sameness of it all—in knowing that there was something in life that could be counted on not to change. To be there, just as it always had been.

She glanced at Jolene, looking beyond the half-hearted smiles and the obvious effort it was taking her friend to keep up a steady chatter. "It's good to be with you, you know?" she said softly.

Looking briefly at Tina, Jolene met her gaze as openly as always. She nodded. "I missed you."

It was first time Jolene had totally connected with her since they'd hugged at the airport a couple of hours earlier.

Tina watched as the hundred-year-old stone cabin came fully into view. As usual, the heavy wooden shutters were down. They'd probably have to chase out a critter or two—if not a mouse, then certainly some spiders. The electrical fuse would have to be put in the pump, the water turned on and beds made before she'd have a chance to pin down her friend about the sadness lurking in her posture, her eyes.

The in vitro must not have worked. She'd been dreading the possibility of hearing this since she'd boarded the plane in Roanoke that morning. For more than five years, Jolene had been putting herself through uncomfortable and embarrassing medical procedures, trying to have the child who'd fill the holes in her husband's heart. For more than five years, Tina had hurt with her friend and worried about her, as Jolene saw each unsuccessful attempt as a personal failure. How long could she blame herself for something that was completely out of her control? At some point, Jolene was going to break. And then what would happen?

Tina's heart pounded as she considered life without her. A world without Jolene would be a world without enchantment.

Jolene turned off the ignition and bent to peer out the front windshield toward the building that had housed both their families for two weeks every summer of their growing up. Tina could feel Jolene's sigh as though the rush of emotion had come from her own body.

Perhaps the work would have to come later.

"You've lost weight."

Always slim, Jolene's five-foot-six-inch frame barely held up her jeans. Her sweater hung loose on her. "A little."

"You didn't need to."

"It wasn't on purpose."

"So, what's up?"

Jolene continued to stare outside.

Trees and shrubs encroached on the small patch of lawn surrounding the cabin. The grass was almost a foot high. Once they got moved in, they'd be mowing.

"Life seemed so clear when we were kids, didn't it?"

"I don't know," Tina said, watching her friend. "Remember the spring our parents told us we were all moving away from Denver, and to two separate towns?" Jolene had gone to Boulder and Tina to Colorado Springs.

"Yeah." Jolene nodded slowly, still gazing sightlessly through the windshield. "I thought I was going to die."

Tina's smile was bittersweet. "Me, too."

"I couldn't imagine not seeing you every morning, noon and night. We managed, though, didn't we?" Jolene said, turning to meet Tina's eyes.

"They thought we'd gradually grow apart, but we showed them."

They'd saved money from babysitting to fund frequent bus trips, wrote long outpourings in daily letters, were on the telephone whenever anything major—or seemingly major—occurred in their lives.

"I called you the second I started my period, even before I did anything about it," Tina said, remembering.

"I cried for two hours straight to get my dad to fund an emergency bus trip that time James Scolaris kissed you," Jolene told her.

"It was our first kiss," Tina added, grinning. *Their* first kiss they'd called it, meaning hers and Jolene's. Because it had been the first for either of them. And that was how it had always been. What happened to one, happened to the other. Perhaps not physically. But it happened just the same.

"All those summers we spent up here, planning our destinies—we really believed we'd do those things, you know?" Jolene said now, her voice sounding far away.

Tina thought about those days sometimes. Occasionally with pride in their efforts or comfort in the sharing, and more often with melancholy.

"We said we'd go to college together. We did."

"Harvard," Jolene reminded her. "We said we were going to Harvard. We went to UC in Boulder."

"You were going to be a social worker. You are."

"Yeah." Jolene turned, a hint of renewed energy in the movement of her shoulders. "And you were going to be a scientist, which you are."

Tina nodded. "I was sure I'd discover a cure for leukemia." She finished describing that particular dream. The disease had robbed Tina of her little brother just months before the two girls had met. "And I haven't."

"Not yet, anyway. And at the rate you're going, you'll kill yourself before you have a chance."

Placing both hands on the steering wheel, Jolene rested her head on them sideways, watching Tina.

"I'm perfectly healthy!" Tina chuckled, a little uncomfortable with her friend's concern. Jolene was the one needing comfort right now, needing a friend. Tina's job was to be that friend.

"I'm worried about you, Teen," Jolene's words carried a lot of impact for their softness. "Ever since you got in the car, all you've talked about is the lab. Every person you mention, every takeout meal you have, the cold you had last month, all revolved around either the lab or your students. Do you ever do anything outside it?"

"Virginia Tech doesn't have many full-time research professorships," Tina explained patiently. "So I have a great deal of responsibility."

"You're telling me that everyone else you work with spends evenings and weekends in the lab? Don't any of them have families?"

"Of course they do, which is why it's natural that I'd be the one to cover evenings and weekends."

"So you take time off during workday hours?"

She could if she wanted to.

"Look," she said, tilting her head slightly as she met her friend's straightforward gaze. "I'm happy living my life in the lab." She checked in with herself on that one often enough. "I know I might never find a cure for leukemia, but the work I'm doing is leading to that end. It's what I'm here to do, Jo. I *know* that."

"I'm not arguing that point," Jolene said, the concern in her expression not clearing at all. "I know that, too. But it doesn't mean you don't have other things to do, as well. Like get married again. Have a family…"

Tina shook her head. "A family isn't as important to me as it is to you," she said, hoping she could make Jolene understand. "I've loved—and lost—as many times as I'm prepared to, Jo. I'm content with my life now. I love what I do. There aren't many people who can say that."

"You're half alive, Teen," Jolene said. "There's a lack of vitality in your eyes, your step, even in the way your shoulders are drooping. I see a difference just since you were out here at Christmas."

"I'm not the one who's lost weight," Tina reminded her, ready to get the conversation back on track. "Maybe what you see as a lack of vitality is really peace and calm."

"Maybe."

Tina had the distinct impression that Jolene didn't think so. But she had the entire next week to set her friend's mind at rest.

"Look, I'll admit that for a long time after Thad was killed in that structure collapse, I was only half-alive." Tina was proud of how matter-of-factly she could say those words now. For years they'd been too painful even to think. "But I've accepted that he's gone. I'm no longer denying it. No longer angry." She sighed. "At least he was doing something he loved—crawling around one of the buildings his family's company was restoring."

"And what about Thad Jr.?" Jolene whispered, her eyes moist.

And just that quickly Tina needed a second to hold back her own tears. She'd never forget that day after her husband's funeral when stress and heartbreak had sent her into premature labor. The little guy, born at five months, didn't have a chance. She'd never forget Jolene there, holding her hand, staying by her bedside nearly twenty-four hours a day until she was once again up and walking around. If it hadn't been for her best friend, if it hadn't been for Jolene's energy being enough for both of them, carrying both of them, she probably would've died right along with her small family.

"He's with his father," Tina finally said, glancing at the woods, the cabin, imagining the stream that trickled lightly behind it. "I'm at peace with that."

"Peace at what cost?" The words were delivered with passion. "Your peace only counts if you spend the rest of your life alone in a lab?"

Okay, time to stop.

Yanking on the handle, Tina opened the door.

"With all the students milling around, I'm almost never alone," she said with unforced cheer. Or almost unforced… They'd talk about Jolene's weight loss later. "Come on, woman, we've got varmints to relocate, shutters to raise, curtains to open, beds to make, groceries to unload and a lawn to mow."

Tina's smile was a little hard to maintain when Jolene hesitated, her expression firm and unrelenting, but the moment passed. Jolene collected the cabin keys from the console of her Explorer and opened her door without further comment.

CHAPTER THREE

THEY'D ONLY FOUND one dead mouse. A can of soda had exploded in the refrigerator. And while sweeping, Jolene had amassed a small mound of spiders and other insects that had expired in the cabin since her uncle's visit earlier that spring.

"Water's on and toilet's flushing," Tina reported, drying her hands on a paper towel. She walked into the front room from the step-down tiled hallway that led back to the bath Jolene's uncle Bruce had put in for Aunt Marilyn fifty years before, when he'd first bought the old stone hunting cabin. "You raised the shutters!"

Jolene, busy with the sheets she'd brought for the twin beds on the porch, nodded. She and Tina had been sleeping there since early childhood.

"Those shutters are heavy! You shouldn't have done that by yourself!" Walking through the archway that led directly from the kitchen into the fully enclosed and screened porch, Tina picked up the pillows Jolene had brought, removing the protective plastic covers.

Jolene yanked at the top of the first mattress, lifting it, maybe a little higher than necessary, to position the fitted sheet around the edge.

"You shouldn't be doing that, either," Tina said. She

grabbed for the sheet, sliding her fingers down until she got to the next corner. "I'll do this."

"I can do it," Jolene replied softly as she stood back and watched her best friend in the world attack their beds as though she could control all of life, make it perfect for both of them, with sheets folded military neat and smooth blankets.

Tina moved wordlessly, only the sounds of swishing material and an occasional pat interrupting the quiet in the old cabin. Jolene let herself escape for a moment into the safe, secure world of "J and T" where there were only the two of them. It was a world filled with the certain knowledge of an unconditional love that would always protect them. A world in which their combined strengths could make anything possible.

"So it didn't work?" Green eyes wide, moist, sparking with anger and sadness, met Jolene's.

Beds made, Jolene went to retrieve the duffel she'd packed, carrying it to the leather luggage stool out of habit. "I don't know."

"You don't *know?*" Tina's voice rose. Her suitcase landed on the lower of the two dressers—just as it always had.

"Uh-uh." It was too early to change into the sweats she'd be sleeping in. And there was no need to unpack.

Tina, standing there with her arms crossed, didn't even unzip her bag. "So you didn't get negative results from the in vitro?"

Jolene shook her head, glanced quickly up at her friend and then away as she slumped on the closest bed.

"Did you start your period?" The bed dipped as Tina dropped softly down beside her. Jolene, eyes locked on the thinly carpeted floor, could feel her friend's gaze.

"No."

"So you could be?"

It was the shorthand of friends who'd been thinking for each other practically since birth.

"I'm sure I'm not."

"But you don't know."

"I know."

"How can you know if you haven't taken the test yet?" Tina's voice wasn't accusing as anyone else's might have been. Her love and understanding broke through the hard wall of numbness keeping Jolene's emotions in check.

"How can I be, Teen?" she asked, engulfed with sadness as she turned to her friend. "We've done this so many times and there's never even been so much as a miscarriage."

The warmth in Tina's eyes calmed some of the tension inside her. "They didn't do anything different this time than any of the others," she went on. "It's just more of the same, with absolutely no reason to believe that anything's changed."

"Then why put yourself through this?"

"You know why."

"Steve."

"I couldn't tell him no."

"What did the doctor say?"

"Same thing she always says. With our history—my problem—pregnancy doesn't seem likely, but it's not medically impossible."

Tina was quiet for a couple of minutes but, as always, her closeness was enough. Jolene sat next to her friend, thankful for Tina, and slowly started to relax.

"We'll get a test in town tomorrow." Tina's words brought back the tension.

"I brought one with me. I knew I could survive the disappointment if you were there. We always cope with everything when we're together, don't we?"

Tina stood. "Then let's get this over with."

"Not tonight, Teen, please?" Jolene followed her into the main room of the cabin. The kitchen was getting warmer now that the propane heater in the middle of the longest wall had been lit. Jolene poured them each a glass of purified water from the bottles she'd put in the refrigerator earlier. "I need some time just me and you, remembering how life used to feel, before I face that."

"Okay, but we're not leaving here until it's done," Tina said, the sternness in her voice belied by the long hug she gave her friend.

Tina might not be able to make Jolene's barren body capable of conceiving, she might not be able to dissipate Steve's lifelong compulsion to have a child tied to him by blood; and she might not be able to find a cure for leukemia. But to Jolene she was all-powerful, somehow making life manageable just because she was part of it.

"WHEN WAS THE LAST TIME you had sex?"

If she'd been with anyone else, Tina would've choked on the iced tea she was drinking with the tuna and pickles and crackers they were having for dinner.

"Two nights before Thad was killed."

Tina popped another cracker in her mouth. The answer was still the same, and Jolene still asked, pretty much every time they spoke.

"Okay. But don't you *want* to now and then?"

It was a new question.

"You really want me to answer that?" No one who knew Tina—private, quiet, calm and studious as she was—would believe she was having this conversation. No one but Jolene. No one but Jolene could get away with it.

"Sure. Why not?"

Smiling, head tilted, Tina studied her friend. "About a year ago," Tina said softly, sobering. "It was the last Sunday I took off work. I'd had some wine late Saturday night, trying to sleep, and had these incredible dreams about Thad." Her gaze met Jolene's. "You know the kind."

Jolene nodded, her expression open, understanding—and tinged with sorrow.

"Anyway, I woke up with all this sexual energy. I *wanted* to have sex—with him. It was probably one of the loneliest moments of my life."

"A year ago, huh?" Jolene asked.

Tina shrugged.

"The dreams, the sexual energy, just stopped?"

Tina didn't lie often—and never to Jolene. She said nothing.

"It's time, Teen." Jolene's soft blond bangs highlighted her candid brown eyes. "Thad's been gone six years."

"And when it's ninety-six, I'll still be missing him."

"I'm not asking you not to." Jolene didn't back down as easily as she had that afternoon. "Only to give yourself a chance to live."

"Thad's death almost killed me," Tina said. The emotion she was usually pretty adept at avoiding came unexpectedly, overwhelming her. "It did kill my son. I can't risk that again."

Jolene watched her, chin on one hand, transmitting the compassion and love that was their mainstay. Tina knew she had her with that last remark; this part of the conversation had happened often enough for her to recognize its end. And yet Jolene, while quiet, never quite gave up. Secretly, Tina was kind of glad about that. Not that she was ever, ever going to be part of a couple again; she just couldn't stand the thought of Jolene giving up on her. Not when she'd already given up on herself.

"Even if you never love someone that completely, your body's trying to tell you it's ready to start living again."

Jolene's words startled her. And were far more of a threat to Tina's carefully maintained emotional equilibrium than anything else that had been said. It was the first time Jolene had pushed her beyond this point. She wasn't ready—even if her body was.

"What are you suggesting, that I go stand on a street corner? Or put an ad in the personals? Hey, these days, I could probably just register on the Internet someplace and have a whole display of men to choose from." The sarcasm wasn't like her. Especially with Jolene.

But her friend had broken the unacknowledged rule—to understand at all costs.

"I'm suggesting you open your mind to the possibility that a less committed but perhaps long-term relationship might be okay."

"It wouldn't be."

"Because you're still hanging on to a six-year-old decision."

"And five, and four and…hell.," Tina gave a grin that was halfhearted at best. "If we're going to get technical, it's probably been about twenty minutes since I decided—once again—that I'm happier single than I would be loving someone. I'd drive us both insane with my worrying every minute of every day that he's going to be snatched away from me."

Jolene's hand slid over hers, fingers wrapping around Tina's palm. The warmth spread through her skin, into her veins, slowly reaching her heart.

"Hey," she finally said. "I'm not asking you to marry him, Teen, or even to meet him yet. I'm just asking you to realize you won't always have to be alone."

It took her a long time, but eventually Tina could meet Jolene's eyes. "I know," she offered, although she didn't need to. Jolene *did* understand. "And I know you're right. I just can't seem to make myself strong enough to actually do what you're asking."

"All I'm asking you to do is think, Teen. Nothing else. Just think about not being alone. If the rest is meant to come, it will. If you meet someone and want to be with him, you'll find a way to deal with the worries. But you aren't ever going to meet him if you don't open yourself to the possibility."

Normally Tina loved it when Jolene was right. This time she hated it. She started to tell her so, but a knock on the cabin door stifled the words.

"Who could that be?" she whispered as she and Jolene looked at each other.

"I have no idea."

"We're sitting on twenty-seven acres of private land."

"Half an hour from the closest town."

The knock came a second time.

"Should we get it?" Tina asked. Both women stood. Moved toward the door.

"It's probably someone from one of the neighboring properties, just checking to make sure we're supposed to be here."

It had happened once or twice in the past. Jolene's uncle Bruce was well liked in these parts. Locals kept an eye on his place. Still, Jolene had called her uncle and he'd told her he'd notify the locals that the place was going to be occupied.

"We're safer here than we are locked in our homes in the city," Tina reminded them both.

She grabbed a poker from the fireplace just in case as Jolene opened the door.

"Steve!" her friend exclaimed.

"Let me get one thing clear, Jolene Hamilton Chambers," Jolene's tall and handsome husband bellowed from the other side of the screen. "You and I are *not* getting divorced."

Tina dropped the poker.

CHAPTER FOUR

DIVORCED?

Jolene and Steve? The two most perfectly suited people she'd ever known?

Did the world make no sense at all anymore?

Even after a night to sleep on it, Tina was still stumbling with disbelief.

"Another deer run." Jolene's voice was only slightly breathless the next morning as she led Tina up the wooded mountain to their most sacred place—a valley of leaves with a treetop roof nestled in the middle of the Colorado mountains.

Tina glanced at the six-inch-wide trail of trampled ground, digging a fallen limb she was using as a walking stick into its loosened earth. She recognized the V-shaped indentations of fresh deer tracks. "It's been used recently."

She, too, was slightly out of breath. The blanket and drinks in her backpack were making the climb a little harder than it would have otherwise been. Still, she'd been making this trek since she was about eight years old—always with provisions on her back—and she'd never been out of breath. Maybe she did need to leave the lab once in a while—to exercise.

She'd finally convinced Steve to go home the night

before, but only after the distraught man had stood outside the screen door for more than an hour trying to get Jolene to let him in—or to come back with him. Tina could hear his passionate confessions of undying love ringing in her ears.

Had Thad loved her that much? Would he still have loved her that much if he'd lived and they'd had six more years of the drudgery of daily life, long hours at the lab, disagreeing about the kids?

"Dammit, woman, get your ass out here and talk to me," Steve had hollered at one point. In response Jolene had climbed under the covers and put her pillow over her head.

That was when Tina had finally been able to talk him into giving it a rest for the night.

"I'm going," he'd said, "but only because I have to work in the morning. But I'll be back. Tell her that."

She'd nodded, watched him drive away so fast the bottom of his car had scraped the dirt track, and then she'd softly shut the door.

Jolene had pretended to be asleep.

"How you doing?" she called to her friend now. Jolene still hadn't taken that test. What if she was finally pregnant? And hurt herself climbing up in the hills? A branch cracked under Tina's tennis shoe and she slid a couple of inches before climbing up the next little bluff.

"Fine." Jolene's voice was muted by the dense trees.

Jolene wasn't fine. The haunted look in her eyes when she'd finally pulled the pillow away from her head the night before had scared Tina more than anything in the six years since her husband's and son's deaths. She'd been shocked by Jolene's whispered "I can't talk about it right now." She and Jolene could talk about *anything*. Anytime.

Tiny rays of sun peeked down through the branches, little spotlights on the carpet of last fall's leaf remains mixed with green summer foliage.

"Remember when we used to try to step only on patches of sunshine?" she called out. Jolene was at least six feet in front of her.

"For good luck." Jolene's reply shot over her shoulder.

If the way their lives had turned out was good luck, what would bad luck have brought? Tina wondered.

With winds and snow and rainfall and wildlife taking their toll, a wild place never stayed completely the same, yet there was no doubt when they'd reached their destination. They'd been climbing for an hour. Tina spread out the blanket and Jolene dug in her pack for the peanut butter and potato chip sandwiches and Rice Krispie treats with chocolate and butterscotch topping they'd made that morning. Eleven-thirty, and she was starved, even after having eggs and toast for breakfast. Tina couldn't remember the last time she'd eaten before one or two in the afternoon.

But then, food sustained life, and when she was with Jolene, life was worth sustaining.

PATCHES OF BLUE and blinding brightness glinted through the ceiling of leaves far above her head. Lying on her back on the blanket beside Tina, roots poking into her backside, Jolene studied the moving patches, astonished that after twenty-five years, they still looked the same. She could count on the dancing movements to be there to play with her, to tease her with a game of hide-and-seek. Could she tell where the shining bright light would appear next?

And what was her reward if she guessed right? One wish or three? Big wishes or little ones?

"I just can't do it anymore, Teen."

Tina turned her head, and Jolene looked in her direction: "Do what?"

"Live with Steve."

"Why?" There was no judgment in the question. Just love and support and everything that defined their relationship—the earnings of twenty-five years of loyalty and trust.

"Every time I think about the look in his eyes when he hears—again—that the attempt was unsuccessful, I feel so trapped I can't breathe. And pretty soon I can't even think straight. All I can do is feel—and what I feel isn't good, Tina."

"What do you feel?"

"Like I want to drive over a cliff."

"And when you picture life without Steve?"

"Incredible sadness—but not trapped…not worthless."

Tina's sigh was enough to tell Jolene she understood. "Have you talked to him any more about adoption?" she asked.

Drawing up her knees, Jolene rested a hand on the waistband of her jeans. "We've talked about it, but since that conversation at Christmas, I know it won't really solve anything. He'll adopt, but he'll still want us to try to get pregnant. Until the doctors say it's impossible, which they aren't going to, he won't give up hope."

"What about the prohibitive costs? Hasn't that become a factor to him?"

She'd thought so. If the doctors wouldn't rule out the possibility, surely their finances would. Shielding her eyes with her hand, she pinpointed the next spot where sunshine would be peeking through the leaves. And waited.

"He doesn't care about the costs," she said, smiling when the sun hit its mark. "This is so much bigger to him than mere money."

"But there's the practical reality of having to pay the bills. Once they aren't paid, the doctors will refuse the procedure."

"He took a second job on weekends—back at that construction job he had in college—to build up enough savings so that won't be an issue." Just speaking the words tightened the imaginary cords around Jolene's chest. Even up here, beneath the clouds and away from her normal daily life, she couldn't find peace. "I hardly see him anymore," she said, hating that she sounded like a shrewish selfish wife. The kind she secretly detested.

She continued anyway. "The free time he does have is spent coaching a kids' team—baseball right now, then it'll be basketball. He's also volunteering at a center for troubled teens."

"Where you work? So at least you see him then?"

"Nope." The ground was hard beneath her head. "A different one."

"Sounds like he's avoiding you as much as you're avoiding him."

"Yep."

"Have you asked him about it?"

"Of course. He refuses to see it. Just makes excuses for—justifies—each incident, rather than looking at the big-picture results of his combined actions."

"So tell him you won't have any more procedures. The man I heard last night would accept that in order to keep you."

"Ah, Tina, if only it was that simple." She turned her head to look at her friend. "He's waiting all the time—waiting and hoping to find out I'm pregnant. It's not just the procedures. It's every month. Not that he says anything, but it's gotten to the point where I feel guilty putting a tampon wrapper in the trash because I know he'll see it—and know that we've gone another month with no success."

"And let me guess," Tina said, her gaze soft as she stared at Jolene. "He denies that he's disappointed."

"You got it. To spare me, I'm sure."

"But it doesn't, of course."

"No." She sat up and again hugged her knees to her chest. "The worst part is, I don't blame him. He can't help wanting a child of his own. He can't help having hope. He can't help his own needs any more than I can help mine."

"And have you asked yourself recently what those are?"

"Honestly?" She frowned at Tina, who was still lying down, but had her arm under her head, watching Jolene. Tina nodded.

"I want to be finished with this. With going through procedures that leave me no dignity. With feeling like a failure every month. With feeling like I'm not good enough. I want to be someplace—in a situation, a relationship—where the abilities I do have are enough."

"Even if it means never having a child of your own?"

"Even then."

"And that'll be worth losing the love of your life?"

She'd been considering that a lot lately.

"What about me, alone in my lab?" Tina went on when she didn't readily answer. "You think *I* should be with someone, yet for *you* the best decision is to walk away."

"I don't want to live my life alone," Jolene said slowly. "But I think it goes deeper than the love of my life."

Tina maneuvered herself into a sitting position. "How can anything be deeper than that?"

Leaves rustled off to the right. Breezes often made their way through the hills. Jolene glanced toward the sound.

"What about love of self?" she asked. "How can you love someone else when you can't stand yourself? If you love him, and you know you're not good for him, and you want what's best for him, aren't you obliged to remove yourself from the relationship?"

"Maybe." Tina glanced toward the right, as well. "Sometimes."

"I can't stand me, Teen." She admitted out loud something that choked her every time she thought of it. "I actually find myself wondering how anyone as good as Steve could possibly love me. I have to get out, get away. I have to find a life where I can like me again, just as I am."

Another rustle off to the right was the only sound during the next several minutes. Jolene shivered. She wasn't really cold; her sweater was thick enough to withstand a crisp autumn day.

This was a first. Being with Tina in the hills wasn't enough. They weren't invincible.

"Maybe if you change your thinking…" Tina's voice faded.

"How?"

"You're blaming yourself for your inability to conceive, and while we both know this isn't about blame, I understand how you feel. But couldn't this just as easily be a genetic incompatibility? Didn't your doctors suggest that? Meaning it's as much because of Steve as it is because of you."

"Genetic incompatibility would be more likely to make me miscarry, not fail to conceive," she said. "And that was only one possible explanation from one doctor a couple of years ago." She laid her head on her knees, staring into the woods. She'd heard another rustle. A little closer.

Was there a deer out there? Would they actually get to see it up close and in the wild?

"Steve's medical reports have all been glowing," she said, subdued. "And I had those cysts in college, remember? They left scar tissue. My periods have been erratic ever since. It's pretty clear the faulty body is mine, but because the evidence isn't conclusive, the doctors aren't going to point-blank say I can't conceive."

"Does Steve agree with you on this?"

She couldn't answer for a moment. And when she did, the word caught in her throat. "Yes."

"He *said* so? That doesn't sound like Steve."

"He was trying to ease my guilt," Jolene said. "He was assuring me that it didn't matter to him. He said we weren't going to let a little scar tissue come between us. And he meant it."

She turned to meet Tina's eyes again. "He doesn't *blame* me. He simply concluded that our problem lies with the state of my ovaries."

The rustling came again.

"That's not just the wind," Tina said.

"It's as if something was sliding." Jolene's heart pounded a little more heavily as she studied the trees.

"Have you heard about any bears being spotted up here in the past couple of years?"

"No." But they were awfully far from home. She stood, began gathering up their things.

"Of course, bears are more afraid of us than we are of them." Tina repeated what they'd been told ad nauseum as children. She shoved the blanket, twigs and all, into her pack.

"Look at us." Jolene chuckled, but didn't slow her step as they scurried down the hill. "We've been roaming these hills alone since we were eight years old. Back when we were kids, we would've been more apt to seek out a sound than run from it!"

Right beside her, keeping up this time, Tina laughed, too. "We've become wimps, my friend."

But neither of them slowed down.

CHAPTER FIVE

STEVE WAS WAITING for them when they returned, sitting on an old wooden bench on the back stoop of the cabin. Tina barely had time to notice him in the distance before he was standing, approaching them as they crossed the bridge over the stream behind the property.

What she noticed more were her friend's faltering steps and sudden intake of breath.

"We'll get rid of him," she said quietly, watching the man. It didn't matter that she loved Steve like a brother. Her first instinct was to protect Jolene.

"He can't do this," Jolene said, sounding close to tears. "This is our time away. He never interrupts or interferes with that."

"I know." Not that she could blame him. He'd just learned that his life was unraveling at the seams. Had she not been hurting so badly for Jolene, Tina would be doing everything she could for him.

"Steve…" she started as they crossed the bridge, since Jolene couldn't seem to find words to say to her husband.

"I know." He held up a hand. "You don't want me here. And I'll go. I just have a question."

"What?" Jolene asked, arms wrapped around her middle as she half looked at him.

"Where's the pregnancy test kit that was in the back of the linen cupboard?"

"In my suitcase."

He frowned. "You haven't done it yet?"

"No."

The hands that had been in his pockets fell to his sides. To Tina, it was obvious. He'd had himself geared up for an answer. He'd been certain Jolene knew, one way or the other, and had been prepared to deal with either possibility.

Also obvious to Tina was the emotional energy he'd invested in the answer. What Jolene had been telling her earlier became much clearer. As much as Steve Chambers needed his wife, he needed a child.

He glanced at Tina. Asking her silently to leave him alone with his wife. She couldn't do that. Not after receiving the plea directed at her from her best friend.

"I won't force my presence on you, Jo," he finally said, turning his body away from Tina as though to shut her out. "I'll leave just as soon as you take that test."

"No."

"I have a right to know if I'm going to be a father."

"Believe me, if that ever happened and I was the baby's mother, you'd be the first person I'd tell."

Jolene's tone was fraught with so much tension, Tina knew her usually calm and capable friend wouldn't be able to handle much more.

"When did you give up hope, Jo?" Steve's voice grew softer.

Tina stood behind her friend as Jolene's shoulders sagged.

"I didn't knowingly give it up," she replied. "I just woke up one day and it was gone."

Steve reached out, apparently to pull Jolene into his arms, but at her slight flinch, he ran the back of his fingers lightly down her cheek, instead.

"This is the part where we're supposed to be living happily ever after," he told her, the softly uttered words filled with a sadness so real and so deep it touched Tina in ways she hadn't felt since Thad died.

It obviously had an emotional effect on Jolene, too. She crumpled to the ground, sitting there in a heap with sobs shaking every inch of her too-thin body.

Steve turned and walked quietly away.

THEY WERE GROWN NOW, his little blond girl-children. His angels. They'd been gone a long time. He'd been a bit angry with them for deserting him. But that was okay now they were back. More beautiful than ever.

He could see their place from the first crest outside his cabin through the old binoculars he'd bought twenty-four years ago. It had taken him an entire week's worth of hauling logs to pay for them, but they were worth it, obliterating the two-mile distance between him and the girls.

With his tongue between his lips, he raised the glasses, anxious not to miss too much time with his angels. He didn't know how long he'd have before they left. Or how he was going to stand letting them go again, now that he couldn't count on seeing them regularly.

His hands got sweaty, and he almost dropped the heavy lenses.

The one with long blond hair was hurt. On the ground. Crying. His angel. Crying. She'd always been his favorite. He'd loved both of them since the first time he'd heard their childish chatter as they crashed through the trees and underbrush of territory he'd always considered his own. But the shorter of the two had been the one he always sought out first, the one who made him feel warmest inside.

He wasn't warm now. No, she was shaking so hard it looked like she'd break something. The other one was there, too, holding her. He couldn't see their faces. If she was that sad here, in the hills, at their cabin, she'd leave.

He had to do something. He had to think.

Lowering the binoculars, he ran back home to make a plan. His tiny cabin was set way back in the woods where no one else had been for almost thirty years.

"THAT WAS STEVE on the phone," Tina said as she came into the cabin's living area just before dinner.

With a cup of hot coffee cradled between her palms, Jolene was sitting on one of the two sofas, staring out the windows at the tall grasses and pine trees swaying in the breeze.

"I figured," was all she said. Jolene had known when they heard the ring that it would be Steve. She'd felt it. She'd let Tina answer it, and then she'd made her mind go blank. Concentrated on the movement of one particular branch, the sudden change in a blade of grass, tried to distinguish between various bird sounds outside the screened windows.

Her love for Steve was destroying her. She had to get away from it—from him—before she lost her health as well as everything else.

They were having a casserole for dinner. The cheeses and tomatoes and oregano smelled just as they always did. They weren't supposed to be making her sick to her stomach. Still, she hadn't had an appetite in months.

"He got a room in Edwina," Tina said.

Only twenty minutes away. Not far enough. She needed distance. Lots and lots of distance. Maybe even a globe's worth.

Tina sat at the other end of the couch, curling her long legs beneath her. Her sweatshirt had a smudge of dirt angling across the left side. "He agreed to leave us completely alone. He won't come out here and he won't call."

"So he says."

"Has he ever lied to you?"

"No."

"He loves you, Jo."

"I know."

"I promised I'd call if you needed him."

"When I find out I'm not pregnant, you mean."

Tina sighed. Ran fingers through curly honey-gold hair that just grew like that naturally.

"He said it, didn't he?" Jolene couldn't let it go. She slid a thumb under the waistband of her jeans, holding the fabric away from her stomach. Even loose, the pressure of the material was uncomfortable. She might have waited too long to take a vacation, however brief. Might already have the ulcer her level of stress was promising her.

She glanced over at Tina, held her friend's eyes for a long moment. "He did." She repeated the words softly, a statement with a hint of question.

Please, Teen, tell me I'm wrong. Tell me his concern had nothing to do with medical procedures and test strips.

Tina's nod almost made her cry.

"WE MUST, WE MUST, we must improve our bust…"

"For fear, for fear, we'll never wear a brassiere…"

Tina grinned at Jolene as her friend, perched on a ladder in the old shed attached to the cabin, joined in, raising her voice to match Tina's.

"…the bigger the better, the tighter the sweater, the boys depend on us! Hey, hey, Ma, Hey, hey, Pa, I think I need a bra, Hey!"

She barely got the last word out through the laughter erupting from deep within her. Jolene's long hair was covered in cobwebs, a smudge of something beige was smeared across her left eyebrow, she had a hole the size of a grapefruit in the knee of her jeans, and her tennis shoes, ironically enough in style now, were the same kind of pointed-toe canvas things they'd worn as kids.

"I can't *believe* I still remember that!" Jolene half coughed through her laughter. "I haven't thought of that song in years!" She was holding a medium-size box she'd pulled down from a shelf near the roof of the shed. And for the first time since Tina had seen her three days ago, Jolene didn't look so fragile. Maybe today she'd be able to talk her into just getting that damned test—and the finality of its results—over with.

"Are you kidding? You don't still hear it in your head sometimes?" On her own ladder, Tina grabbed the next can of paint on the shelf, checking to see if it was worth keeping. "I sang it to Thad on our honeymoon. He'd been, uh, enjoying the tightness of my sweater and I told him you'd taught me how to please boys."

Jolene sat on top of the ladder, ripping open the lid of the box, and laughed again. "I taught you a *song,* woman!"

"Yeah, well, I had him going for a second there…."

The lid on the can was rusted. Tina dropped it into an old wooden crate that used to hold deer bait. They'd converted it to a trash bin the previous morning when they'd decided to tackle the shed, clean it out and organize it, as a way of thanking Jolene's uncle for the use of his place. They'd call someone to haul away the crate when they were done.

Thad had laughed at the song, his voice deep and rich with life. And then he'd taken her sweater-covered breasts reverently into his palms and held them. Simply held them. As though cherishing them as a part of her, not as a toy for him…

"Hey, look at this!"

Open box in her lap as she sat, still perched on the ladder, Jolene held out a bent and yellowed paperback book. Tina recognized it instantly.

"Our first romance novel!"

"I had no idea it was up here."

"Do you remember what it was about?" Tina asked, wishing life could feel this full, this right, on a regular basis.

"Of course!" Jolene thumbed through the pages. "He's a landowner and he forced her into a loveless marriage…."

"But damn he was sexy, wasn't he?"

"He sure taught me what I wanted in a man," she said in a light voice. But then she grew quiet, staring down at the book.

Tina sat on top of her own ladder. "And did you find it?" she asked.

"Yeah." Jolene looked over, telling Tina something she already knew. "I did."

"I did, too."

"So that's it?" Jolene asked, tossing the book into the trash bin. "We found it, and now we're done?"

"For me, that's it."

"We're only thirty!"

"You ready to take that test?" Tina regretted the words instantly. She'd been hoping to show her friend that she didn't *have* to be done, through, finished. To remind her that the man who'd filled her romantic girlhood dreams was still here—still wanting her.

Jolene's expression, changing from sudden outrage to insecurity, reflected the delicate balance inherent in any happy moment for either of them.

"I'm ready to take a walk. How about you?" Jolene climbed down from the ladder. "We've made a great start here, but I'm tired of hiding out inside because noises in the woods scare me now."

Tina joined her. She was tired of being afraid, too.

CHAPTER SIX

THEY HEARD NOISES. RUSTLINGS in the debris of last October's fallen leaves. But Jolene did her best to ignore them. If she couldn't find the courage to walk in woods that had always been a piece of heaven for her, then how the hell was she ever going to convince herself she could face that stupid little test strip back at the cabin? Or a life without Steve?

They walked alongside the stream, taking off their shoes and socks, rolling up the legs of their jeans to wade across to the field on the other side. And they found the big old fallen tree that had served many summers as a balance beam. All the times they'd tripped along that tree in their bare, little-girl feet…

"I dare you to walk across it," Tina said midafternoon on Thursday as they faced the gnarled and grayed old trunk spanning the rapid, six-foot-deep stream.

"Yeah, like you dared me to get wet that summer you fell in?"

"I didn't want to be the only one in trouble! Being grounded together would've been fun."

"Instead, I get pneumonia and spend the rest of the summer in bed." Jolene glanced at the log. Remembered the girl she used to be. "I'm game if you are."

They made it across. Twice. And halfway across

the third time, Jolene's right foot slipped. Not much. Just enough to make her stomach jump and take her breath away.

"Whoa, baby!" Her voice was shaky as she quickly lowered her butt to the tree. Once she was safely straddling the trunk, she looked up at Tina and grinned when her friend joined her.

"Does this mean we're back to living life in fear?" Tina was smiling, her voice light.

"No," Jolene answered slowly. "But growing up means losing the illusions, you know? We're no longer invincible."

"Danger's not just out there, it's hit home."

Exactly. "It's funny, though," Jolene said. "I would've understood fear of being raped or murdered or poisoned by chemical warfare. I never would've figured being afraid of myself, afraid for my mental and emotional stability, afraid of noises in the woods."

"You're much stronger than you think, my friend."

Sitting there, watching a light green leaf fall and get swept away by the tiny whitecaps of water, Jolene didn't *feel* strong. She felt more like that leaf. Poised above the rapids, waiting to fall, to be pulled under by the current.

"It's Thursday, Teen," she said, head bent. "We only have three more days together, and I'm not ready to have you go."

She wasn't ready to hurt Steve any more than she had already, either. "I have no problem facing life on my own," she continued. "I'm ready for it. And in some ways, I'm looking forward to the freedom of being enough just as I am, of not constantly worrying about disappointing the person I love. I…" Her voice trailed off.

"*Are* you ready, Jo? Really ready?"

Hands on the rough bark between her legs, Jolene stared up at the woman facing her. "Is anyone ever completely ready for anything? How can we be when we don't know what's coming next?"

Tina studied her for a second. Shook her head. "You want to know what I think?"

Jolene's stomach twisted. "Of course."

"I think part of the reason you're so reluctant to take that test is that you aren't ready for it all to be over."

Maybe. A little. But who could blame her? Endings were hard.

"Well, Teen, if you're anything to go by—and in my world you always have been—it's going to take me a lifetime to get over him."

An animal scampered in the trees behind her. Jolene flinched, she wanted to turn around and assure herself that no danger lurked at her back, but she didn't. She was strong. She had to be. Or the next few weeks of her life, the next months, were likely to reduce her to nothingness.

"You know, I think I've realized something, coming here to the cabin," Tina said, her knees almost touching Jolene's.

"What's that?"

Tina's short curly blond hair was windblown. Her sweater was oversize and her jeans baggier than she'd worn them in high school, but she still looked every bit the gorgeous cheerleader type that had garnered her any boy she wanted.

"I don't miss Thad as much as I used to."

It was a bold statement. A life-changing one? Jolene was afraid to move, to distract her from a revelation that had been years in coming.

"All the talking we've been doing here about Thad, the remembering—there used to be an almost debilitating pain associated with it. I feel sad, don't get me wrong, it's just…more distant now."

"And that's as it should be." Dare she hope that Tina was finally going to move on? There was still time for her to find someone to love, to start a family, to have the full and happy life Jolene had always imagined for her.

"I'll tell you what I really miss, though," Tina said, her chin resting on Jolene's shoulder.

"What?"

"What Thad and I shared—that togetherness—that knowing there was someone out there who knew where you were, who expected you home, who helped pay the bills and cared if you bought new towels for the bathroom."

"Someone to have cereal with on the nights you're too tired to cook or go out or even be sociable," Jolene added, refusing to turn around when the breeze, or a bird, knocked a twig down from a tree some distance behind her. She could do this.

Tina's gaze was sharp, her hazel eyes unrelenting as they met Jolene's. "You can still have that, Jo," she said. "It's not too late."

For a second there, she let herself pretend, imagine, believe. And then she shook her head. "You saw him, Teen. You heard him. Do you really think Steve will ever be happy without a child of his own? A biological child?"

"He's been happy with you all this time."

"But do you think he'll ever give up hoping?"

Tina didn't reply. She didn't need to. They both knew the answer.

"And that's why I can't stay," she said, standing. "I can't live the rest of my life disappointing him. I'll end up hating him for the way I feel every month when I start my period."

"But what if—"

Jolene held up her hand. "I can't live my whole life in fear of what might happen," she said, waiting for Tina to stand, to turn and head back across the log the way they'd come. "Tomorrow morning, first thing, I'll take the test."

Instead of scaring her, which the thought of that pregnancy test had done almost constantly, the plan, clearly stated, gave her a measure of peace.

"I'm going to hold you to that," Tina warned, taking one careful step and then another, in front of her, causing a slight swaying.

"Up in the hills," Jolene added, not quite as confident as she'd been. "At our special place. Up there it's easier to believe that life is manageable."

Tina reached the bank. Hopped off the end of the log. And Jolene stepped forward, the bark solid and scratchy beneath her bare feet. She could do this. Had done it a million times before. Just one small step. And then another.

Lift a foot, put it down. Lift a foot and—

Something scampered behind her and Jolene jerked, arms flying up as she struggled for balance.

"Jo?"

Tina's cry was the last thing she heard before she landed in water so icy she couldn't breathe. And then, for a split second, as shock and numbness took hold of her, she was content just to be.

"It was a squirrel." With both arms wrapped around Jolene, trying to impart some warmth, Tina moved them awkwardly through undergrowth and fields knee-high with weeds, back to the cabin half a mile away.

"S-sounded b-bigger than a squirrel." Jolene's teeth chattered so hard, understanding her was a challenge.

"I saw it," Tina assured her. If they came back to this place in another twenty-five years, would they find as many changes in themselves as they were finding this silver anniversary? "He ran up that double-trunked oak just near the bank."

"C-close then," Jolene stuttered. "No wonder so loud."

Huddled against her, soaked and small, Jolene had never been more precious to Tina. Or as delicate.

"We're going to be fine, you know," she said now, as though she was back at the university speaking to a room full of students, needing to convince them that if they'd dedicate their time to research, they would eventually find a cure for cancer. "We made it through separation, starting our periods, acne, and being dumped a week before prom. We'll make it through this, too."

If this stage of life required them to be afraid, so be it. "We're going to face our fears, you and me, Jo, and we'll be back here fifty years from now, looking back and applauding. You mark my words."

"I'm marking." What she was doing was shaking, from head to foot.

"You aren't going to get sick on me, woman, you hear?" Tina admonished her.

"Nope. Just cold."

And underweight. And run-down. And as a robust child, she'd had pneumonia for more than a month after an unexpected plunge in the stream.

Not a believer in much anymore, for the first time in more than six years, Tina sent up a tiny prayer.

TINA WAS SITTING at the kitchen table, two cups of hot chocolate before her, as Jolene came around the corner from the bathroom forty-five minutes later. She felt warm and cozy in a pair of black sweats and an old black-and-white Colorado sweatshirt. Her hair was still damp and she wasn't sure she'd ever wipe the memory of that freezing water from her mind, but she was pretty much recovered from her tumble. Sitting down opposite her friend at one end of the scarred solid-wood table, she took a long sip of chocolate. It was her second cup. Tina had left the first one on the bathroom counter for her to drink when she got out of the shower.

"Someone's been here."

Tina set her cup down, frowning. "What do you mean?"

"It dawned on me while I was in the shower," Jolene told her friend. "That towel that was outside on the pump when we walked up…"

"Yeah?"

"I had it in my hand when we were leaving this afternoon, so I dropped it on the table out on the porch, right next to the water bowl. I knew if I forgot it, I'd find it there when I emptied the dishwater tonight."

"You're sure about that?"

"Positive."

Tina didn't say anything. Her thumb tapped a rapid pulse against the rim of her cup.

"I'm sure it was Steve," Jolene told her. "No one else is around and if they were, they'd either leave a note or wait for us to get back."

"You aren't scared?"

"No!" She had been. A little. Before she'd thawed and figured it out. "He couldn't even keep his word to stay away for two days! His need to know about that test is so great, he's driving himself crazy with it."

"He sure wasn't himself the other day."

"I know!" Jolene wished she was sipping something a little stronger than hot chocolate. "This is precisely what I mean! He gets like this every time!" She could feel tears gathering behind her lids, and wished they wouldn't. Tears made her feel so weak. "I just can't live with that tension anymore."

"I know, hon," Tina said, reaching over to cover one of Jolene's hands with her own. Her thumb reassuringly stroked the back of Jolene's hand. "I understand. I've only caught a glimpse of it and I don't see how anyone could handle that for long. At least he left before we got back."

He hadn't found them. Or an empty test box in the trash. Had he found the unopened one in her bag? Would he really go that far?

"What am I going to do?" The cry was soft, but burned her inside.

Tina shrugged, held her gaze. "You're going to take that test in the morning, give Steve his answer, and move on with your life."

"Alone." It sounded so final. So real. "Once I see that the test is negative."

"If that's what you have to do to be healthy."

Healthy. She couldn't remember the last time she'd associated that word with herself. She took a deep breath.

"How would you feel about the two of us living to-gether?" She'd been toying with the idea on and off for more than a year. Still, hearing herself voice it out loud...

"You're kidding, right?" Tina said, but there was a

hint of energy about her, the almost imperceptible lifting of her shoulders, the glint in her eyes.

And Jolene's words came easier. "I've been thinking about moving to Roanoke."

"You're serious?" Tina grinned, although she looked as though she was trying not to. "I mean, you really shouldn't do anything rash...."

"You want to live with me or not, Teen? We got along okay in college."

"We got along great in college!" Tina said, smiling outright. "Of course I want to live with you! There's no one else I'd rather live with...."

And suddenly Jolene was grinning, too. Finding within her friend's unconditional love the peace and acceptance she'd lost over the past few years. Life would go on. And she would go with it. She knew that now.

CHAPTER SEVEN

THE NEXT MORNING, Tina busied herself looking out at the horizon through the woods while her friend went behind a tree and took care of the personal business of conducting a home pregnancy test. True to her character, Jolene hadn't wavered from her decision to get the test over with once she'd made up her mind. It was reassuring that *something* was normal.

Jolene was going to be fine, either way. Her friend was resilient, a fighter. She'd never backed down from a challenge in her life, not from Tommy Borcher in fourth grade when he'd grabbed her and kissed her and she'd bitten his lip and kicked his shin. And not when Tina had been ready to give up her own fight for life after Thad had died and she'd lost the baby and Jolene had sat there day after day, fighting for both of them. She'd been so certain that love—the love of a best friend—would be enough to pull her through.

And she'd been right.

Tina's love would do the same for Jolene now.

She knew that. She knew they'd be okay. That Jolene would be okay.

So why the hell was she shaking inside? Why was she so damned worried?

Jolene would call out when she was done. She was

going to leave the stick on the box and Tina was going to read the results. Jolene had planned it all when they'd gotten out of bed this morning. She'd rather hear the results from Tina than read them for herself. She'd looked at so many test strips she hated the sight of them.

Tina waited another couple of minutes, trying not to pace. Jolene was nervous, probably having a little trouble making herself go. The least Tina could do was keep enough distance to leave her friend a little dignity. Not that they hadn't shared a bathroom a hundred times before.

Sixty seconds more, and Tina was hearing leaves rustle constantly. A squirrel. Or three. She glimpsed a cottontail scampering between the trees about halfway down the hill. The wind was blowing. She and Jolene had decided late last night that *no fear* was their new motto, unabashedly stolen from a famous tennis-shoe maker. They were going to town later that morning and both of them were going to buy shoes and a sweatshirt of the no-fear brand. They'd turned over new leaves.

No pun intended.

Tina tried to chuckle at herself, but the sound caught in her throat. She *was* afraid. Jolene was taking too long. Had her friend passed out? Was she feverish from her fall in the icy water the day before but hadn't said anything? Had she seen the answer and done something drastic? Turning, Tina climbed quickly back to their sacred spot, frantically searching for Jolene. She wasn't anywhere around.

"Jo?" she called, hurrying over to the tree she'd seen Jolene heading for almost ten minutes earlier. "Jo?" She ran to the other side of the tree and stopped cold.

The pregnancy kit was there. The little cup was full. The strip had been used.

And Jolene was nowhere in sight.

THERE HAD TO BE A TRAIL. Jolene would've left one. Their parents had always told them to leave a trail if they got lost. The girls had played the trail game countless times as kids.

Yes! That twig wouldn't have fallen like that naturally. It must be the first sign. Tina glanced desperately around, looking for the next sign, for any indication of which way to go next. She ran several yards in one direction, circled around, came back.

Downhill and up, Tina scoured a half-mile radius.

Maybe the twig wasn't a sign. Maybe a deer had kicked it last night while roaming for food.

Oh, God. Food. Bear.

How could a bear have carried off Jolene without Tina's hearing a thing? No—it was impossible. Running back toward their sacred spot, she tripped on her own foot and fell. She barely registered the bruise on her hip from the rock she'd hit. She scrambled back up. Kept running. She had to get home. Call the sheriff.

And Steve.

But first she had to get that stick. She shoved it in the back pocket of her jeans. She couldn't leave it up there. It would be like leaving Jo.

And she wasn't going to do that.

She had no idea what had happened to her friend, couldn't think of a single reasonable explanation, a single thing that wasn't horrible beyond words.

Had she chickened out at the end? Been too afraid to hear what Tina would say? Had she run off?

Would she be back at the cabin when Tina came bursting through the trees on the other side of the stream? She put all her hopes in that thought, strained to see long before the cabin was in view. And almost fell stricken when she arrived at an empty yard. An empty house.

STEVE CHAMBERS STOOD at the foot of the cliff, staring up at the craggy rock and variegated browns and greens that covered the landscape just outside Edwina, Colorado. A man used to constant activity, to being aware of hundreds of emotionally intense lives unfolding around him all day every day, Steve was finding the self-imposed halt nearly impossible to endure with anything like his usual calm. Here he was, just two days after parking himself in a small hotel at the edge of town, ready to scale a wall that would challenge experts. And he'd never done any rappelling in his life. It was either that or hit something. Hard.

How else did a man rid himself of a tension so great he felt he could incite an entire army to battle?

The ringing of his cell phone was a relief, bringing him out of the private hell of his own mind to the outside world. His assistant principal was completing the week of new-teacher orientation for him. And she'd called about six times a day.

Still, for her he had answers. Every time.

"Steve Chambers," he said, so eager to connect with a sane human being that he didn't even notice the incoming call number.

"Steve?"

The voice was only vaguely familiar. The panic unmistakable.

"What's wrong?"

"Steve, it's Tina!"

Yes. Steve gritted his teeth. He should've known that. "What's wrong?" he asked again, forcing himself not to holler.

"Jo's missing, Steve... I have no idea where she is... I can't find her... There's no trace... It doesn't make sense... She went off to do it... She was there and then she wasn't..." Tina laughed. Gulped. Sobbed. And continued rambling.

"Okay, Teen, calm down," Steve said, adrenaline kicking him into save-the-world mode. He strode to his car, climbed in, remembered to buckle his seat belt and then pulled slowly into traffic before accelerating to a higher-than-legal speed.

"...peeing and I didn't...a cottontail...and then... and a twig was...I thought..."

The closer Steve got to the cabin, the more panic threatened to overtake his rational mind, and the more unintelligible Tina became.

"I'm almost there, Tina. Calm down. You went up into the hills together?"

"Yeah!" Tina's voice rose on a wail. "And then..."

"What time was that, Teen, do you remember?"

"Morning." She hiccupped. "It was morning."

It was still morning. He ignored the squealing of his tires as he took the next corner. Any cop who tried to stop him be damned. Or better yet, if a cop showed up, he could lead the way.

"Did you call the sheriff?"

"Yes," Tina said, her enunciation too emphatic. She was rational enough to try to calm down. That was good.

"Is he on his way?"

"Yes."

Okay. The first problem was solved.

"I'm almost there, Tina," he said again, his heart beating so hard he didn't think he'd make it unless he focused on her. Not himself. "Just stay on the phone with me until I get there. I'm sure there's a logical explanation…."

He had no idea what he said after that—just a steady stream of nonsense intended to keep him and Tina from going into shock.

But in the back of his mind, as he drove the last miles in record time and blew through the trees and dirt of the private road leading to the cabin, was only one thought.

He couldn't live without Jolene.

Period.

WELL, HE'D TAKEN CARE of things. His angel wouldn't lie on the ground and cry anymore. He'd made a miracle. He should probably do more. Honor the moment. Touch. Feel. Have pleasure.

He'd touched himself before. Not often. On his birthday.

He'd do something. Soon. For now, it was right to sit with his bottle. Drink. And know.

TINA RANDOLPH REMINDED Sheriff Tom Hunter of his ex-wife. Except for the clingy part that had driven him not to fight her when she'd told him she wanted a divorce. Tina Randolph didn't cling. On the contrary, she took charge of the world around her as if she owned every square inch of it.

Or her best friend's uncle did.

"So let's say she left a trail," he said now as he and

Tina and the missing woman's husband, Steve, walked up to the hills where Tina had last seen Jolene Chambers. "What would she use?"

"Twigs, her ponytail holder, tissue from her pocket…"

"Jolene always has a tissue in her pocket," Steve interjected. The poor guy looked wretched, tight-lipped, pale skinned, and he was climbing with enough brawn to move the whole damn mountain. He hadn't said much, except to answer Tom's questions about Jolene's habits—and to produce a picture of his missing wife from his wallet—but Tom liked the way he'd been staying one step behind his wife's friend, ready to catch her if she fell.

"The search dogs and handlers will be here sometime tomorrow. Hopefully we'll have found her long before then." He stopped at a tree about halfway up the wooded mountainside. "Looks like someone slid here, saved themselves by grabbing the trunk of this tree."

"That was me," Tina said, panting as they climbed. "When I was running home a little while ago."

The hills were vast, covering miles of woods—and she'd brought them to the exact spot she'd traveled earlier. Tom was impressed.

"IS THAT ALL the drink she had with her?" Tom asked when, an hour into the search, they'd reached the tree where Tina had last seen Jolene and he saw the bottle of water Jolene had apparently left.

Along with a box for a home pregnancy kit.

Steve Chambers shrank visibly when he saw that box—raising questions Tom would need to ask. But not yet.

"Yeah," Tina said. "We didn't plan to be up here very long."

"Did she have any food?"

"No." Tina couldn't seem to stand still, walking over and over ground she'd already covered, as though her friend would magically appear from beneath the old leaves and summer ground cover. "That won't be a problem. Jo could live out here for days. The water in the stream is crystal-clear, and she knows every edible plant and berry in the state."

"So what's she going to do if we don't find her by nightfall?"

"If she's still out here, you mean?" Tina sounded as if she didn't consider that feasible.

Avoiding Steve's eye, Tom nodded.

"She won't be," Tina said firmly. "No matter how lost she is, she knows to follow the stream until she eventually finds a cabin."

Tom didn't like the feeling he was getting. No visible sign of a scuffle. Nothing to indicate that the woman hadn't just disappeared into thin air. No clues at all.

"She might have slipped, hit her head." He hated the part of his job where he had to be the bearer of bad news. But if there was a hope in hell of finding the missing woman alive, he needed the help of her friends. His instincts told him they didn't have much time.

If any at all.

"She might not remember to walk along the stream," he muttered.

Or to eat berries, not that starvation was a great concern at that point.

"She'll remember," Tina and Steve said together, sharing a look, a brief, sad smile. "She caught pneumonia up here one summer," Tina said, glancing at

Tom. "She didn't want to miss out on our time together, so she didn't tell anyone she felt bad. We came up here the next afternoon, and I guess the climb was too much for her. We were reading and I drifted off to sleep and when I woke up, she'd wandered off. By the time I got down off the hill, she was home in bed, delirious with fever. I've never been so scared in my life."

Until now. Tom heard the unspoken words.

"You said you were over there—" he pointed to the south of them "—so let's head north and see what we find."

"SHE FELL in the stream yesterday." Tom was only half listening to the intermittent conversation between Steve and Tina as they slowly canvassed the trees. Steve split off from them occasionally, but Tom kept Tina close. In just a few short hours, he'd begun to rely heavily on what Tina knew about her missing friend. People wandered off in the woods fairly regularly up here. Unless they were dealing with a small child, it usually took a twenty-four-hour disappearance to warrant a search party.

"Just like last time?" Steve asked. Even a hardened cop like Tom, a total stranger, could hear the desperate note of hope in the other man's voice. Hope that Jolene had wandered off in a feverish delirium and they'd find her any minute, bedded down in leaves.

"No," Tina said. "We got her right home and into the shower," she said. "Back then we hid out until we dried so we wouldn't get in trouble."

"And this morning? Was she well?"

"Not even a sneeze."

Tom had already gathered that the two women had

been up at the cabin alone—a celebration of twenty-five years of friendship. But he wasn't sure why the Boulder high school principal had been so far from home—and just twenty minutes away.

AROUND DINNERTIME, when her feet had grown as numb as her emotions, Tina's heart suddenly stopped and then picked up at breakneck speed. "Look, that's Jo's!" she said, grabbing at the small piece of clear plastic that she'd almost stepped on. Only half an inch long, maybe an eighth of an inch wide…

"Don't touch it!" Tom said before she could pick it up. He pulled a clean handkerchief out of his pocket, collected the minute piece of plastic and put it in a plastic bag. That done, he held it up to the light, glanced at Steve—and then looked at Tina.

"What do you think this is?" he asked her, doubt clear in his voice in case she'd missed the skepticism on his face.

Tina took a quick peek at Steve. His eyes held the same near-pity the sheriff had just bestowed on her.

"It's that little plastic piece that goes on the end of a shoelace," she said without wavering. *Oh, ye of little faith.* "I can't believe I saw it," she said, although she'd known that if she studied the ground hard enough, covered all of it, eventually she'd find a sign from her friend. That she'd been there, in that place. That she was alive.

She stared at the contents of the bag, barely perceptible in the fading light. "The leaves shifted right as I was walking by and the sun glinted off the edge of the plastic." She was talking too fast. And couldn't stop herself. "When we were kids, playing the trail game,

Jolene used to come up with the most bizarre things to leave behind. She talked one time about stepping on her shoelace, leaving part of it behind, because if you were in trouble and a captor had your hands tied and was watching you, you'd still be able to step…"

Her voice trailed off as she heard her own words.

A captor.

Something bad had happened to Jolene. Someone bad.

Tina would have fallen to the ground if male arms hadn't slid around her from either side, holding her up.

She supposed that the two men carried her down the hill as well. She didn't remember much after that.

CHAPTER EIGHT

SOME TIME LONG AFTER DARK, Tina woke from a restless and confused sleep to dim light from the kitchen shining through the door of the enclosed porch. Tom Hunter must still be there. The old alarm clock with glow-in-the-dark markings by Jolene's suitcase showed that it was after two. She'd taken a sleeping pill around ten but had been awake as much or more than she'd slept. And every time she regained consciousness, the feeling of dread and loss was heavy within her. Her first thought now was of the sheriff. In her mind he'd become the only hope of seeing Jolene again.

Throwing off the covers she sat up, taking a minute to let the dizziness subside. She'd showered earlier, while Tom and Steve organized a formal search to begin as soon as dawn broke, and was still wearing the sweats she'd put on then, wanting to be dressed just in case.

No one was talking in the other room. Had Tom left? When was he coming back? Was Steve asleep? He'd collected his stuff from the motel in town and was staying at the cabin with her. Had they left the light on for Jolene?

Had they heard something and not woken her as they'd promised they would?

Torn between hugging Jolene's possessions to her chest and avoiding them altogether, Tina walked quietly to the door, just to make sure there wasn't something going on that she should know about. Then she'd lie back down, make herself sleep.

They hadn't called Jolene's parents yet. There was nothing they could do at this point, and as Jolene's father had just had open-heart surgery the year before, they didn't want to worry him unless they had to.

Only the light over the stove was on, giving the kitchen a lonely glow amid the shadows. The counters, canisters and bread storage bin, the paper towels and the coffeepot were all just vague shapes in the dimness.

Steve was awake, his short sandy hair mussed. Still dressed in the jeans and long-sleeved T-shirt he'd had on that afternoon, he was sitting at the table, forearms resting on the scarred wood, staring down at his thumbs, rubbing them back and forth in a repetitive, mindless motion. Tears were falling slowly down his cheeks.

Seeing the depth of his pain, Tina found a strange kind of strength—enough to propel her to him and, when he stood, to put her arms around him and hold on. She was trying to give him something she didn't have, and needing from him something he could never give her, but she held on anyway. There didn't seem to be anything else to do.

"Where's Tom?"

"Home. Sleeping."

Steve knew he should let go of Tina, but he held her for a moment longer.

"Talk to me, Tina." It was late—after three in the morning. They needed rest. He stood by the long wooden table in a cabin he'd visited a dozen times or more, searching for answers that weren't there.

"I don't know what to say," Tina told him, pulling away. She ran a hand through her hair. "I've been over yesterday morning a million times. I keep thinking I must be missing some important fact. Some clue. But no matter how many times I replay everything, I don't see anything."

"I need to talk or risk going insane with the scenarios my mind keeps inventing. Where is she right now?" Steve sat down and glanced over at Tina, her sleep-tousled hair, makeup-free skin, the pain shining in her eyes, and felt tears fill his own eyes again. "What's happening to her?" He said aloud the question that was torturing him.

How did a man sit calmly at a table while God knows who was doing God knows what to the woman he loved?

"You can't think like that," Tina said, joining him at the table. "I know it's hard, but we just can't. She has to be okay. I have no idea where or how, but she *has* to be okay. Until we know differently, that's what we believe."

There was no factual basis for her statements, but Steve nodded anyway. He needed the hope.

"So…" Tina said, looking at him and then away.

"So…" he repeated. There was so much he wanted to ask her. And yet, nothing he could say.

"She loves you."

Steve slid down in his chair, resting his head along its back edge. God, what a mess his life had become. Where had he been? Why hadn't he seen?

"Tell me something, Tina."

With an elbow on the table, Tina rested her head against the palm of her hand. "What?"

"Do you think she ran away? That she left of her own accord?"

He knew what she'd told the sheriff the previous morning. Had it been the truth?

"Absolutely not."

"I saw the box there."

"I'm pretty sure she doesn't know the result, because the stick was facing backward in the cup. But she was prepared. Either way."

Relief flooded through him. He'd been so afraid she'd run because he'd forced her to face a situation she didn't feel ready to face. He could be so damned pushy sometimes. He tried to temper his reactions, not get ahead of himself, but sometimes it was too difficult to sit back and wait. Sometimes, because he was driven to move on, he forgot.

"I know the result." Tina's words were like a shotgun blast in the darkened room.

"I don't want to know," Steve said immediately, before she said too much. "Not without Jolene." They'd tried for a baby together, and they'd deal with the result together, too.

Tina's lips curved upward just slightly at his reply. Nothing close to a smile, but he seemed to have pleased her somehow. She sat up.

"What if you had to choose—Jolene or a child of your own. Which would it be?"

Steve frowned. *What ifs* were beyond him at the moment. "I can't have a child of my own without her." He stated the obvious.

"She thinks you can. With someone else."

Steve leaned forward until his eyes were level with hers, staring her straight in the face. "Jolene is my life," he said. "I want us to have a family, yes, but without her, that's a moot point to me. She is the breath in my life. She's that vital."

Tina blinked, and blinked again. Her lips turned down and her chin stiffened. When tears appeared, she quickly wiped them away.

"Do you know that every single month, when she has a period, she hates herself for her inability to give you what you so desperately need?" she asked softly, her voice thick. "The weight of the responsibility she feels for disappointing you has become so heavy it's crushing her. Do you have any idea how much her heart breaks every single month when she sees that she'll have to hurt you again?"

He couldn't believe it. That wasn't how it had been at all. It wasn't even close. Steve shook his head.

Jolene hadn't disappointed him. Ever. Most of the time he wondered what he'd done to deserve her, to be the lucky man she'd chosen, above all others, to share her innermost thoughts with, her moments of playfulness, her insights, her inadvertent spurts of ridiculous humor, her gorgeous body.

How could he have put that kind of pressure on her and not even known he was doing it?

"She's not hurting me," he said softly. "Seeing Jolene, talking to her, is what I most look forward to each day."

"Then why have you been spending so much time apart from her?"

Good question. Hard to answer.

"Seemed easier." *Cheap, Chambers, really cheap.*

Tina's raised eyebrows compelled him to say more.

"Sometimes it felt as though she was withdrawing—emotionally." Words were difficult; Steve wasn't in the habit of explaining himself. Even *to* himself—when it came to matters of the heart. If he became aware of them, he worked more, filled up waking hours with distractions that moved him forward.

"So you withdrew, too?" Tina was frowning at him.

"I figured the less time we had together, the more that time would mean. To both of us."

Or something of the sort. He'd never actually formulated the concept.

"I want children," he said, his eyes once again meeting Tina's. "But I can live without them. I can't live without Jolene."

Tina's gaze changed, clouding with fear and he knew what she was thinking. That he might not have a choice about living without Jolene.

She had to be wrong.

"REGION FIVE reporting in...nothing..."

Tina took another step up the hill, and another deep breath, as the radio at Tom Hunter's belt crackled yet another negative response. The search had been on for more than two hours, and so far there wasn't even a hint that Jolene had been anywhere in the vicinity.

She'd paired up with Tom, and the two of them had spent the early hours of the morning scouring the area where Tina had found the shoelace tip the day before.

"I'm sure she must have left another sign on the trail," she said again, scared to death that Tom was going to give up on her—on Jolene.

Tom, who'd started the morning optimistically, sent her a quick glance that could have conveyed anything from pity to impatience.

Peering up into the mountains, he started off.

"Where are you going?"

"It's a long shot," he called over his shoulder, "but I'm going to O'Reilly's place."

Tina sped up, slipping in the leaves as she hurried after him. "Who's O'Reilly? We've been roaming these hills all our lives, Tom. There's no one up there."

"Benton O'Reilly grew up on a remote farm about five miles from here." Tom didn't even sound winded as his long legs took the hills as easily as if they were city sidewalks. In full uniform he looked out of place in the woods. Or maybe he just made Tina uncomfortable because she'd never, in a million lifetimes, thought she'd be climbing these hills with a cop—searching for Jolene.

"He went away to college after World War Two but I'm not sure he graduated. He spent five years trying to educate the public about the degradation of the environment. Very few people were ready to listen. Word is, he eventually grew disillusioned and returned home to Colorado in disgust. He bought some land from the state during an auction some forty years ago. It's up here, on the remotest part of the mountain."

Tom glanced back at her as he spoke, as though to see if she was still with him. He needn't have worried. Until they found Jolene, she was going to match him step for step. Even without any sleep.

"He lives up here?" she asked. "In what?"

"He carved a cave of sorts out of the side of the mountain, then built quite a nice cabin by himself, from logs that he sawed manually. He's been here ever since, logging his land and ignoring a world that's slowly killing itself. Most of the locals know him by sight, but few have spoken with him."

"We've never seen or heard of him."

"Well, he definitely exists—no mistake about that," Tom told her, veering off to the right, further and further from the cabin. As kids, she and Jolene had never been permitted to wander this far away—or any distance further than the sound of their fathers' car horns—and as adults, they'd only revisited their childhood haunts.

And then it hit her.

"You think he's *got* her?"

Oh, God. A man who'd been outside society for more than forty years? Tina started to feel nauseous. And cold.

"No," Tom said, digging his foot into a sand pile for leverage as they came to a six-foot wall of mountain that was almost straight up. For every step he climbed, he turned and took Tina's hand, to help her up behind him. "O'Reilly's a gentle, if disillusioned, guy who just wants to be left alone. Our best hope is that your friend stumbled onto his place and he's keeping her safe until help arrives, or until he can go for help."

He pulled her up to more level ground, then released her hand. Tina wished he'd held on. "You think she's hurt then?"

He stopped, shook his head. "I don't think anything," he told her, his expression dead serious. "In my job, committing myself to any one way of thinking means closing my mind to other solutions."

Tina nodded, stayed half a foot behind him as they

started up again. She'd much rather he'd told her that in his job he saw this kind of thing often and that it always turned out just fine. Or even that it sometimes did.

THE OLD GUY WAS much as she expected after what Tom had said. Soft-spoken, gentle, with stooped shoulders beneath thin, long gray hair and a beard that reached down to his chest.

"I haven't seen a woman such as you describe," he told the sheriff outside the open door of his cabin. After a thorough once-over when O'Reilly had first come outside to the sheriff's call, the man had not looked at Tina again, but spoke directly to Tom.

"Were you out yesterday?" Tom asked.

"Yes, sir." The man nodded, pointing to a large flat-bed wagon on the side of the yard, half-filled with freshly cut logs. "I'm working the south forty this month."

The southern forty acres of his land, Tina surmised, based on the earlier conversation with Tom.

"Did you notice anything amiss?"

O'Reilly shook his head. The man's overalls and flannel shirt were clean, though worn almost colorless.

Though she kept trying to get a good look inside the cabin, Tina could only see the first few feet of wooden floor. There were no windows—being built into the mountain precluded them anywhere but the front—and the place couldn't be more than one room. A wooden bookshelf stood along the wall she could see and seemed to be overflowing with tome-size books and manuals.

"No gunshots? Screams? Nothing?"

The weight inside Tina increased when she heard

Tom's words. Wouldn't *she* have heard Jolene's scream? Had there been one?

"You mind if I take a look inside?" Tom asked after the other man once again shook his head.

O'Reilly winced. "I wish you wouldn't."

"I know we agreed I'd check in once a month and never trespass in the cabin, but these are extenuating circumstances, Benton."

"You doubting me, Sheriff?"

"Not at all, just doing my job. Surely you wouldn't expect me not to?"

O'Reilly gave Tom a long stare. "I suppose not." He sounded resigned. Bowing his head, he said, "Come in. But not her." He didn't even glance at Tina. "And wipe your shoes."

When Tom complied and disappeared inside, Tina stood in the yard, wishing they could just get out of there and continue searching.

It didn't take long for the two men to return, Tom standing tall with his steady and sure gait and O'Reilly, several inches shorter, beside him, shuffling like a man who wasn't confident of much anymore.

"…what would be your guess?" She caught the tail end of the sheriff's question.

"That she's unhappy with her life as it's being lived and sought the opportunity for a clean and utterly complete escape."

Tom stopped a couple of feet outside the door, and Tina joined him. "Why do it right then?" he asked with narrowed eyes. "Why here? Why not just drive off into the sunset?"

"You'd trace a car in a second," O'Reilly said. "But out here? It's hard to search and nothing to fingerprint.

And there's as much chance of natural danger as anything else." He nodded once, as though pleased by his explanation.

Tina didn't much like O'Reilly.

CHAPTER NINE

ABOUT A QUARTER OF A MILE down from O'Reilly's place, Tina stopped. Dizzy with fatigue and shock, she needed a moment to register the tiny piece of dirty tissue lying on a leaf, off to her left.

"Tom! Here!" she cried. She wasn't imagining this. She wasn't. Reaching for the tissue, Tina laughed, choked back a sob. "She's been here!"

"Don't!" Tom yelled sharply when she would have picked up the blessed little piece of paper. Leaves crunched beneath his feet as he strode to her side, crouching down with his little plastic bag to store the tissue.

And when he held it up, he frowned. "This isn't tissue," he told her. "It's a piece of web from tent caterpillars. It's been knocked loose. Look." He pointed above them, to the off-white substance growing in the V between the branches of a huge tree. Though most of it was firmly attached, a corner of it had pulled loose and was moving slightly in the breeze.

"It's tissue from her pocket," Tina insisted, but staring at that little bag, she wasn't sure. It *could* be a piece of tree disease. Or, for that matter, a sun-bleached piece of leaf. Or the top layer of skin from a mushroom.

Tom's silence scared her. She couldn't look at him.

And then she did. He was staring right back at her, his brown eyes warmer than she'd seen them. Tina recognized that expression. And hated it. She didn't ever want to see it directed at her again.

"Don't pity me." The words were sharp out of necessity. Sharpness would kill softness before softness could kill her.

"I can't tell you what you want to hear."

She didn't like his honesty any better.

"You think she's dead, don't you?" Tina whispered, the words scraping her throat.

Tom studied the sky for a moment, then gazed somewhere over Tina's shoulder. He slid his hands in his pockets, shrugged. "I don't think she's okay."

She took a step back. Meant to take another, but her feet weren't steady on the rough earth, her knees weren't strong. Tina had no intention of falling against this man, any man, didn't even know she had until her head hit his chest.

His arms came up around her shoulders. She didn't want them there. It was wrong and dangerous for her to lean against him—against anyone. Dangerous to need anyone. Perilous to her future.

"Shh, everything's okay." She barely heard the words at first. And when she did, they made her cry harder for their delusiveness. He didn't think everything was okay at all.

"I lost my husband." She couldn't believe she was saying the words. She didn't speak of Thad to anyone—except Jolene. It was the number-one unwritten rule of her life. "I lost my s-s-son." She expanded on her error. "I can't lose Jolene, too. I just *can't*."

It was something Tina knew from the bottom of her

heart. If Jolene didn't survive this, Tina wasn't going to survive, either. They were *best friends,* not meant to live in this world one without the other.

That knowledge had been present the day they'd first met. It had been the glue that kept them together through the separation years in their teens and brought them back together for college. It had been the strength that had seen her through Thad and Thad Jr.'s deaths.

It wasn't debatable.

TOM HUNTER DIDN'T LIKE unanswered questions. He didn't like disappearances without explanations. And he didn't like hearing Tina Randolph cry. Tears didn't usually bother him. He'd heard enough of them during his marriage to make him pretty much immune.

He got quite a few of them on the job, too. From teen-agers who'd been caught speeding, doing drugs, being out after curfew, teenagers who knew there was going to be hell to pay. And from the families of accident victims.

But nothing compared to the wrenching of his gut as he held one very strong woman in his arms and heard her let go of an anguish that was too big for her to bear.

Because he didn't know what else to do, didn't feel there was any other choice, he held her close. Something about his life was changing in that instant. Something he didn't particularly want to have changed. Still, he was as powerless to stop this event as he was to find Tina's best friend. He was missing something but had no idea what.

He stroked her short, honey hair. Rubbed his hand lightly over the sweatshirt covering her back. He bore all her weight. And thought over the meager clues he had to help her.

Two small plastic bags. One he'd turned in to the lab late last night with a tiny unidentifiable piece of plastic. And the other one was in his pocket. He swore silently. How the hell did a man pull a miracle out of a tiny unidentifiable piece of plastic and a—

"It's ironic, you know," Tina said, her voice muted against his chest. "Jo and I have been acting like scaredy-cats the whole time we've been up here, getting spooked by things that never bothered us before. We were berating ourselves for being scared and letting it interfere with our lives—and then this happens."

Tom's cop instincts were screaming. But he couldn't turn down the noise enough to know what they were telling him.

"What kind of things spooked you?" he asked Tina, all the while searching his mind for the clue he felt was there.

She talked about squirrels, Steve's knock on the door… "And the other day, when we got back from the hills, there'd been someone at the cabin. Jo noticed that a towel had been moved from the pump outside the back door. It didn't take us long to get over that one, though," she said. "Jolene figured out Steve had been there and—"

"Wait!" He pushed Tina away so abruptly he barely had time to catch her shoulders before she fell.

"What?"

"You heard rustling in the leaves, sounds that didn't blend in like the rustling you've been hearing all your lives…."

"We decided we're just wimps now," Tina explained,

her head against him. "We've grown up and discovered that we're not invincible," she was saying.

"And someone was at the cabin...."

"Yes. Steve."

"He told me this morning that he hadn't been to the cabin since the afternoon you two came in from the hills and found him waiting there."

"Tom?" She stared up at him, her fingers clawing into his back. "You think someone's got her?"

And just like that, it all fell into place. "O'Reilly!" Tom blurted. "He could've been up in the hills, watching you."

"But we just talked to him. You were even in his house...."

Adrenaline flowed through Tom. "What you said, about the pump..."

"What?"

"O'Reilly's a stickler for order. Everything in its place. There wasn't so much as a dish out of order. The washrag was hanging neatly on the pump by the sink, perfectly folded. I asked if I could wash my hands, and he was meticulous about refolding it when I was through."

"I'm not sure I'm following you," Tina said, her voice uneven.

"Like I said, I know he's obsessive about order, down to the smallest thing, like his washrag. But I realize now that something was off."

"What?"

"There's a well beside O'Reilly's cabin—it serves his pump. Its cover is made of sawed-off two-by-fours covered with roofing shingle, and it sits snugly in a four-by-six cement hole in the ground."

"And?" Tina asked. Her eyes, rimmed by lashes still wet from her tears, were studying him intently.

"It was askew today. I've been visiting Benton O'Reilly since I took office three years ago. I've never seen that cover anything but snug."

Taking another step back, Tina frowned, her eyes dark with concentration. "So there's something about his well. I'm not following you."

Tom's mind was racing. If it *was* tissue in his pocket, if Jolene Chambers *had* been this close to O'Reilly's place, he had to get back there. There was no way anyone would get this close without the old man's knowing about it. Which would mean he'd lied....

He had to call for backup.

"There's a six-by-six-foot cement crawl space between the cover and the well itself," he told Tina.

"Six by six..." Tina's shoulders straightened. "Big enough for a person..."

Or a body.

Pulling the radio out of his pocket, Tom issued a string of orders.

"I KNEW YOU'D be back, Sheriff."

Benton O'Reilly sat on the front porch of his log cabin, protected by the mountain into which his home was built and by a series of log supports between him and anyone who could be out there in the woods, pointing a gun in his direction. He was rocking in a double-size chair he'd carved himself. Across his lap lay a rifle that Tom would bet was loaded and cocked. He'd underestimated the old man.

The well cover had been moved again. It was securely in place.

Tom stopped half a dozen yards away, a signal to those behind him to spread out through the woods around the cabin. Steve Chambers, several of his deputies and Tina Randolph were out there, unseen. With his eye on that rifle, he kicked himself for allowing Tina to come up the hill with them. Not that she'd have stayed behind, no matter what he said.

Keep back like I told you, he willed, mentally measuring the distance between O'Reilly and the well.

"I'm going to have to kill you now," O'Reilly said without emotion. "And I'm sorry about that because I like you, Sheriff."

"I like you, too, O'Reilly."

The old man nodded, one hand on the barrel of his rifle, the other on the trigger. "I know."

There wasn't any stress to calm, anger to pacify or panic to assuage—no obvious way to disarm the situation. O'Reilly lived in his own world, under his own law, and Tom had entered that world.

He could let the old man take him. His men would get to the well, save Jolene Chambers. Or her body.

"You have the woman." O'Reilly didn't seem averse to conversation—more time for Tom's men to get into position.

"I saved her from a misery worse than death."

He'd killed her. *God, please don't let Tina be in hearing range.*

Tom caught a glimpse of beige moving up the mountain over the roof of the cabin. "Why?"

"She's my angel," O'Reilly said as though stating the obvious. "For twenty-five years she's been showering these hills with her angel dust."

Tom slowed his breath, focusing on his subject.

Benton O'Reilly was far more deranged than he'd supposed. Was there a way to work that in his favor? Could he get everyone out of there without any more bloodshed?

"You've been watching her for twenty-five years?" he asked.

"About that," O'Reilly said, a distant smile on his face as he slowly rocked.

"But you never spoke to her."

"Didn't need to. She and her friend spread their joy all by themselves."

"So what changed?"

"She lost her joy." The rocker stopped abruptly. "Your world is a doomed place, Sheriff. The pollutants, the population, the noise—it's bringing the earth closer and closer to hell and destruction. Eventually it sucks all beauty out of everyone who lives in it."

The man stood, his mountain home at his back, positioning himself carefully beside a log support column. Slowly, raising his rifle deliberately, he aimed it straight at Tom's chest. A quick vision of his ex-wife came to mind. She'd feared this moment during their entire marriage. At least she was free of him now and would be spared.

"You won't get away with this," he said, though not for any reason other than that he was still alive and *could* say it. His men were in place. They'd get to the well—or to O'Reilly.

He'd been prepared to die since signing on with the sheriff's department at eighteen, but he hadn't expected it to happen.

"A hundred people know where I am. They'll come for you."

O'Reilly scowled. "They won't find me." He sounded certain of that.

Tom took a step forward. "Are you willing to take that chance?" he asked. "If you shoot me, and they do find you, you'll be in prison for the rest of your life. You can't do that to yourself, Benton. Being locked up would be a hell worse than death for you. Nothing is worth that."

The man tightened his grip on the rifle. "They won't find me," he repeated.

Tom took another step forward. "Give it up, Benton. I'm going to get the woman, one way or the other."

"Won't do you no good."

She was dead then.

Tom stood still, his mind whirling. Was he willing to die to recover a body?

O'Reilly could be bluffing. What if the woman in that well was alive?

Even if she wasn't, he couldn't walk away and let a murderer go free.

He moved forward again. One more step. Holding his breath against the possibility of a loud crack in his ears, searing pain in his chest. Better him than Steve Chambers, who was on the periphery of the woods, waiting.

"Let's make a deal," he said, having completed the step and finding himself still alive. "I can ensure that you're taken care of."

"No deals."

"What then, Benton? What can I do to save my life?"

The man didn't want to kill him or he'd already have done so. But that didn't mean he wouldn't.

"That's the damnable thing, Sheriff," he said, the rifle moving slightly as if to punctuate his words. "There's nothing. I'm going to shoot you. And anyone else who gets close to this cabin. No one can get behind me. I don't care if there are ten or a hundred of 'em, I'll take them down, one by one."

"What if they storm the porch?" Tom asked, lifting his right foot only enough to push it slightly forward.

"They'll blow up."

Tom froze. Glancing down, he noticed the small ridge in the sand surrounding the porch. It hadn't been there two hours before. The old man had his place wired.

I'll be damned.

Tina Randolph was out there in the woods. Her short blond hair would be lifted by the slight breeze. Her sweatshirt would be bundled beneath her ribs where she had her arms wrapped around herself. He would've liked to ask her out.

"You'll blow up your mountain."

Another step closer, longer, faster, staring at the barrel of the rifle. It jerked and Tom's heart skipped. But there was no blast. No burning in his flesh. Not yet.

Only a couple of yards away now, he started breathing again.

"Nope. Individual detonators, like land mines. They're set to blow to the south."

His direction.

O'Reilly bent down to the scope. And the tip of the rifle pushed outward, just over to Tom's side of the lethal ridge in the dirt.

Without thought, he crouched, darted, grabbed for the barrel. A woman screamed. He heard the deafening crack of a fired bullet. A sharp push against his arm. Another shot.

Benton O'Reilly fell to the ground.

And Tom was still standing.

CHAPTER TEN

TINA HADN'T MEANT to scream. Hadn't realized the in-
human sound came from her until it was all over and
her throat was burning and raw. Seeing the blood
staining the upper sleeve of Tom's beige work shirt,
she ran forward from the edge of the clearing just as
Benton O'Reilly fell to the ground. He'd been shot
by a deputy .who'd come into the clearing right behind Tom during the single second Tina's scream had
distracted O'Reilly's attention from killing Tom
Hunter.

The plan had been in place all along. Hunter was
going to sacrifice himself to allow a second man behind
him—in the one corner of the yard they'd have the shot
at O'Reilly—to take out the old man. In the end, Tina
couldn't stand to see it happen.

"The well!" Tom hollered, as Tina reached the yard.
She turned and ran with the rest to the six-by-six-foot
lid. Steve ran up beside her, sliding an arm around her
waist as they watched a deputy lift the lid.

"I see something!" The deputy's voice was lost as he
disappeared into the hole, with Tom right behind him.

Steve was shaking. Tears streaming down her face,
Tina held onto him, willing them both to remain standing no matter what they saw.

"She's alive!" The shout came up from the darkened hole long minutes later.

Tina was seeing stars as she felt Steve falter beside her and stumbled, too. "She's going to be okay," she said through the darkness. She regained her balance and her eyes once again focused on the hole at their feet.

There'd been no sound from Jolene yet.

"She's alive," Steve said with strength in spite of the shakiness of his voice. "Anything else we can deal with."

He was right. And still, as they heard the murmuring from below, watched as the law officials' shirts moved in and out of view, Steve's words conjured up horrible pictures in Tina's mind.

Would she be naked? Bleeding? Bones twisted and broken? Raped?

Would her spirit be able to recover?

Please let her be okay, Tina prayed. They'd get her through this. No matter what he'd done to her.

"We're bringing her up." Tina couldn't tell a thing from Tom's voice. She knelt with Steve, ready to help pull Jolene up from her grave.

The tennis shoes appeared first, still on her feet. Tina grabbed one while Steve took the other. A deputy slid his arms around the jeans that appeared next, taking hold of Jolene's calf. She wasn't moving.

Her thighs were lifted up. Steve was there, beneath her hips, supporting his wife's weight gently as they raised her upper body in the sweatshirt she'd been wearing yesterday, through the hole. Tina began to cry again at the first glimpse of Jolene's beautiful long hair, now dirty and mussed.

And then they saw her face. Smudged. Pale. But

unbruised. Her eyes fluttered open briefly. She blinked, squinted at Steve, at Tina, before her lids drifted slowly shut.

"I knew you'd come." Her whisper was hoarse.

But it was Jolene.

She'd come back to them.

AN HOUR AND A HALF after they'd pulled her up from the ground, Jolene started to feel like herself again. An emergency medical team had checked her over—blood pressure normal, heart rate strong, pupils dilating properly. No signs of dehydration.

"He didn't hurt me," she told the female officer across the table from her. She'd insisted she was well enough to go straight to the police station, compelled to get this over with so she could go home.

Home.

The cabin. Boulder. Roanoke. It didn't matter. Steve mattered. And Tina. She'd had a lot of time to ponder life during her time with O'Reilly. Two days, they'd told her. It felt like seven.

"Your arms are bruised," the woman said, pen poised over her report.

So were her legs and ankles, but no one had seen those yet.

"I'd just finished, uh, filling the cup and I was fastening the button on my jeans when he grabbed me, covering my mouth." She took a moment to catch her breath. "I fought him, but he dragged me over the next hill. He tied me up. Carried me up the mountain and lowered me into the well. For the next two days, he just kept coming down there, sitting on a little stool, staring at me."

She couldn't help the shudder that passed through her. Steve's warm hand on her back moved, rubbing gently. Tina squeezed her hand. Her friend had been holding it since they first sat down. Jolene didn't ever want her to let go. That time alone in the hole, mostly in complete darkness, unable to differentiate between night and day, she'd known she had to survive. She and Tina were a pair. That wasn't how it was supposed to end. Not until they were both old and gray. Not until they'd supported each other through every stage of life.

"He fed you regularly?" the officer asked. Jolene had already told her story; the woman was just going over the report, verifying facts, though with O'Reilly dead, Jolene didn't know what difference any of this made.

"I lost track of time pretty early on." Jolene repeated what she'd told Tom Hunter earlier, before the sheriff had disappeared to have the wound on his upper arm tended to.

She hoped he came back. She hadn't had a chance to thank him yet.

"I just know I never went hungry. But if I never see another peanut butter and jelly sandwich in my life, it'll be too soon."

He'd given her water, too. Lukewarm. He'd held the glass rather than untying her. He wasn't good at it. Kept tipping it too fast. The water had dripped off her chin and down to her chest, dampening her sweatshirt every time.

He'd had her pee in a pot. He'd pulled down her pants, waited for her to finish and then pulled them back up. Panic rose to the surface again at the thought and she concentrated on Steve's touch, Tina's hand. She was safe. Honored. Respected.

O'Reilly was dead. Tina had seen him on the ground. That was enough. It was over.

"TINA?"

Spinning around, Tina saw Tom Hunter standing in the doorway of an office at the other end of the station. He'd changed shirts. Beneath his sleeve his left arm was bulky, probably from bandaging. His arm was in a sling.

"You're back!" She was about to return to the interrogation room from a trip to the vending machine to get Jolene the diet soda she was craving. They were almost through in there. "What did the doctor say?"

"That three stitches wasn't much for a gunshot wound." Tom's half grin made Tina smile. "Thanks to you, the bullet barely grazed me."

She wondered if she should apologize for breaking his rules and coming closer to the yard. "I wasn't supposed to be there."

"I have my life because you were."

Well, good, then. She didn't know what to say, felt stupid standing there grinning, even stupider because she *wanted* to stand there grinning. And talking to him.

"I have to get back," she said, holding up the can of soda. "Jolene's having a caffeine attack."

It was more a case of Tina doing everything in her power, as quickly as possible, to reintroduce Jolene to all the normal and loved things of her life.

Tom nodded. Turned, as if to go back to the office from which he'd come, stopped. "You leaving soon?"

"My flight back to Roanoke isn't until next Monday."

"How about dinner one night before you go?"

She backed up, trying to keep her smile intact. "I'd

like to, but…really…I don't have any idea what's going on with them, what we'll be doing. But…I'll let you know."

Tom nodded, said something she couldn't quite hear as she fled. He'd accepted her prevarication kindly. So why wasn't she relieved about that? Why did she almost wish he'd pushed?

Jolene was standing as Tina pushed through the door. All thought of Tom Hunter fled. Her best friend was back. And based on the facts they'd heard so far about Jolene's experience, based on the shadows lurking in her friend's exhausted eyes, that was where Tina's heart needed to be.

IT WAS ONLY THREE IN the afternoon by the time Steve pulled up to the cabin, with his wife beside him and Tina in the back. Seemed like days had passed since just before dawn that morning, when the small place had been crowded with searchers gathered to receive instructions. Of course, he was going on almost no sleep in close to forty-eight hours. Not that he felt ready for sleep. Not yet, anyway.

"You hungry?" Tina asked Jolene as the three of them walked into the cabin.

Jolene dropped onto a kitchen chair, subdued but not devastated. After doing a mental check of her color and the dilation of her pupils, as explained by the doctor who'd climbed the mountain and been waiting in the woods not far from O'Reilly's place to tend to Jolene, Steve sat down beside her. He couldn't relax yet. Wasn't sure he'd ever be able to completely relax again.

"I could use something," he said now. "You got any of that casserole from the other night?" His gaze never left Jolene.

"Sure." Tina hurried to the refrigerator, busying herself with preparations.

Jolene hadn't answered. She hadn't said much of anything, other than one- or two-word answers to questions since they'd driven from the station.

"You okay, hon?" he asked.

She smiled at him. Nodded. "Just feel…odd," she said. "Like I don't know who I am or where I belong."

"Disorientation," Tina said, her voice strong, matter-of-fact. Reassuring. "It's to be expected."

Jolene smiled at her friend. "I guess we should have a toast, huh?" she asked. "To my safe return. I brought a bottle of champagne up with me." She made to rise from the table.

"Stay put," Tina told her. "I'll get you some soda. I don't think champagne's such a good idea."

Steve wasn't so sure about that. He'd welcome some help relaxing and imagined his wife could use the same. Soon…

"Jo?" he began. "I suspect now isn't the best time— and yet maybe, so you know where you're heading, there's no better time…."

"What?" He hated the fear in her eyes. Especially now.

Steve glanced at Tina, saw her nod, and continued.

"I've learned some things during the past forty-eight hours." Dishes rattled on the counter. Water ran. The oven opened and closed. Jolene's eyes were weary, guarded as she watched him.

"I thought we were in the baby thing together," he told her. "That your disappointment and mine were the same, that we shared it equally." How did a man go about undoing this kind of damage?

"I had no idea that my disappointment was putting pressure on you."

There was no change in her expression as she stared at him. His entire future depended on these moments. The thought that he might be too late weighed heavily.

Taking Jolene's hand, Steve leaned against the table. "I love you, Jo. Even if I spend the rest of my life completely alone, I'll still have had all the family I'll ever need in having shared a home, a life, with you."

She blinked. Nodded. Swallowed. He waited, but that was all there was.

"I want a baby, but only because I want a part of you and me joined together, a blood tie between the two of us. If we can't, then *that's* our tie, the loss of something we both want. That's what we'd share. And it'll bring us every bit as close as raising a baby together would have done."

"When Tina and I were about nine we became blood sisters." Jolene's words seemed to come from deep inside her. She was speaking slowly, almost as though she was in a trance, yet her eyes seemed to focus on him completely.

Tina had stopped moving. She was looking at Jolene, her eyes moist.

"We pricked our fingers and smeared them together until neither of us could tell whose blood was whose. I swore I could *feel* when her blood entered my body."

Tina turned back to the sink.

"Do you understand?" Jolene asked him.

God, he hoped so. "What you and Tina shared, even back then, was thicker than blood," he said, her gorgeous brown eyes guiding him. "The ritual was a promise made, but it was the love you have for each other that gave the promise life."

Jolene nodded. And watched him.

"You married me," he told her. "That was our ritual."

"Yes."

"We don't need a baby, or a prick of the finger, to bring us any closer. To make us more than we already are."

"Yes."

Steve took a long breath, let it out. Did it again, and with the exhalation released a tension he seemed to have been holding most of his life.

"God, I love you," he said when he could.

"Oh, Steve…" Jolene tumbled from her chair into his lap, burying her face against him. The sobs that tore through her were painful to hear, filled with an anguish he suspected he was only just beginning to understand. She'd have to talk about it all eventually—the past years living with the pressure of feeling she wasn't enough, and the past days locked in a grave with a madman. And Steve would have to listen to it all, let his love show her how precious she was.

And he'd have help. Glancing toward the sink and the woman who'd not only saved lives that morning, but who'd just saved his, he frowned. Tina was gone.

"TINA GORDON RANDOLPH, come out here right now!" Jolene wasn't sure how long she'd cried in her husband's arms, she only knew, when the sobs finally subsided, she felt better than she had in years. Until she noticed that her friend had disappeared.

"Tina!" she called again when there was no movement in the cabin.

"Tina!" Steve added his voice to her own.

"What!?" Her voice raw with fear, Tina came racing around the corner from the bathroom wearing clean jeans and a white blouse, with a towel draped over her shoulders absorbing the drips from her wet hair.

Jolene grinned. "Nothing," she said, feeling a bit stupid. "I just didn't know where you'd gone. I didn't want you to think you weren't welcome."

"Hey, we're blood, remember?" Tina said, grinning back. "You two have had a rough time, and I needed a shower," she said, joining them at the table. "So, all better now?"

Jolene looked at Steve and then back at Tina. "Better than it's ever been, I think," she said, including both of her best friends in her smile. "You know," she said, growing serious as the effect of the past days and weeks pressed on her heart, "bad as the last forty-eight hours have been, they taught me just how rich I am. I could easily have gone crazy sitting in that hole, unable to see or even hear anything outside my own breathing. Instead, I thought of the two of you constantly." She wasn't going to cry again. She just wasn't. "And I found a sense of humor, Teen, just like you always have through even the worst times. I could hear you making jokes about the hole, telling me I'd do anything for some time off. And Steve, I could hear you telling me that we could make it through anything. I heard you both telling me over and over again how much you loved me. And you know what else?" Still perched on Steve's lap she glanced from one to the other.

"What?" they chorused.

"I had so many memories of times spent with the

two of you that I was never alone, never without a story in my head to keep me focused on life rather than death...."

Tina leaned forward, looping her arms around their necks. "I love you, guys," she said. Three foreheads touching, they were silent for a moment—a perfect moment.

And then Tina kissed each of them on the forehead, stood and headed back to the bathroom.

DINNER WAS a time of laughter as Jolene and Tina sat at the table, regaling Steve with stories from their illustrious past, all things that Jolene had relived in the past two days.

"Sing him the song, Jo," Tina said, fork in hand.

"Only if you sing it with me," Jolene said, tired but not wanting the evening to end.

"We must! We must!" They were screaming more than singing and barely heard the knock at the door.

Jolene glanced at Tina, then at the door. It couldn't be Steve. But they didn't have to worry, either. The two of them sat at the table, still smiling while Steve went to the door.

"The bakery in town told me this was on order for delivery here today...."

Jolene raised her head, startled, when Sheriff Tom Hunter came into the kitchen carrying the twenty-fifth anniversary cake she'd ordered for her and Tina. She'd forgotten all about it.

But why would the sheriff be delivering it?

Jolene didn't have to wonder long. When she looked at Tina, to tell her about the cake, her friend was staring at the handsome officer.

"I was afraid to wait for you to let me know," he was saying to Tina, "in case you didn't."

"I…"

"So what do you say, Tina Randolph? Will you have dinner with me before you go back to Roanoke?"

Tom Hunter was asking Tina for a date? And Tina wasn't immediately shutting him down?

Jolene sat back, grinning again. Was it possible that more good than she'd even known, a real-live miracle, had taken place as a result of her ordeal?

"I don't think I'll be going back to Roanoke," Tina said slowly. The surprises just kept adding up. "At least not permanently. After almost losing Jo…" The smile she sent Jolene was warm and tremulous. "I realized that no job is worth being so far away from the land and home and people I love."

"Does this mean you'll go out to dinner with me?" Her heart jumping with joy at the news she'd just heard, Jolene still had focus enough to hand it to the sheriff. He was persistent. And exactly what Tina needed.

"I think so," Tina said, but her smile was a lot more definite than her words.

"This calls for a toast," Steve said, standing behind Tom Hunter. "Jo, where'd you say that bottle was?"

"Wait!" Tina stood up, crossed to Steve, took his hand and then grabbed Jo's. "I don't think that's a good idea," she said, just as she had before.

There was such an odd look on her friend's face, Jolene frowned. What was wrong?

"The day Jolene disappeared, she took a test," Tina said quickly. "Neither of you have asked about the result."

"Teen?" Jolene looked up at her friend and burst into tears.

"Congratulations, my friends," Tina said, tears in her eyes, as she raised their hands to her lips. "It was positive."

For my parents

WADE IN THE WATER

Margot Early

Dear Reader,

I loved working on the twenty-fifth anniversary project in part because I am the same age as the heroine. It has been fun to look back and remember what was happening twenty-five years ago. For instance, I love making Ryan a *Star Wars* fan. Also, age forty (or so) is a notoriously tumultuous time of life. Parents may be sick or dying, the relationship between husband and wife may change. Equally, the teenage years are harrowing. I would not be fifteen again for any amount of money.

This is the first of my stories to come into print since the death of my father. In the past, as soon as an author copy of my latest book arrived at my parents' house, my father, then my mother, read it immediately. Both of them always encouraged me and praised my writing. My belief is that my father still watches my career, observing, enjoying and cheering me on, through a power stronger than death. This novella is dedicated to him and to my mother with great love.

Sincerely,

Margot Early

CHAPTER ONE

Santa Barbara, California

WHEN SHE WAS UPSET, Lily Moran took her mind off whatever had upset her by trying to prove the Riemann hypothesis. Someday, perhaps, she would solve this or another great unsolved math problem, but she didn't expect to. She simply preferred to put her mind to things that made sense to her. Math made sense. It was *predictable*.

Her ex-fiancé, Drake Norms, who had just left her an appalling phone message on the subject of her "inflexible" and "controlling" personality, had *proven* unpredictable, which was the main reason she'd broken their engagement. Regrettably, his sour grapes attitude was all too predictable, and when the phone rang again, she spent a moment debating whether to stay inside and listen to the message or go out onto her balcony and watch the waves strike the offshore oil rigs. Since a second message from him would no doubt provide further evidence that they shouldn't marry, she stayed inside to hear what other insults he had to direct toward her via the highly controllable medium of her answering machine.

But the number caller ID announced was not

Drake's local 805 number. Rather, it began 218—northern Minnesota.

Her parents.

She stepped toward the phone, not because they were easier to get on with than her ex-fiancé—they weren't—but because she was a good daughter and owed them attentiveness and caring, having caused them the most painful experience any parent can know. She owed them a debt that could never be repaid. Not even a debt. Beyond that. Because of what had happened long ago on Swan Lake in Minnesota's north woods, where her parents still chose to live, she always answered the phone when they called. Those long-ago events had mapped her life; she was in her parents' thrall and stayed that way. Willingly.

It was the least she could do.

It was all she could do.

Though she declined to live with them. Or visit them at the lake. Minnesota had fifteen thousand lakes, but Lily only knew one, and it was *the* lake.

"Hello?"

"Lily?"

Her mother's voice first, then her father's. They asked her about school, if final exams were through, if her grades were in. The questions spun a web of control around her, and within it she grew irritable. She was forty years old, and they still checked up on her, not to applaud her but because they expected her to fail. Philosophy, differential equations and number theory meant little or nothing to them. But if they knew she taught the wildly popular class "Death and Philosophy," that *would* mean something to them, all the wrong things, which was why she'd never told them. She taught at the community college on the mesa overlooking the Santa Barbara Channel. The salary earned her enough to afford rent on this tiny—very tiny—studio half a mile from campus.

"How are you?" Lily asked them. "Ready for the summer season?" Her parents, when they'd decided to live at Swan Lake year round, had bought up property on the western shore of the lake and built several small cabins, which they rented to vacationers from the cities.

"Oh, sure," her father said. "Glad you asked, though."

Why wouldn't she?

"Yes, Lily." Marie Moran paused, and Lily held her breath and wondered why she should feel so apprehensive. "We're really hoping you'll come out this summer—"

"Oh, I—"

"—because we're going to scatter Ryan's ashes in the lake."

She just stopped herself from exclaiming, *You mean you haven't done it yet?*

But of course they hadn't. They would've told her. She used to ask about it, back when she was in high school and once in college. Eventually she'd stopped asking.

This was a parental request she could not refuse. Oh, her therapist would tell her that she could indeed refuse it, just as she often pointed out that Lily *could* choose not to answer when her parents phoned. But Lily's own sense of decency, of minimum things due, would not allow her to deny her parents this one thing.

After all, it was her selfishness that had lost them their only son.

FOR THE NEXT WEEK, the first week of June, she puzzled over how to arrange her life so she could spend as little time as possible at Camp Death—as she tended to caption the place they'd named Camp Boreal. This process, figuring out how to flit in and out of Minnesota without mortally offending her parents, involved many hours trying to prove the Riemann hypothesis. In other words, wishing the other problem, the more difficult life problem, would go away. Lily could say she'd be teaching the summer quarter, but this year that wasn't true. She was editing a textbook. *Number Theory.*

If she let her parents know that, she might be stuck at Camp Death all summer. Sitting on her balcony, using a towel to create a canopy over the screen of her laptop, she reminded herself again to think of the place as Camp Boreal so that she didn't accidentally call it Camp Death in front of her parents or some weekend camper.

Camp Boreal was born the year after Ryan died. It was twenty-five years since his death. *It's time,* her parents had said.

Just about, Lily had thought, then felt guilty for even internally criticizing anything her parents did. They had suffered the loss from which no one can really heal.

And it was her fault.

But I can't think about it, definitely can't dwell on it, or I'll go crazy.

She'd been living with her own guilt since she was fifteen. Her parents had never blamed her. Not in words, at any rate. They'd blamed Colin Gardner. Lily had no idea if he blamed himself, not having seen him or spoken with him for twenty-five years.

She'd been in therapy most of her adult life and had come to certain conclusions.

One: Therapy could not absolve her of her own sense of guilt in Ryan's death.

Two: She could feel compassion for her parents and work toward what she thought would make them happy without actually liking them.

Three: She was under no obligation whatsoever to subvert her experience of losing a brother, of having failed to prevent his death, to her parents' way of dealing with their loss. In other words, she never had to visit Camp Boreal, never had to return to Swan Lake.

Except that now, twenty-five years after the death of their ten-year-old son, Patrick and Marie Moran had decided to scatter Ryan's ashes on Swan Lake. *And Helen's going to come,* they'd added. In the years since Ryan's death, Helen, Lily's perfect—to her parents' mind—cousin had become the daughter the Morans wished they'd had.

Lily had never really figured out how to like Helen—or why her parents did.

It was at such times that she most wished Ryan had lived. She didn't believe for a moment that if he had, her parents would have become sensible or anything less than thoroughly strange. But if he'd lived, she would've had someone to talk to about her dysfunctional family, someone who could understand as only another family member could.

As it was, her parents were united—not against her but rather in some fierce possessiveness and protectiveness and censure toward her.

Yet she had not lived with them since the summer when

she was fifteen, and they had neither protested her choice nor opted to go where she was. What would she have done, Lily had sometimes wondered, if she'd been them?

Her mother's hysteria had taught her, as no later wisdom would, what the loss of a child was to a parent. No later wisdom would teach her because she had chosen never to have children and never to have them in her life—other people's children, for instance—for a whole scope of reasons she could not articulate. Maybe, her therapist had suggested, it was because Lily had witnessed the intensity with which a mother could love her child and had consciously decided never to risk loving—or losing—so much.

Lily had decided to drive to Minnesota. Her therapist had been stunned by this news, saying, *Alone?* That was, of course, the point. Part of the point. The main idea was to be able to escape—from Camp Boreal, from Swan Lake, from her parents.

She called the textbook's contributors to let them know she'd be in Minnesota. They could leave messages on her cell phone. If there was no service at the lake, she could retrieve her messages from her parents' phone, with a calling card. Her car was a used two-year-old BMW she'd gotten cheap from a dealership who couldn't get rid of it fast enough. Lily thought it was a silly car. She was herself a practical person, and she thought any car that required expensive or difficult-to-obtain parts was ridiculous. However, it was a two-seater, and she enjoyed that. No station wagons with three children in the back seat for her.

And it was reliable. Predictably so.

The drive took her two long days. As she headed

east, particularly after crossing the Rockies, she found herself running the air-conditioning, closing the windows to fight off midwest humidity, running the windshield wipers full blast against downpours like she never saw in California. When Minnesota's rolling hills of wheat appeared before her, she felt the first thread of disquiet. Her CD player was blaring Led Zeppelin. She'd never outgrown what Drake had called "music that wasn't good the first time around." But it was music Lily liked nearly as much as she loved differential equations. In some real sense, she understood it. "Black Dog" and "Stairway to Heaven" provided unchanging insulation against an unpredictable world.

And this world, the world into which she had returned, seemed increasingly impossible to predict.

She drove up between fields, into the trees, among lakes, into the north woods that were her parents' home.

Twenty-five years since she'd been to Minnesota.

Twenty-five years ago, they were a half-dozen families enjoying the same Minnesota lake for the summer months. On music nights, Lily had played an out-of-tune upright piano; her mother had played a Celtic harp, her father—to Lily's shame—the accordion, and Ryan had played the violin from the time he was five. For drama nights, they'd planned puppet shows, told ghost stories, memorized poems, made up skits or dances.

She'd loved those childhood summers till the summer she'd arrived to find that her childhood friend Colin Gardner, whose music-night instruments had been made from discarded coffee cans or fallen tree branches, whose most beautiful instrument was always his voice, had sprung broad shoulders and his voice had deepened. Suddenly, she was willing to do nearly anything to have his attention. Unfortunately, Lily had not been blond, beautiful and free of teenage awkwardness like Megan Wright or Samantha Cole. She had been—and still was—fair-skinned, red-haired and brown-eyed. Ballet lessons and a tiny "willowy" figure had not compensated for what she saw as an underdeveloped body and a total inability to tan.

But Colin had said, on one memorable evening, that she reminded him of a fairy princess. He'd said some other things, too, over the next thirty-six hours, right up until that July third afternoon.

Now it was twenty-five years since she and Colin Gardner and Ryan had crossed Swan Lake and tied up the canoe on the other side. Lily had accepted Colin's suggestion that they "look inside" the ice-fishing house stuck back in the woods. He had given Ryan a kazoo to play, and she, Lily, had said Ryan could take off his lifejacket as long as he didn't go near the water. She had said this because of her knowledge that at any moment the little fiend might lapse into a spontaneous Yoda impression: *Grow your breasts won't. Ugly are you, Lily.*

It was the last time she'd seen her brother alive.

Her life had changed forever that day.

She had learned, the next morning, what the body of a person submerged in the lake for an afternoon and a night looked like. She had heard her own mother's voice keening for her drowned child. It was a time of horror she would never forget or get over.

And it had been her fault.

How could her parents bear to live here?

It was just before 5:00 p.m. on Tuesday when she

drove beneath the stockade sign reading CAMP BO-REAL. It was recognizable, barely, as the driveway she and Ryan and her parents had used to get to her folks' house on Swan Lake all those years ago. Stands of white and black spruce, paper birch, so many other trees she couldn't name but recognized from her past. She didn't know the first cabin she saw along the road nor the second. Her parents had sent her pictures over the years, but she hadn't spent much time studying them. She'd been annoyed that her parents always seemed intent on reminding her of Swan Lake, which she would never forget.

Their house looked unfamiliar. When Lily had stayed there during the summers, it had been one story, with just three bedrooms. But her parents had added on. Now the first floor had sprawled out along the lakeshore and a second sat atop it. It was just short of vulgar, but her parents would love telling anyone, interested or not, how they had salvaged every bit of material. A railing from a Second Empire Victorian in Minneapolis, a roof from a shed in Bemidji. The thought of listening to the litany made Lily tired. Both of her parents were from moneyed backgrounds—old money in her father's case, new food industries money in her mother's, all now duly inherited. Lily supposed that pathological thrift was her parents' signature form of rebellion against their affluent roots.

She parked behind a truly ancient Toyota Land Cruiser in the carport beside the house. Heading around to the front porch, she caught her first glimpse of the lake. Some people were out in a canoe. A woman and child walked along a new dock to the south. There were several new docks.

Was it this obvious evidence of change that had finally inspired her parents to scatter the ashes of their only son, twenty-five years after his death?

As soon as the thought crossed her mind, she felt ashamed—and guilty.

Who was she to say what was the right way for a couple to mourn the loss of a ten-year-old child?

My fault. My fault.

"Lily!"

Her mother ran down the porch steps, her blue-gray hair in two braids. She wore jeans and a flannel shirt with the sleeves cut off; her earrings were beaded, her feet bare and calloused, with the nail of one big toe badly cracked.

Again, Lily felt ashamed of her own thoughts.

"Well, look at that sporty new car." Marie Moran embraced her. "Fancy."

Lily felt her molars grind and attempted to stop the grinding, which she knew would cause her gums to recede.

"I'm surprised you can afford that on a teacher's salary," her father said before he'd said hello. He'd appeared almost soundlessly, melting out of the side of the house. His hug seemed almost an afterthought, but he exclaimed, "It is wonderful to have you here."

"The car was used and a bargain," Lily felt compelled to say and wondered why she was justifying herself to them.

"Oh, I meant the upkeep," he said.

"A fair point." Lily attempted grace as her self-esteem plummeted. *It's not about me. It's about them.*

Her father wore the kind of knit sports shirt with a collar that often had an alligator on it. But his was some generic brand and came with a sailboat instead. His shorts were denim cutoffs, and he'd gathered his thick white hair in a short ponytail.

In her childhood, she had visited Swan Lake every summer, but the rest of the year she'd lived with her family in a conservative suburb where having wealthy vegetarian academic parents who dressed like hippies, a mother who was so tight she squeaked when she walked and who'd sooner slit her own throat than buy either of her children clothing anywhere but at a thrift store, not to mention a father who played the accordion, was—well—weird. Lily frequently told herself that at the age of forty she was *over* her childhood stuff.

So why did she feel an old sting of resentment that her mother and father had both criticized her car? She glanced at her watch, deciding to count the minutes until they took issue with her clothes, the silver clasp binding her long red hair, her computer, her luggage—and everything else she'd brought with her. Her parents had spent their lives together pursuing an existence they termed "real," they had lost a child, and yet, as far as Lily was concerned, they were still completely immersed in a very external reality.

A reality made up of judging everyone who wasn't like them—which was practically everybody.

I can't stand these people. They make me insane.

"Can we help carry up your bags?"

"No, I'll take them. And let's not worry about them now."

"But don't you want to see your room?"

She wanted to climb back in her BMW and drive away. "Oh, whenever. There's no hurry."

"We're dying to show you."

This filled her with trepidation. It would be a lesson in economy, she was sure.

The inside of the house smelled as she always remembered her parents' homes smelling, whether in Illinois or here at Swan Lake. A faint whiff of patchouli, fresh-baked bread, herbs, wholesome cleanliness.

The anger she felt toward them abated. They had been good parents, good people, and still were. Eccentric, yes. A bit thoughtless—definitely. Intentionally cruel to their offspring, no.

And how they'd loved Ryan.

Well, in truth, she, Lily, had always been her father's favorite. But it was no secret that her mother preferred Ryan, smiling at him indulgently as he made fun of Lily's nail polish, of her clothes, her body, her personality and any attempt she made to be attractive.

She still remembered the first time she'd told her therapist, *He was really a little beast.* Her therapist had not been shocked but had given her an empathetic smile that said it was okay to call the brother she'd let die an insufferable brat.

"Look at this couch," said Marie. "Someone just left it by the roadside up near Lake Meredith."

"I can't believe it," Lily answered, noticing that one of the lodgepole pine legs must have been missing. Someone, her parents undoubtedly, had replaced it with a smooth maple leg, which did seem to give the piece extra character.

Her eyes strayed around the room, looking for something that might contain Ryan's ashes.

She saw no urn.

A large photo of her parents dancing in a group of people wearing kimonos sat on the woodstove—unused at this time of year. The occasion, Lily remembered, was Obon, in Hawaii. Three years after Ryan's death, they'd gone to the islands together, the three of them. Her parents collected grieving rituals from around the world—another way they dealt with Ryan's death.

In the hall, her mother pointed out a mirror she'd found at the Salvation Army store in Bemidji. The frame was copper with a patina. Her father led them upstairs. The staircase banister looked like a salvage item, too, though it hadn't been used as a railing in its previous life. It was a wooden mast from a sailboat.

"Ingenious!" she said approvingly. Charming her parents was sometimes the way to stop them from criticizing her. She could compliment their thrift and originality, and perhaps they would perceive her as thrifty and original.

Why does their approval still matter to me?

It did; that was certain.

The stairs led up to a large, open room. A piano—not the out-of-tune upright of her childhood but a different upright—stood against one wall, beside a large talking drum. She saw a violin case—Ryan's, complete with a Darth Vader sticker. A file box containing sheet music sat beside her mother's Celtic harp. Before the great window overlooking the lake was a makeshift stage.

"This is the music and drama room. We've made extra money hosting workshops."

Since Ryan's death, her parents had rented out cabins on the lakefront, much of which they now owned. No doubt they were still working to make the property pay even bigger dividends.

"Groups sign up," her mother continued, "and run the whole thing themselves. It's been very profitable."

Imagine caring about that. Of course, they didn't hoard their money. They gave something like twenty-five percent to Amnesty International and Sea Shepherd and the Dalai Lama and whoever else they thought deserved it.

Her room was off the music room. It, too, had a view of the lake, and French doors led onto the deck above the carport—or rather, it formed the roof of the carport. A patchwork quilt—a green and brown log cabin pattern—covered the bed. "This is beautiful. One of Grandma's?" Marie's mother lived in Canada with her brother; they'd gone there when his draft number came up in 1971.

Marie nodded. "She and Bobby were down this spring. She made that especially for you. It's a surprise—for your birthday. Of course, you're free to take it back to Santa Barbara."

Which made Lily feel decidedly unfree to do so. What a tactful, emotionally intelligent person would have said was, *Grandma is really hoping you'll take it home with you.*

But her mother seemed constitutionally incapable of making that sort of statement.

"I love it," Lily replied. "I'll write her first thing. And maybe I'll paint some of the trees. I brought my watercolors."

"Did you?" exclaimed Marie. "I'm so glad. You know I've always hoped you'd do something with your art."

In a moment, no doubt, she would begin holding forth on what Lily had done with her life *instead* of pursuing art.

What you really *hope is that I'll be someone alto-gether different, someone you like.* "I don't have that kind of passion for it," Lily replied. And she'd always preferred modern art to landscape painting. "Not the kind required to make it a career."

"I don't understand where your fascination with math came from."

"And philosophy," her father chimed in. "But that's easy, Marie. My father was, after all, an engineer by ed-ucation, and his brother is a theologian, which isn't the same as a philosopher but *is* related. I prefer philoso-phy myself to theology. And Lily's musical because of me."

"*Or* me," Marie answered.

Lily barely heard. She was staring at a photo on the chest of drawers, her childhood chest of drawers, part of an old bedroom set that had been painted white with lilacs on it. The photo was an eight-by-ten in a wooden frame, clearly a thrift-shop find. The photo showed her and Ryan lying on their backs in a pile of newly raked fall leaves. Her hair had been and still was the bur-nished red of some of those leaves, while Ryan's was quite dark, as her father's had been when he was young.

"Thank you," she said. It didn't bother her to see this picture of her and Ryan together. It didn't suffuse her with guilt. Instead, it seemed somehow just right, just the thing for her bedroom here at Swan Lake.

"Now, it's music night this evening," said her father, "and we do have a workshop going on here. They're a women's prayer group. But we'll join them for music, and we'd love it if you would, too."

"I will," Lily said, trying to sound happy about the

suggestion. "I might like to go for a swim or go out in the canoe before then. If that's all right."

"It's fine," her father said very quickly, as though to show that he trusted her now, now that she'd reached the age of forty, now that his only son had been drowned through her carelessness, now after everything. No worrying now.

"Oh, and Helen called," her mother said. "She and Bert should be getting in tomorrow night. They'll take the other two upstairs rooms, of course."

It was all Lily could do not to cross her eyes. Her forty-three-year-old cousin was *not* a virgin, but she and Bert, whom she'd been dating for years, could not bring themselves to share a bed. Lily sometimes found herself speculating on what Bert saw in the situation. Had he no interest in sex? Or an aversion to sex with Helen in particular? Had they taken vows of celibacy? She said, "Still not sleeping together?"

"At least she doesn't practice *serial* monogamy," replied her mother.

That was for those of us who've slept with more than one man. Lily carried her bags upstairs and changed into the swimsuit she'd brought with her, a white maillot, then coated herself with sunscreen, SPF 45. She braided her long hair, grabbed a beach towel and went downstairs. "Where are the life vests?" she asked her mother, not because she couldn't have found them but because she wanted to reassure her parents, who must still worry about some things they needn't have worried over.

"There's a light blue one that'll fit you out on the porch railing."

"Thanks, Mom." And Lily went over to her mother and hugged her.

Her mother said, "Pretty suit," in a way that meant she was thinking something critical as well—but restraining herself from voicing the thought.

Lily left before Marie could overcome that self-control.

The life vest did fit her. She fastened it as she walked down to the water.

An aluminum canoe—not the green wooden one she and Ryan and Colin had taken that July day twenty-five years before, the canoe Ryan had then taken out alone, to his death—was upside down on the beach beside the dock. Hastily, Lily rolled it over, dropped her towel inside and shoved it into the water.

She picked up the paddle that had lain beneath the boat, waded into the lake and climbed into the canoe, as steadily as if she'd been out on a canoe every day for the last quarter century, instead of never setting foot inside one since Ryan's death.

The mosquitoes whined in her ears as she dipped her paddle over the gunwale. She'd been told that taking lots of vitamin B complex would discourage mosquitoes—and make her stink. Both seemed to be true. Nonetheless, she'd brought some light cotton pants and a blouse and hat to put on if they started biting too greedily. The mosquitoes at Swan Lake had, in some years, been measured in numbers per square inch.

Ryan? she thought, reaching out in her heart, remembering a strangely tall and skinny boy who'd been such a pest that long-ago day. He had *known* of her crush on Colin, and he'd made the most of his power—of any power to tease her, to bother her. Where was he now?

Her take on death was informed by the subject she taught so well—because, she supposed, she'd experienced the death of someone close to her when she was so young. But what she *felt* about death, what she supposed she *believed,* had more to do with spirituality than philosophy.

Philosophically, Ryan's death had taught her that she was mortal, that her parents were, that every living thing and person would eventually die. This was a mortality she really wouldn't completely accept until she herself died. But spiritually, she wondered if Ryan's soul was immortal, as Plato would have argued. And she studied the elaborate rites of people since the Cro-Magnon, rites designed to appease the spirits of the dead.

Her brother's spirit had never come to her, to communicate either forgiveness or condemnation.

Even to talk like Yoda and tell her she was ugly.

Lily paddled across the lake alone, wondering again why she felt guilt toward her brother. Socrates had envisioned a soul that could both endure and think. Didn't sound too bad, except here in this familiar humid heat, with the canoe weightless on the water and even the mosquitoes so profoundly *alive.*

Yes, to cheat someone of life was a great crime, and she must answer for it, certainly until she died and maybe afterward.

The old dock drew near. She didn't mind recalling because she would never forget. Following Colin Gardner into the ice-fishing house, a shell its owner would carry onto the ice in winter. Colin had kissed her and felt her breasts, such as they were, through her bikini top. They had kissed with tongues. *French kissing,* she'd called it.

She'd done one thing right, though not right enough, and that was to say, *Wait,* and to peer outside, primarily to see that Ryan wasn't creeping up to spy on them.

And he hadn't been.

It had happened so fast. The canoe wasn't far from the dock, drifting but still on the water, not rocking at all. They'd heard nothing. Ryan must have tried to get into the canoe and slipped into the water. At first, she'd been certain he was hiding, playing a diabolical trick on her—then on her parents, too; it was the kind of thing he'd do, just to see what everyone did. When his body was found, there was no indication that he'd struck his head. He had drowned.

The dock drew closer, and she steered the canoe alongside it and leaned forward for the chalky cotton bowline. She made it fast to a cleat that looked new.

Had someone bought this property?

Incredibly, the ice-fishing house was there. It had been repaired, then allowed to decay. Yet it still looked as though someone used it regularly. And not far away, hanging from a magnificent red maple, was a tree swing. In an adjacent ash was a primitive tree house. Nonetheless, the shore looked very wild—and quite deserted. Lily stepped onto the dock in her bare feet, liking the warm feel of the wood, the water in the air.

She knew she'd like the ground, too, damp and warm, spongy, humus-like, beneath the paper birch lining the shore.

The place of her guilt.

This shack.

Feathers erupted from the undergrowth beside her feet, and she jumped, heart pounding, and sprang back.

Yellow eyes, yellow beak, and gray feathers, great wings lifting. Or one lifted. The other dragged limp.

The face was a lunar circle.

It was an owl, and Lily knew immediately, as she'd known with certainty few things in her life, that it was here in her life for *her*; that this bird was part of her destiny, part of her past, part of her future.

It was an owl, the bird of death, and it could not fly.

CHAPTER TWO

THE BIRD WAS HURT and frightened. It was also huge, more than two feet tall. A Great Gray Owl. Lily suspected it had been surviving in its injured state for some time, days rather than hours. She didn't know why she thought this. She'd seldom seen animals in the wild, never come across even a small bird that had been injured or was sick. Dead animals on the road—yes.

But this owl. A Great Gray Owl.

She wished she'd brought her cell phone across the lake. She could call someone. Her parents would know where to take a wounded raptor.

But if she left the owl, she might not be able to find it again. Were they endangered? Was it even legal to pick up an injured owl and take it to help? It seemed to her there were laws against helping eagles and peregrine falcons.

If I don't help….

She decided. She would get her beach towel from the canoe and throw it over the owl and pick the owl up. If she could do this easily, she would. If it seemed as though she was hurting the owl, possibly making the injury worse, she would not.

She figured she would get one try.

The yellow eyes, a light lemony-yellow, gazed at her.

"I'll be right back," she said and crept away through the undergrowth, her toes and the pads of her feet imprinting themselves on the moist, deep earth.

She glanced over her shoulder at the owl. The creaking of the old dock seemed too loud. *Don't go away, owl.*

How far could it go?

Irrelevant. She had no doubt that if any owl, even an injured one, did not want to be caught by her, it could manage not to be caught.

She had to surprise it. If it had no idea what she intended, if she was fast, she could capture it. Years of ballet had made her an athlete. She would never stop dancing, because dancing was her meditation.

Her steps now were dance upon mulch, dance into forest earth turned forgiving in the place where she would be forgiven at her own death.

God, she was sure, forgave her.

But she had made a deliberate choice not to forgive herself the one mistake of leaving her ten-year-old brother unattended by the canoe; part and parcel of that choice was that she'd never make such an error again. She did not live with recklessness, nor with unpredictability. She did not continue relationships with people who were wild cards—and too many were.

Colin Gardner had been.

Not *especially* wild. He hadn't, she understood, gotten on well with his father, with whom he'd lived during the school year. His father, she'd been told, had been glad to send him to live with an aunt and uncle, and Colin had been glad to go.

None of that made what had happened with Ryan his fault. The fault was hers, and she accepted it. But she'd never again make the mistake of being around someone like Colin, someone with that charged, creative energy, a way of being that ducked out of and denied basic human responsibility.

She approached the ice-fishing house again. The owl had not moved from its place.

Yes, she'd throw the towel over the bird and herself upon it.

But what if she squished it? Were they delicate, owls? Lily realized she had no idea.

Pale yellow eyes gazed at her.

One chance was all she had, because after that chance the owl would be frightened and much harder to catch.

No hesitation. She held the towel at her waist, spread out like a net she could fall upon. She dove down the instant she dropped the towel, using her falling body to make the towel's shape more netlike. She needed to make sure the feet didn't get her; they could probably rip open her hands, her arms.

She had it.

The shape trapped within the towel, trapped against her middle and her thighs, was both smaller and lighter than she'd expected. She tried to feel for the feet and grabbed the owl's leg instead and decided that was better. But the free foot tore the towel and her skin. She grabbed at it awkwardly and couldn't catch it. Then she managed with the hand holding the other leg.

The hand not holding the legs was sticky and she saw blood oozing down her thigh, too, from a gash there.

Would she need antibiotics? Lily didn't care. She had the owl, and she held it against her, not releasing its legs, as she stood. How could she paddle and hold the owl? Her hand was already beginning to cramp.

What had it been doing here, anyway? Here, where she'd failed. Ryan had died in the lake. It was where she, Lily, had lapsed and changed so many lives forever.

She carried the owl—the incarnation of feather-light—over the creaking dock. *I caught a wild raptor. I did it.*

She would take it back to her parents' house—to Camp Death—and they would tell her who to call, where to take the bird.

Without using her hands, busy with the owl, Lily stepped into the canoe. She sat on one of the seats and arranged the owl so that one arm held it, the same cramped hand clutching its legs.

Swan Lake was half a mile across and one mile long. The trip to her parents' beach was just over a half mile.

The owl must really be mostly feathers to weigh so little, Lily reasoned as she paddled. It moved not at all now, or not so that she could feel any movement.

They made good time.

She stumbled getting out of the canoe, her bare feet slipping in the shallow water, in the mud, over smooth rocks. The bird stirred and she said, "It's all right, owl friend."

For the first time, she knew comfort in being back at Swan Lake, back in the North Woods. She was used to the world of beach tar, to swimming in the Santa Barbara Channel every day. She never told anyone where she was going, and she swam alone. In doing so, she was endangering no one but herself. However, she felt divinely protected. Because Ryan had drowned, she would not. She was certain of this.

This was another world, this place of wet air and mosquitoes and heat, heat that Santa Barbara did not know. But nature soothed, a balm.

Rather than remove the towel from the bird, she decided to take it as it was to someone who could help. Someone else might have to drive her.

Her hand, holding the owl's legs, shook, numb.

Her father stood just below the porch, facing the lake, with a couple of women in motorcycle leathers—part of the prayer group?

Lily supposed she could put the owl in a cardboard box to transport it wherever it needed to go.

"Lily!" Her father called her over, and she trudged toward him, keenly aware that she was scratched and bloody from the owl's talons. But her parents, too, would understand the need to get the owl to a wildlife hospital.

"Dad, I found an injured owl. I think its wing is broken."

Her father and the bikers gazed at her with interest.

"You should have those cuts seen to," her father said. "I'm sure they can get infected. It looks like you might need stitches. Is the owl under there?"

"Yes. I found it over by the old dock. I'm fine."

"An owl," said one of the women.

"Ask your mother to find the number of the Aerie for you."

"The Aerie?"

"The North Woods Aerie. They rehabilitate sick raptors and provide a refuge for those that can't be released. Colin Gardner runs it."

Colin Gardner? Not— But it had to be, or her father

would have explained that it was a *different* Colin Gardner. And hadn't Colin always been fascinated by every hawk and eagle and owl he saw, and when they were children hadn't he said that he was a Scottish chieftain galloping across the highlands with a falcon on his arm?

"I thought he left. I thought he lived somewhere else." She mustn't let go of the owl's legs, or she was sure its talons would get her again—and it could get free and injure itself further.

Were her parents on speaking terms with Colin Gardner? They had so thoroughly blamed him for Ryan's death—had blamed him and held Lily blameless—or forgiven her, at any rate.

Her father must have noted her expression. He assigned it his own explanation. With an unenthusiastic look, he told her, "Well, he lives here now. He owns some of the property across the lake, actually. His place—and the Aerie is part of it—extends north quite a ways, I think almost to Canada."

Her father's tone lacked acerbity. What did that mean? And what was Colin Gardner like now? He'd been part of the biggest disaster of her life—may no greater catastrophe ever touch her. *No mistakes* was Lily's rule in life. So—had she made a mistake by picking up the owl instead of leaving it to its own devices or calling a professional to pick it up?

No. This time she'd gone on instinct, and she'd done well. Could she switch her right hand, holding the owl's legs, with her left?

She took the owl inside and very carefully changed the way she was holding it. Relief. Her numb hand trembled against the towel.

Marie came down the stairs and said, "Lily, what have you done to yourself?"

After learning about the owl, her mother said, "Well, we'll have to take it down to the Raptor Center at the university."

Lily perched on the edge of one of the mismatched—but beautiful—chairs near the maple table that had been part of her childhood. "Dad said there's a raptor center nearby."

"If you can call it that. It's just him and one very messed-up child and an elderly woman who comes and helps, I believe. Maybe a few other people. They're not *professionals*."

"Is there a veterinarian?" Clearly, Marie would prefer to drive all the way to Minneapolis rather than deal with a person whose name she couldn't bring herself to utter.

"Well—he has *some* training of that kind. It's up to you if you want to take it there. It makes me absolutely sick to see how he's raising his son. I think homeschooling's all right if a child has siblings, but they are *so* isolated."

So Colin Gardner had a child. And a wife hadn't been mentioned. Immediately, a scenario sprang into Lily's mind. Colin was divorced and had bullied his wife so that he received custody of his son. Of course, that didn't *have* to be the picture, but she thought it often was with custodial fathers.

Her mother's view was no kinder. "It's no surprise how the man's turned out. Not that he hasn't *changed*. But he's grown into exactly the kind of person I thought he would. All friendly on the surface but very angry underneath. Of course, he was a very angry young man."

Lily did not remember this.

"If you're going to take the owl there," her mother continued, "I think *I* should make the call. And I should drive the bird."

"Why?"

"Well, you can do as you like—you always do. I just assumed you wouldn't want to have to speak with him or see him."

"The owl is important, Mom." She'd told her how the Great Gray had erupted from the ground, demanding her. "I want to take the owl myself, wherever it goes. We could take it together."

"If you *want* to take it, you may as well go yourself. I get no pleasure from seeing Colin Gardner. To come back here and buy *that property*. Taunting us. It was very cruel."

Lily considered this in silence.

"I'll call him," Marie repeated, reaching for the princess wall phone. Lily noted that it had buttons and wondered if her parents still had any rotary phones. They did have an answering machine—with a message about Camp Boreal.

"This is Marie Moran."

The chill silence that followed matched her mother's unwarm tone. Lily felt a strange respect for her mother's powerful grudge toward someone only tangentially involved in the death of her son. *It's the anger they should feel toward me and maybe do feel, but they won't admit that even to themselves, so they treat him this way.*

What if her parents ever woke up to *her* part, her bigger part in Ryan's death?

Into the phone, her mother said, "Our daughter, Lily, is visiting, and she found an injured owl…. It's here. She put a towel over it and picked it up…. Well, I'm sure she didn't want to leave it for predators."

Odd, Lily thought, how her mother could find fault with everything she did—but let someone else criticize her daughter and the fur would fly.

"Surely that's moot?" her mother was saying. "The owl is here. Do you want to help, or should we find someone who does? It would probably be better off at the university Raptor Center, anyway."

Lily blushed, listening. But perhaps the person at the other end was being more no polite than Marie.

"We'll bring it over, then," her mother said stiffly and hung up the phone, her lips tight.

"Mom, is there a cardboard box around?"

"Yes. And thank you, really, for taking it yourself. I really prefer it. I detest the man—and not just because of Ryan. I wouldn't have cared for him in any case, and I just worry about that poor child with only an angry man for a role model."

They found a big box that had once held bottles of organic apple juice, and Lily put the owl inside, still wrapped in the towel, and carefully released its legs. Its talons moved before she closed the lid.

"Will it jump out of the box while you're driving?" her mother asked.

"I hope not. Maybe we should put a piece of tape on the lid." It was a strange moment, putting the owl in the box with her mother's help, the two of them united in caring for the injured animal that Lily had found where she'd last seen Ryan alive.

"Will you let me wash those cuts? And are you going to put on more clothes?"

She had never told her parents that she and Colin had gone into the ice-fishing shack to make out. Her mother's remark about clothes brought it to mind, where she knew it would linger. The guilt of that secret could not be lifted now, it was that heavy.

"I can wash the cuts myself."

"Your leg looks as though it could use stitches."

Lily agreed but didn't want to go. "Let's see if some butterflies do the trick."

She cleaned the cuts made by the owl's talons, and her mother poured hydrogen peroxide and Betadine over them. "Thank you again for taking the owl over to that place. Now, you know you just drive around the lake road? There's a sign on the right that says North Woods Aerie."

"How long have you been neighbors?" Lily asked, knowing she should run upstairs for more clothes, to get out of her torn swimsuit.

"Four years," her mother said tersely. "The Aerie should've been a good thing. We need something like that up here. But your father and I have never liked him. No personal skills. You *know* that."

Yes, Lily knew. Her parents had liked Colin Gardner fine before Ryan's death, before he had become their scapegoat, substitute target for the hatred they should have sent toward their own daughter and for some reason could not.

"You should hear what he said to Helen. Well, really it was to Bert."

Lily gave her a look of interest.

"I can't remember the circumstances, but it was quite bad."

On the money, then.

"He won't be friendly to you, either," Marie said. "He's quite nasty. You'll see."

Lovely, Lily thought.

Her wounds bandaged, she ran upstairs, snatched up a black cotton, above-the-knee, wraparound skirt and tied it over her swimsuit.

"Don't handle that bird again," her mother said as she came down the stairs, car keys and cell phone in hand. "You're taking your cell. Good. In case you have trouble. You should have coverage on the road, at least." There was none at Camp Boreal. "I'm sure you'll be back soon."

Lily had expected her mother to scorn the expense of a cell phone. Clearly, Marie's dislike of Colin Gardner was overriding all other rules of life.

Lily carried the box out to the BMW and put it in the passenger seat. She had rescued the owl, and now she would turn it over to a person who could care for it.

But it didn't seem that simple to her.

She noticed, for instance, that this was the first time she was driving away from Camp Boreal, and she wasn't doing it because she was sick of her parents and couldn't bear to be in their presence for another moment. Also, she'd found the owl—and the owl *was* a symbol of death in so many traditions—at the place where she and Colin Gardner had acted in a way that had resulted in Ryan's death.

And she was taking the owl to Colin Gardner to be healed.

She'd seen the wing, though.

Would it ever fly again?

There's the metaphor. Nothing would bring Ryan back. Nothing would allow her parents to get over his death, because one didn't get over such a thing. It was normal *not* to get over it.

Maybe, Lily thought with a flash of insight, it was even normal to hang on to his ashes for twenty-five years, to refuse to release that last part of him to the earth or the water or any of the elements, to let go.

Yes, maybe her parents' reaction had been the most normal one of all.

She had driven only three miles on the road around the lake when she saw the sign that read NORTH WOODS AERIE. It was stenciled in bright red on a white background and the name wasn't all the sign proclaimed. Beneath the name in black: VISITORS BY INVITATION ONLY. A phone number and NO TRESPASSING. VIOLATORS WILL BE PROSECUTED.

Good grief. Well, she'd been invited, she supposed. In a manner of speaking.

There was no gate, just a muddy drive. More signs. SLOW.

Funny how somebody who, at sixteen, had been sexy as hell, appealing to every girl he met, could be, at forty-one, a person who hung signs that made him sound like a man who'd appear on his porch with a sawed-off shotgun if anyone came too close. Somehow, she doubted it was the death of her brother that had affected him this way.

He'd shown horror, too, when they'd seen the canoe, when they'd been unable to find Ryan. Unlike her, he had not believed her brother was playing a trick on them, and he had dived into the lake at once, around and under the dock, searching the murky water.

They had searched together for two hours.

Colin had told her that if they found Ryan in the lake even after all that time, there might be a chance of reviving him, because of something called the mammalian diving reflex. Later, she'd read about this. She didn't know whether Ryan had been young enough for that to help him survive.

Ryan's death had been a life-changing event for Colin Gardner, she was sure of that—and just as sure that he'd gone on to kiss other girls, to love and find love, and to enjoy being alive.

SLOW, another sign cautioned.

A huge building appeared, sided in a combination of weathered wood and the kind of corrugated tin that's made to look old. It was as big as an events center, she thought, like one of those places at fairgrounds where people showed livestock and dogs.

There was a very old fifth-wheeler, used for she couldn't guess what, another building, smaller than the big one but of similar construction, and a very small cabin, undoubtedly an old summer place built in the fifties and remodeled to withstand four seasons.

She shivered in her car's air-conditioning, in the security of her rolled-up windows, safe from mosquitoes and this strange world of Colin Gardner. She decided that living in northern Minnesota made people strange but reflected again that it had become a refuge for her parents, who had lost a child, and for a man who, as a teenager, had been instrumental in that loss.

Yes, it was her blame.

But it wasn't as though he owned *none* of the blame. Even he had shown anguish at the time—and remorse.

The cabin door opened, and she saw a figure behind the screen, masculine and indistinct, in fatigues and a T-shirt, with a plaid, maybe flannel, shirt over that.

She parked outside the cabin, opened her own door and made sure her skirt was straight before she got out. "Hi," she called and immediately walked around the car to open the passenger door, to give a clear message that she wasn't remotely interested in trespassing on his privacy or feeding the bears or whatever it was that made him so prickly.

She heard the screen door creak but didn't look over her shoulder, just lifted the box holding the owl from the front seat.

A small dog darted from the house, barking. "Thank you, Winky. Quiet." His voice and footsteps behind her. "It's alive?"

She turned. "I think so. It was definitely alive an hour ago. I think it's been hurt for a while." The Jack Russell terrier sniffed her, then sprang away. The last thing she would have expected Colin Gardner to have was a small dog.

He took the box from her hands, and she glanced up at him for the first time.

Different. The same person, but different. Gold threaded his tousled, rather curly hair the color of a walnut shell. Thick eyebrows, a straight nose, green eyes, and a handsome, laughing face. He wasn't as tall as six feet, nor particularly heavy. Strong, though. Lily remembered all about that. At sixteen, he'd looked great with no shirt, and she suspected nothing had changed.

He wasn't especially clean, and she decided his close beard must require less effort than shaving. She wondered if he drank but didn't think so. He seemed feral and unlike the teenager she had known. Where was his son?

Lily was unafraid of questions, afraid neither of asking or of answering. She had been told that she was fear-*less* but that wasn't true. She feared repeating the mistake she had made twenty-five years earlier, feared making another like it. "What brought you back here?" she asked. "I thought you left. Or lived somewhere else—during, you know, the off-season."

He carried the box away from her, toward the huge barn. It was corrugated metal on the outside, utilitarian-looking, almost like an airplane hangar.

"Neighbors," he said. "I came back for the neighbors."

"My parents say that's why they like it here, too."

His lips twitched, which she remembered was how he'd sometimes smiled. It had seemed sophisticated when he was young, as though he had seen things, learned things. It still seemed that way.

But his *real* smile—she recalled that as something with much greater impact.

Although once she would've made an apology for her parents' attitude, to do so now seemed pointless. She didn't care about currying favor with this man—or any other. Why should she apologize for the rudeness or prejudice of others? After all, it wasn't her fault, and what good could it do?

She followed his fluid strides, not willing to let her owl out of sight that easily.

The owl was wild of course—not really hers. Presumably, Colin had some training and probably state permits for handling it.

"How did you catch it?" he asked.

"I threw a towel over it and kind of hugged it, and then I reached through to find its legs."

He nodded at the gash on Lily's thigh. "Looks as though you got footed."

"Well, yes."

"You're lucky. If it'd grabbed hold, it could have taken a couple of people to pry the talons off."

That had to be exaggeration. Lily looked up and remembered those eyes behind eyelashes so long and thick you could lose your way in them. But now there were laugh lines, too, the kind that only came with age—and life.

"That's the possible danger to you," he said. "I've had a talon through my palm. But the bird's at risk, too. If you grab a leg above the hock you can bruise it. Hold a raptor the wrong way, you can break feathers."

Her teeth clamped tightly together. "I did what I thought best. I found it where—I found it by the ice-fishing shack. It seemed—" She decided not to try to explain. What did it matter?

"The owl is considered an omen of death in some cultures, a messenger from the dead in others. Is that how it seemed?"

She shrugged. "Something like that."

"I hear you do philosophy and math."

She crouched down to pet the Jack Russell terrier, which had returned. "I teach philosophy and math. But philosophy is not my religion, if that's what you're implying." *You little preppy snot,* she wanted to add, abruptly recalling where he'd spent each school year. At some prep school, rowing sculls, playing lacrosse, sailing and alpine skiing. Or at least she supposed that was how it had been, not really remembering the details. He hadn't gotten on with his father, which explained why he'd chosen this back-to-nature existence that he might or might not eventually outgrow.

Her thoughts reminded her of her mother, and she fought a blush.

"What sort of philosophy?"

In all the years Lily had been teaching, her parents had never asked this. "I teach one class on Nietzsche and one called 'Death and Philosophy.'"

He shot another glance at her from under the brim of his very frayed and faded baseball cap. The cap, she saw now, had a patch of the yin-yang symbol sewn on the front. The patch looked as worn as the hat.

Colin led her toward the corrugated building, and she saw that the side that hadn't been visible from the road was covered, in many places, by grating. He opened a door at the corner of the building. "The rehabilitation mews and clinic are on this edge. The rest is our flight barn," he said. "Put together with funds raised by the local elementary school. We have another mews for long-term residents. Education birds. A mews," he explained, "is a room where we keep the raptors."

She'd known this already. "Why no visitors?" She gazed down a long hallway of unfinished wood. The wall on her right had many windows and doors and was topped with more grating. There was a door for each mews.

Colin shut the door behind her. "Sometimes visitors disturb the birds or surprise us in the middle of a difficult task. There are juveniles here that we try very hard not to let see humans at all so they don't imprint on us."

He opened another door into a stall-like area surrounded by bars that reached to a ceiling lower than the roof of the barn. Probably above the stall—or mews, for that was what it appeared to be—there was a storage area.

As Colin led the way down the hall, a figure emerged from a doorway on the left, and Lily's heart stopped and restarted.

He was very small—almost delicate-looking, like an elf—but wild and healthy-looking too. But it wasn't the mop of pale hair, or the baggy cutoffs and T-shirt that could almost have fit his father, that fit more like a dress, or the bare and very dirty feet. It was that he wore a heavy glove like a gauntlet, like a welder's glove, on his left forearm, and on that very small arm perched a bird that must have been a foot and a half tall. On his right hand, he also wore a glove, but to Lily the elfin child seemed incredibly exposed.

Lily had felt the force of just the tip of the talon that had torn into her leg—and now the wound had begun to ache. In light of Colin's graphic warning to her, how could he let his son handle a bird like that? What could that huge bird do to that boy?

Colin said, "Hello, Sharpe. Sharpe's a red-shouldered hawk and one of our permanent residents. And this is my son, Luke. Ah. And Mosi, our veterinarian."

A young black man with dreadlocks gathered low and loose behind his neck had come through the door behind Colin's son. He wore scrubs. His bearing was regal, his smile comfortable.

So much for my mother's information, thought Lily. "It's nice to meet you all," she said. Then, "Do many people work here?"

Colin and Mosi and Luke all seemed to consider the question.

Colin said, "Several. We have four volunteers and two paid employees besides Luke and me."

Her eyes strayed again to the raptor on Luke's arm.

"Would all of you like to come to Music Night tonight at my parents' house?" The impulsive invitation was unlike her. Why she'd offered it, she couldn't have said, except that she was curious about this man who had been as much a part of Ryan's death as she had. She was interested for more misanthropic reasons, as well. In speaking with a man she'd liked when he was a sixteen-year-old, she could congratulate herself on not getting what she'd once wanted—because, in the long run, it would surely have made her miserable. There would be satisfaction in that.

Strange, this summer was the twenty-fifth anniversary of Ryan's death. Lily supposed it was also the twenty-fifth anniversary of the first time a male she liked had returned her affection. More than that, too. First real kiss...

Which shouldn't be a chilling memory but always was, because of Ryan.

"Music night." Colin seemed thoughtful. Was he remembering nights of their childhood when he'd made musical instruments from empty coffee cans? He walked into the clinic, trailed by the others, and set the box on a ledge just below waist height. "Do you have a hot date tonight, Mosi?" he asked, almost under his breath.

"As a matter of fact I do." The veterinarian grinned.

"Lily, we're going to ask you to step back into the hall,"

Colin told her. "You can watch through the glass until we've restrained the owl. Then we'll come and get you."

"I'll put Sharpe away," said Luke helpfully and walked down the hall to one of the mews.

Lily wondered if she was allowed to follow *him*. She opted instead to watch Colin and the veterinarian through the bank of windows, which were marked at intervals with pieces of tape, perhaps to keep the raptors from trying to escape through the panes.

Colin donned a welder's glove like the one Luke had worn. Mosi reached into a cupboard, taking out a thing that reminded Lily of a stocking mask. He rolled it carefully while Colin opened the box.

Lily saw him groping for the legs before lifting the owl.

The door of the mews down the hall shut, and the small blond boy suddenly ran past her, opened the clinic door and stepped almost silently inside.

The men removed the blanket, and Colin held the owl while the veterinarian dexterously rolled the stocking-like thing down over the owl's head and partway over its wings.

Lily, immersed in the feeling that this was *her* bird, that it had come to her for a reason, saw the owl's distress, saw it struggle at this treatment. But surely Mosi had noticed the injured wing?

Luke opened the clinic door again. "My dad says you can come in."

Lily wasn't sure why she found this child so endearing. She wasn't *good* with children. She didn't like most children.

Well, certainly he was an attractive child and he seemed intelligent, but what did that mean, really? Very little.

Mosi appeared to be counting feathers. He looked up and caught Lily's eye.

"Is the wing broken?" she asked.

"It was, but it appears to have healed—incorrectly."

"Can you break it again and fix it?"

Mosi considered. "Best not. I don't think he's in pain—the physical kind. He may have been hit by a car while hunting. He'll make a good education bird."

So the owl was male. "Does that mean you'll take him to schools?"

"*We* will," Luke said. "My dad and I do that."

So the owl she'd saved was to be taken in by Colin Gardner, fostered by him and his son. It would become theirs.

Well, the Aerie's, which amounted to the same thing.

"Do you need to be licensed to take care of an injured raptor?" she asked.

"Our volunteers aren't licensed," said Colin. "The facility is. Why?"

"Oh—I just want to—" She couldn't say it. It would sound too naive. "I'm just…interested. I—well, I found this owl, so I'm interested. In it. Of course, I'm only going to be here for a couple of weeks."

"Of course," he echoed.

Was he mocking her for not wanting to live in Nowhere, Minnesota? *Well, be my guest.* She didn't want to live in the North Woods through the freezing winters. She wasn't afraid of the cold, but she'd go nuts being so near her parents. They'd have their fingers in every aspect of her life.

"Well," Colin shrugged. "If you want to help take care of him while you're here, that would be all right."

It would provide a way to escape from her parents.

"Thank you. I would like that."

"I'll show you around," Luke said.

Colin's glance at his son seemed to Lily to be nearly indifferent. "And then she can come back tomorrow," he said, "after the owl's had a chance to settle in."

"Does that mean you don't want to come to Music Night?" she asked innocently, knowing the answer perfectly well. She could tell without asking that he had no hot date.

"Our bedtime is pretty early," he said, with more grace than she had anticipated. "Thank you anyhow."

In other words, thanks but no thanks.

Lily nodded and followed Luke Gardner's small blond head out of the clinic.

CHAPTER THREE

SHE DROVE HOME thinking about Luke. He'd shown her the raptors in each mews for long-term residents. Then he'd shown her the room full of cages containing various live food for all the raptors. Luke, who was eight, he said, seemed to have no trouble at all with the idea of feeding a cute bunny rabbit to an eagle or a Great Horned Owl. Lily thought she might; would the owl she'd rescued eat live food?

The Jack Russell terrier, it transpired, was Luke's, and Lily wondered if *it* was in any danger of being carried off by any of the Aerie's residents. She hadn't asked Luke.

Instead, she'd asked him if he liked to read.

Yes. Harry Potter. *But* The Hobbit *is my favorite book. You're reading it yourself?*

I've read it twice by myself.

That wasn't necessarily true, but Colin did seem to be fulfilling his parental duties to some degree. For instance, Luke seemed to know a great deal about raptors and trees.

He could name several of the trees around the buildings, which was better than she could do. But as he introduced her to one of his favorite resident birds, a Harlan's hawk that had been raised in captivity and had imprinted on its human owner, he'd asked, *Do you know where people go when they die?*

Lily had shaken her head. *No. I don't think anyone does.*

He hadn't answered.

When she'd left, Colin had been inside making dinner. She'd looked in the door, which Luke had opened, and he'd said, "Oh. Goodbye. Ready for dinner, Luke?"

Luke, like Luke Skywalker.

Of course, it was unlikely Colin even remembered how her brother used to love *Star Wars*. Probably his son had been named for the Gospel-writer or just because Colin and his wife liked the name.

No more information about that wife. Perhaps Lily's parents would know the story.

But she shrank from the idea of asking them—or letting them know she'd be returning to the Aerie to look after the injured owl.

It occurred to her suddenly that she might actually be *wounding* her parents by going back to the Aerie, even to take care of the owl. She and Colin, together, were the reason Ryan had died—the means to his death. Her parents might take it personally, very personally, if she chose to spend even a second more than necessary in the company of Colin Gardner. Which meant she should be careful what she said upon her return home.

But neither of her parents asked even one thing about her trip to the Aerie; they didn't even encourage her to share negative impressions of Colin as manager of the Aerie and as a parent.

Nor was anything said the next morning, while she fished with her mother from their old dinghy and caught a couple of walleyes. They cooked the fish, her catch and her mother's, for breakfast, and afterward Lily swam across the lake and back. As she neared the far shore, she wondered if she'd see Colin or Luke, but neither appeared. While she swam, she wondered what to tell her parents when she left to take care of the owl. Afternoon seemed the best time of day to go—especially since she could put off telling her parents until then.

That afternoon at about three-thirty, when she came downstairs in pale green capri-length pants, a white tank top and white platform sandals, her mother said, "Where are you going? You look like you're going to the city."

Lily wore her backpack-style purse with her cell phone clipped to it. If she told her mother the truth, Marie would never let her hear the end of it.

Shopping. The lie was on the tip of her tongue.

But she was forty years old! She should either not do this thing that would trouble her parents so much or she should face up to their reaction. Deceit would only demean her.

And spare them pain, perhaps.

I shouldn't have said I wanted to take care of it.

"I'm going to help look after the owl I rescued."

"Like *that?*" exclaimed her mother. "You've dressed like you're going on a date."

"I have a work shirt in the car," Lily assured her.

"Why you? Can't he take care of it?"

He.

"I *want* to help. It's going to be a long-term resident. His wing—it's a male—can't be fixed."

"Are you going to feed it? They eat live food. You know that, don't you?"

"Yes." She didn't want to think about it, but she'd do what she had to.

Marie Moran put her hands on her hips. "I'm astonished by how little you've changed, Lily. Have you forgotten that Helen and Bert are coming tonight?"

I tried to forget.

"You're forty years old," Marie went on, "but you're still chasing after Colin Gardner as though he cared about you at all. He's on the make and always was."

Lily didn't know where her mother had gotten that mean streak. Lily felt no need to protect Colin from her mother's meanness. But she wished she had as little feeling about the mother-daughter digs that were always so close to the bone.

"I'm not chasing Colin Gardner." Lily hated the way her voice shook. "I have chosen to take care of the owl I found at the place where I last saw Ryan alive. This has always been about the owl. But I don't know why you blame Colin for what happened to Ryan when you should blame me. It was my fault. You know it was. I was Ryan's babysitter. I let it happen. There's no point pretending any different. And yes, I was the sort of silly teenager who paid more attention to boys my own age than to my little brother when I was supposed to be taking care of him. If St. Helen had been available to babysit instead of dutifully helping at the church luncheon for senior citizens, Ryan would probably be alive today. I really am the terrible person you think I am. Let's just accept that. Blame me. Blame Colin, too, if you like, but why blame him instead of me?"

Marie had frozen. "Ryan died a long time ago," she said. "You were very nearly a child yourself. Colin was older."

"By one year! And I was fifteen. Anyhow, it *was* a long time ago. Can't we all move on?" As soon as the words were out, she heard how unthinkable *and* how thoughtless they were.

But her mother showed no reaction to her plea, the plea Lily knew to be appalling in its insensitivity. "I'm sorry," Lily whispered quickly.

"I don't suppose he told you how his wife died."

He hadn't even told Lily that his wife had died; nor had Luke told her. She opened her mouth, but nothing came out.

"It sounded to me like the same sort of thing as Ryan's death, another drowning, another accident," Marie continued. "You don't like careless men, Lily, so I'm surprised you're spending time with him."

"I'm spending time with the owl," Lily repeated. "It's a Great Gray Owl. It seemed to me like—"

"A sign from Ryan?" Marie's face changed, softened. Her mother's features actually lost their sharp-boned tension, but at least she looked interested, lively with the urge to share something positive. "He sends us messages, you know," she told Lily. "There are things that always remind us of him. The loons, when they come back."

Lily nearly swayed with exhaustion. She had hoped her parents were truly ready to put Ryan's death behind them, that this was the meaning behind their decision to finally scatter his ashes. It no longer seemed likely.

"Yes," Lily said. "I guess that's what I mean. A sign from Ryan." It wasn't precisely the truth, wasn't the truth because she did not believe that Ryan, wherever he was, would send a message to her, Lily, or to any of them. "And that's why I'm taking care of it."

COLIN CAME OUT of the cabin when she drove up. He wore jeans and a flannel shirt. To Lily's surprise, he smiled when he saw her. It was a rugged, attractive smile, and she wondered how she'd find it if she were the sort of woman, like so many of her friends, who could actually become significantly sexually excited by a man, by any man.

Why were they all such a huge disappointment? Helen, her cousin, bragged incessantly about Bert, the incredibly boring man she'd been seeing for years, and the whole thing made Lily's stomach churn. In addition to not sleeping together "until we're sure"—Helen's suspect explanation—they seemed to be in a tiresome, never-ending competition to see if they could spend even less money than Lily's parents. For Christmas, Bert had given Helen a wallet that looked like it had come from Wal-Mart.

That was all! Lily had exclaimed to one of her girl-friends, feeling petty and furious at the same time over how cheap Bert was and how proud Helen was of his cheapness.

Would Colin Gardner be cheap?

Lily doubted it. Not extravagant, but not cheap. Cheap wasn't practical, and Lily felt certain that, if nothing else, Colin was practical at heart.

He walked with her toward the row of mews housing long-term residents.

Lily, as though determined to put her foot wrong everywhere she could, to bring up every painful and awkward subject for perusal, said, "My mother told me your wife died. I'm sorry."

But it wasn't the wrong thing to say.

An Important Message from the Editors

Dear Reader,

If you'd enjoy reading novels about rediscovery and reconnection with what's important in women's lives, then let us send you two free Harlequin® Next™ novels. These books celebrate the "next" stage of a woman's life because there's a whole new world after marriage and motherhood.

By the way, you'll also get a surprise gift with your two free books! Please enjoy the free books and gift with our compliments...

Pam Powers

Peel off Seal and Place Inside...

THE EDITOR'S "THANK YOU" FREE GIFTS INCLUDE:

▶ Two BRAND-NEW Harlequin® Next™ Novels

▶ An exciting surprise gift

YES! I have placed my Editor's "thank you" Free Gifts seal in the space provided at right. Please send me 2 FREE books, and my FREE Mystery Gift. I understand that I am under no obligation to purchase anything further, as explained on the back and opposite page.

PLACE FREE GIFTS SEAL HERE

▶ DETACH AND MAIL CARD TODAY!

356 HDL D74U   156 HDL D726

FIRST NAME

LAST NAME

ADDRESS

APT.#

CITY

STATE/PROV.

ZIP/POSTAL CODE

Thank You!

(HN-HF-11/05)

The Reader Service — Here's How It Works:

Accepting your 2 free books and gift places you under no obligation to buy anything. You may keep the books and gift and return the shipping statement marked "cancel." If you do not cancel, about a month later we'll send you 3 additional books and bill you just $3.99 each in the U.S., or $4.74 each in Canada, plus 25¢ shipping & handling per book and applicable taxes if any.* That's the complete price and — compared to cover prices of $5.50 each in the U.S. and $6.50 each in Canada — it's quite a bargain! You may cancel at any time, but if you choose to continue, every month we'll send you 3 more books, which you may either purchase at the discount price or return to us and cancel your subscription.

*Terms and prices subject to change without notice. Sales tax applicable in N.Y. Canadian residents will be charged applicable provincial taxes and GST.

"Thank you." He paused, squinting up at the trees.

She followed his gaze to a tree house, another tree house, as ramshackle as the one on the lakeshore. But Luke was sitting on a platform on this one, high, high above the ground.

Her heart pounded.

"Hi, Lily!"

"Hi, Luke. Be careful," she called, watching the tiny bare legs and bare feet. "Doesn't that scare you?" she asked Colin.

He didn't answer immediately, and Lily was left looking at him, admiring his features. "If it does, is that a reason to make him come down?"

"Yes!" exclaimed Lily, quietly. "Fear—that kind of fear—is part of our survival mechanism. Genetic survival, too. *I'm* scared looking at him."

"He'll be fine," Colin said, as though he knew something about it that she didn't. Then he changed the subject. "Do you dance anymore?"

"Not really." She stole another glance and saw Luke reaching for another limb, pulling himself higher. He must be twenty-five feet or more off the ground.

"You wanted to dance with one of the ballets."

She'd almost forgotten that. Still watching Luke, she said, "I suppose I changed after Ryan died. I went to live with my grandparents, because my parents wanted to live here full-time. I couldn't stand being here after what happened. This is the first time I've been back," she admitted.

"I couldn't stand being in Utah," Colin said. "After Marisa died. I came back here…."

The sentence drifted off.

Luke hoisted himself higher in the tree. She longed to make him come down, to climb safely down to the ground. Colin was insane to let him do this.

"How did she die?" She jerked her head quickly to see Colin. "If you don't mind my asking?"

"She drowned. In a flash flood. She was trapped beneath debris and broke her leg. She'd been hiking alone, looking for a falcon we'd lost. She headed a raptor center where I volunteered—that's how we met." He paused. "You know, her death felt to me like payment of a karmic debt that I incurred when your brother died."

It was impossible to keep looking at Luke and impossible *not* to watch the small boy.

"Is that why you think your son's in no danger up there?" She almost whispered it, shocked that their conversation had reached such an intimate level so quickly.

"I didn't say I think he's in no danger."

"You're a fatalist," she exclaimed, turning on him then. "Hugo called it 'that stigma of crime and unhappiness.' And he was right."

To her surprise he smiled again, and the smile was even more attractive than she remembered. Wolfish. He was a very handsome man, more so in maturity than as a teenager.

"And you're not a fatalist?" he asked.

"How could I believe that Ryan's death was fate? That would deny *my* responsibility." A pause. "You think it was?"

"I'm not a fatalist," he answered. "The Greeks may have believed that we can't escape what fate has in store for us, but I think we affect everything around us, even the smallest things."

Then why do you let your son climb that tree?

At that moment, Luke began to slide expertly down a long thick rope whose upper end was fastened to a bough above him.

But at least he was coming down. Winky the Jack Russell terrier barked up at him as the boy descended and wagged her tail as he touched down.

"Hi, Winky," he said and petted her, then ran to his father and hurled himself into Colin's arms. The soles of his bare feet were black with grime, and Lily saw knots in his shoulder-length blond hair. He then turned to see her face. "Hi, Lily," he repeated. He looked at his father and whispered something to Colin.

Colin looked at him and shook his head. "You can."

Luke, suddenly shy, buried his face in his father's shoulder.

Colin said, "We named the owl." He carried Luke toward the mews, and Lily walked beside them.

When Colin said nothing else, she put the question to Luke. "What did you call him?"

"Socrates," Luke said.

"I told him you teach philosophy, and that philosophers are thinkers, and he asked for the name of a famous philosopher."

"That's a great name," Lily told Luke. "I couldn't have thought of a better one."

Luke slid out of Colin's arms and ran ahead. "Mosi said you could feed Socrates a rat today."

"Great." Would she have to pick it up?

"There's not much to do for one bird," Colin said.

"Would you like to learn about the others while you're here? And we have some eaglets that are a lot of work. We use a blind and hand puppets to feed them. We also have a falcon we think we're going to be able to release—at least we're working in that direction."

Lily saw this, not as an attempt to secure another volunteer, but as the generous gift he no doubt meant it to be. "Thank you!" she said, meaning it. "Yes. I'd like that."

Colin's answering glance held surprise, although it wasn't unflattering. More…speculative.

No other volunteers seemed to be around that afternoon. No Mosi either. Lily half expected Colin to make an excuse and leave her with Luke, but he stayed with them instead, giving her advice on entering the mews, watching Luke show her the supplies to clean the area, showing her later how to push or let food into the mews through a one-way food flap.

She used heavy gloves to pick up the white rat. At least it wasn't cute.

After they'd fed Socrates, they watched him through the glass.

He sat on a perch high in one corner. Lily thought of the way Great Gray Owls dived in winter for prey, dived into snow. This bird would not do that again.

Luke wandered down the row of mews to visit the Harlan's hawk that was his favorite. "No dancing with a famous ballet," Colin said, almost to himself. "What are your dreams now?"

To answer that question truthfully would be sad. She knew the sadness of the answer every day, not just today because he'd asked. But it was just growing up, wasn't it? "Dreams are different when you get older," was all she could say.

He looked at her. She felt it.

His silence compelled her to say more. "I wouldn't say I have dreams now. It's enough that nothing like that—like Ryan dying the way he did—has to happen in my life again. I mean, that's a dream right there. There is no horrible thing that categorically *can't* happen to us."

Socrates seemed uninterested in the rat. It was a safe change of subject. "Will he wait until night to eat?" she asked.

"Maybe. But probably not."

"How will he catch the rat if he can't fly?"

"Mosi thinks he can fly well enough to catch a rat in the mews."

Lily remembered a piece of rhyme about dreams dying. Without them, life was "a broken-wing bird that cannot fly."

Her wings weren't broken, except in her mind.

When she'd gone to live with her grandparents in Chicago, the stated reason was so she could dance, and so she had danced. She'd gone to a performing arts high school and had danced every single day. But while her classmates were ambitious, anything resembling ambition in herself had made her feel vaguely ill.

Her teachers were initially puzzled by her lack of fire, lack of engagement. Until, undoubtedly, someone mentioned that Ryan had drowned because of her.

"What was your wife like?"

He turned from the mews and didn't answer at once.

"Smart," he said finally.

Lily waited.

Nothing.

"She was a veterinarian," he said next.

"What did you do in Utah?"

"I had a business. I designed some shoes for boatmen to wear on the river. Colorado River Toed. They were popular."

So that was how he'd financed the Aerie—and bought the land. "You sold it? Or you still own it?"

"Sold it."

"Did you blame yourself—for what happened to your wife? Besides what you said—that you thought it was a karmic debt?"

He considered, then shook his head. "Sometimes I blame *her*. It was pouring, she was walking in a wash. She knew better."

"Well, you owe no karmic debt for Ryan's death," Lily told him. "That was my fault. He'd be thirty-three now. He might have married. He might have had children of his own."

"I don't think that alternate reality exists," Colin responded, "except in our imaginations."

"Believe me, it exists in my parents' imagination."

He said, "Want to walk down to the old dock?"

"Why?"

His eyes flickered. "Why not?"

"I just wondered if you had some reason for wanting to repeat the past," she replied.

"Well, since you're no longer a fifteen-year-old virgin and I'm no longer a sixteen-year-old one, we can't, in fact, repeat the past—any part of it."

What did *that* mean? "I don't mind looking at the water," she said.

"Luke, we're going down to the lake," Colin called to his son.

"Okay," Luke shouted back and ran down the aisle toward them.

Her shoes seemed especially silly on the walk to the lakeshore, and she took them off and carried them. The feel of the bare earth reminded her of the moment she'd found Socrates. And of older events.

Mosquitoes whined around them and began biting before they reached the water. Twenty-four hours on Swan Lake, and Lily's arms and legs were dotted with red bumps.

At the water, Lily asked, "Is this the same ice-fishing shack that was here back then?"

"I think so. But I'm not sure. We use it."

"I'm going up in the tree house," said Luke.

"Okay," Colin answered.

"Is that safe?" Lily squinted up at the structure overhanging the lake.

Colin's expression as he studied the tree house made her wonder if the question had ever crossed his mind before.

Luke had already disappeared into the undergrowth between them and the tree house tree.

"How can you just let him *do* things like that? Carry around raptors that you've told me could tear out my muscles. Climb in tree houses that look like they're about to fall down. Aren't you at all concerned? Accidents happen. *You* know they do. And you told me you're not a fatalist."

He tipped back his head, and she thought he had the profile of an Odysseus. A man a woman would wait for, wait twenty years for, or maybe more.

"If I tell you," he said suddenly, "you need to understand that I've never told anyone else."

Everything about his saying this surprised her, most of all that it was an admission from a man she didn't know—and yet knew better than any other. He knew *her* in a way no one else did. Simply because of the crime they shared.

She nodded.

His voice lowered beneath the whine of the mosquitoes. The scent of the raptors was still in her nostrils. The owl stank like a skunk, which Colin said was its favorite food in the wild. But Colin's earthiness, his son's wild hair and bare feet, enticed her, seemed comfortable. "I believe," he said, "with absolute certainty that Luke will not be injured and will not be taken from me. It's kind of about the odds, and it's kind of superstition. Maybe you'd call it fatalistic."

"I call it silly," she said without hesitation. "And untrue. I think it's far more likely that you're scared to death he'll die as your wife did, as Ryan did, so you can't even acknowledge it by trying to protect him in any normal way."

The green eyes stared.

She felt his hand as it caught hers.

"I'm going! Watch, Lily!"

She started as the small body hurtled down from the tree house on the rope as it swung out over the lake, and Luke splashed in, perhaps six feet from the dock, perhaps sixty feet from where they'd found Ryan.

She couldn't stand it and ran barefoot onto the dock and sat down on the edge as Luke, so terribly small with his sleek wet head, the blond hair now looking light brown, stroked toward the dock.

He clasped the dock and said to her, "Lift me out."

She reached down and lifted the very small boy onto the dock beside her. It was hot, and the water felt good on her feet and ankles. "Luke," she said earnestly. "Be very careful. Please don't go swimming without your dad or someone watching you."

"That's the rule," he said. "Because I can get a cramp. Have you ever gotten a cramp? I saw you swim by yourself today."

"My parents knew I was going. They were watching."

Though she swam alone in the ocean without a lifeguard. She shared Colin's logic, she thought. She swam alone because Ryan had drowned and so she could not.

"I'm going back to the house. You want to come see my room?" asked Luke.

"Yes. Thank you."

He jumped up and ran down the dock and past his dad. "I'm going to show Lily my room."

"We'll be there in a minute," Colin said.

Lily knew. She knew before she stepped off the dock and over to the ice house, to the spot where Socrates had sprung from the ground, the broken-wing bird that could not fly, the death that would never leave by its own power.

His voice was very quiet. "May I kiss you?"

It bore no resemblance to what had happened when they were teenagers, and that fact was cleansing, saving. He was a man.

"Yes."

It started as a simple kiss, lips against lips, warm and interesting. She liked his scent, touched the cotton of his shirt.

It went no further.

Just a kiss.

Looking into each other's eyes.

"Two weeks," he said.

She could not answer. She could not say, *Yes. Just two weeks.*

She wanted to say, *Forever.*

She had no idea where the tears came from or why. She picked up her shoes, which she'd dropped when Luke swung down from the tree house.

She put them on and followed Colin's son back toward the house, each step uncertain.

CHAPTER FOUR

HER COUSIN, Helen, had what Lily instantly decided was one of the ugliest haircuts she'd ever seen. She disliked her own pettiness, and she disliked Helen for turning her into a person she disliked.

Lily couldn't stop thinking about Colin and Luke. Luke's showing her his bedroom, his Harry Potter Lego sets, then perhaps the biggest surprise. *These are my dad's poetry books. He writes poems about the raptors and we sell them to make money for the Aerie.* Lily had started reading the poems, when Luke rambled on. *I usually sleep with my dad in his room. Come see.* Colin's room. She had sat on the bed, and Colin had come in and sat on the bed, and Luke had bounced on the bed, which had a quilt in a plaid flannel cover.

Colin and I have business on that bed.

She felt the future looming, massive and definite, and hadn't even gritted her teeth when her mother had said, *You were gone long enough. Helen's been looking forward to seeing you.*

Helen had looked her up and down and said, "Cute outfit. Santa Barbara?"

"Yes." *I'm projecting. I'm projecting onto her and*

Bert and my parents that everyone is assessing how much money I spend on every little thing.

It seemed to Lily that Helen spent more time with Lily's parents than with her own, who lived in Florida and liked to play bingo, but maybe it was just that Helen's parents couldn't stand her, either.

Bert, tall and mustached, with that slight belly hanging over his belt but still managing to look fit, stood with Lily's father, discussing the cheapest price on tires.

"I'm sorry to hear about your engagement," Helen said. "Oh, Marie. Can I help with dinner? Too bad it didn't work out, Lily."

She wandered from the big front room into the adjoining kitchen, where Marie was taking a loaf of bread out of the oven.

No bread machines for the Morans, reflected Lily. "Don't be sorry," she told Helen.

Colin. Colin, Colin, Colin. She had never felt for Drake what she felt now, in this brief time, for Colin. One kiss. And it wasn't just Colin. She felt bound to him and Luke.

She felt that a winter in the North Woods wouldn't be so bad.

She could go ice fishing.

"Lily, you could start on the salad," Marie said, ignoring Helen's offer of help. "What's wrong, Lily? Are you all right? Did something happen over there? Did he say something horrible?"

Why not? Why not say it here, while her father and Bert wandered into the kitchen, now discussing Bert's inexpensive car insurance? "No." Lily moved closer to her mother. A stain on the floor that turned out to be a knot in the wood leaped up at her. She made herself meet Marie's gaze and thought how she had inherited her mother's long thin nose with the beaklike bump at the bridge. "He was very nice. And I like his son. I'm having dinner there tomorrow night."

Her mother peered under the lid of the pot on the stove—one of her soups, the smell filling the house, gorgeous as morning. Like the bread. And unlike the cloud of hatred billowing in her black eyes—dark, dark brown—the eyes she'd given Lily. Now Lily wondered if she was going to look like her mother, sharp-faced and angry, when she was older. If she was beginning to look that way already.

Marie said nothing.

Nothing.

The lid banged back down.

Lily's mother opened the refrigerator door, began taking out vegetables.

Lily swiftly grabbed the cutting board.

"I'll do it," Marie said.

"I can help," Helen chimed in, touching Marie's back, soothing.

Lily ground her teeth and thought of receding gums and didn't care. She wanted to scream at Helen, *Get out of this house. It wasn't your tragedy. That's* my *mother, and we need to sort this out!*

But she couldn't.

And Marie touched Helen's arm, motherly, sisterly.

Marie said, haltingly, to the organic celery she'd pulled from a plastic bag she had reused and would use again, "If you're not busy—we're going—to scatter Ryan—we've planned the ceremony for Saturday."

Two days away, and her mother had shed a tear, and Helen put an arm around her shoulders.

Lily stepped forward, ignored Helen, tried not to touch her or smell her generic soap and shampoo, and embraced her mother, who seemed thin and who turned, not to her niece, but to her daughter.

Lily looked into her mother's face, and the dark eyes looked at her. Marie's skin hung loose on her bones, aging, autumnal. "I forgive you, Lily. I have never blamed you. But I don't understand you. How can you repeat the very thing that lost us Ryan?"

SO HER PARENTS KNEW. Well, it wasn't rocket science, Lily reflected again as she drove up the Aerie's road the next afternoon. It wasn't hard to figure out why sixteen-year-old Colin and fifteen-year-old Lily had been so remiss that day.

How can you repeat the very thing that lost us Ryan?

Lily had spent her life, since her brother's death, being attentive to safety, determined not to create another situation like that, not to preside over another accident that needn't happen.

This was not repeating what had happened before.

It wasn't the same at all, or she wouldn't do it.

Winky greeted her at the door of the cabin. Inside, she found Mosi and Luke lying on the faded Navajo rugs on the living room floor, engrossed in a game of chess. Colin came out of the bedroom. He had recently showered, his hair still wet, pulling on a T-shirt over the chest that had filled out and sprouted curly dark hair.

"We're having homemade pizza," he said, walking into the kitchen. The pizzas were on the counter, and the oven was hot; he put them in and set a timer. "Feel like a walk?"

Luke sat up. "Are you going to show her the blue tree house? Can I come?"

"I'll save that for you," said Colin. "You finish your game. Someone has to beat Mosi."

THEY CLIMBED UP into the tree house that Luke had swung from the day before and stared down on the lake.

Lily felt freer than she had since Ryan's death. She had lost childhood that day, lost the paddling of canoes and the climbing of trees and bare feet on damp spongy ground beneath spruce and maple and birch. Sitting beside Colin, she told him what had occurred the night before. She concluded, "She forgives me, I suppose, but she doesn't forgive the act. And she shouldn't, in some way. I was thinking about something I wanted at that moment, and I neglected a sacred trust."

"Lily, if they hadn't believed I was levelheaded, they would've made you stay home to watch Ryan."

"Yes, right. Maybe my mother even forgives you. She just hates the idea of my being in your company." She chose the last words carefully, words that wouldn't assume too much.

"It's not the same."

"No," Lily agreed. "How long were you married?"

"Four years."

Lily gazed across Swan Lake at her parents' place. His aunt and uncle had always rented the cabin next door to the Morans'. Now her parents owned that property in addition to their old house. It had become part of Camp Boreal. She gazed down at toenails painted pale pink. Her mother had commented on it the night before and asked if she'd "paid someone" to do that. "It was such a freak thing," Lily said, "the way he died."

"I'll never forgive myself."

Lily frowned. "It wasn't *your* fault."

He didn't answer.

"*I* was the one babysitting. My mom said, 'Take your brother, Lily,' and she told him to mind me, though I doubt she remembers that." A breeze blew one of Colin's wavy locks of hair. Did he really blame himself? But he would. Of course, he would. She muttered, "I was so sick of the little twerp." She fell into one of Ryan's Yoda impressions. "The dark side of the Force is Lily. Ugly she is. Kiss her no one will.'"

A genuine grin cracked Colin's face, erasing the troubled expression he'd worn moments before. "That's what I remember most about him. And that once he told me that if I gave him money, he'd arrange for me to see you naked."

Lily's jaw dropped. She was tempted to say it was good the little pimp had perished, but it didn't come out, because her annoying pest of a brother *had* drowned and it had been *her* fault, and the money-making scheme he'd tried on Colin was so profoundly *Ryan*. She had a sudden image of him practicing his violin. Condemned to oddity by her parents—but possessed of genius. No one had ever doubted his brilliance. She told Colin about the plan to scatter Ryan's ashes. "You should be there," she said.

"Your parents should determine who's there. Anyway, it wouldn't make a difference."

"To what?" The wind gusted over her ankles. She'd

actually worn denim overalls to this dinner, with a white tank top underneath. Swimming kept her arms in good shape. She was, she thought, a young forty. She tucked her feet up against her, clasped her arms around her knees.

Colin didn't answer. Not at first. He looked at her, his expression surprisingly earnest. "Have you forgiven yourself?"

She shrugged. "In a sense. I'm still *guilty*. But I've determined not to make that kind of mistake again. That's why it frightened me so much seeing Luke swinging in the trees."

He scooted back, resting his spine against the trunk of the tree. "I'll never forgive myself. And that's a choice. But I don't have the kind of peace you have with it. Marisa—I had nothing to do with that. I wish I could go back in time and stop her going after that bird. But it wasn't my fault. Ryan's dying was. I was a lifeguard. What your mother said was true. You let him take off his lifejacket, and one of us should've been watching him, and *my* choice, my leading you away—allowed it to happen. It's my fault."

My parents should hear him say that. Would it make a difference to them? Or to Colin?

He was easy to talk to. Near him now, she felt as though she'd been waiting lifetimes to finish a conversation with him. *This is the one.* Every time their eyes met, she knew—and knew that he knew, as well.

Beside him in the tree house, she laughed about Helen, about her persistent hatred of her cousin, their rivalry for the mother Lily sometimes thought she also hated. It was confessional; her mother had pointed out just that morning that Lily seemed to have no trouble laughing at things, but was she able to take anything seriously? Lily told him this and told him the answer she hadn't given her mother: she took seriously the business of going through life without making mistakes.

"That's a tall order." His long lashes blinked once, reflectively, as he watched a loon on the lake.

He told her about homeschooling Luke, about the schedule they maintained, and the fact that Luke clung to him even more than Colin did to his son.

Finally, he said, "You haven't been married."

It meant something, this question, from him. "Engaged. Twice."

The twitch of the mouth. "Married to your job?"

"Not." For the right reason, she could walk away from teaching. Not from the book she hadn't touched since arriving in Minnesota; that was a commitment on which she must follow through.

"Do you want children?" he asked.

"I like your son." Lily stood on the plywood roof of the tree house and stretched her arms above her head, thinking that the wind made the trees dance and trying to move like them, swayed by the wind. "Why did you name him Luke?"

"Why do you think?"

She stilled. "Really?"

Colin nodded. "Ryan was a hero. He was on his journey." Abruptly he put a hand to his face, rubbing his jaw.

"Colin, what caused this break between you and my parents? Really."

"Well, you know they didn't forgive me for what happened—Ryan dying. More than didn't forgive. You remember those few days."

She did. Her parents had turned on him. Her mother had shouted, *And what were you doing, Colin? You're supposed to be a lifeguard, aren't you?*

"Right," Lily said. "Did you come back here after that? Before you moved back."

"No. I did the same as you. Avoided the place like the plague. When Marisa died—things looked different. I came back then. I think your parents resent Luke."

Colin's son wasn't anything like Ryan. Ryan had been dark-haired, awkward, gifted and maniacal. Luke was blond, appealing, athletic and *normal.*

But perhaps the point was simply that Colin had a son. And, in her parents' eyes, particularly her mother's, Colin had cost them a son.

Lily stretched again, swaying like the trees. She had braided her hair before coming over, in part to look as though it didn't matter to her that she was having dinner at his house.

Now he said, "You're beautiful. You dance like the trees." And when they climbed down from the tree house, he went first and then helped her as she came down, barefoot, into his arms, where he kissed her against the trunk, and she felt bark on one side and Colin on the other. He was clean from the shower, but a smell of woodsmoke and raptors lingered around him. His lips against hers said what they both already knew. "You don't like Santa Barbara that much, anyhow."

"DO YOU THINK Socrates would like to eat more than one rat a day?" she asked Luke. The pizza wasn't quite done, so Colin's son had suggested they go out to the mews to feed the owl.

"We should ask Mosi," he answered, "but he'll probably say no. Socrates doesn't get much exercise, seeing he can't fly. It changes his metabolism."

Lily beamed down at him. They'd given Socrates his one rodent and walked down to look at Sharpe, who was Luke's favorite. "Do you learn about raptors from Mosi? Or when you homeschool?"

"From Mosi. And I read about them."

They fed the other raptors together, taking them rats, hamsters, mice, rabbits, and in the case of two of the eagles, chickens. Some of the raptors, Luke told her, required specially cooked food. Mosi or Colin or the volunteers fed them.

"Once," Luke said, "one of the eagles got out and flew up in the trees and we didn't know where she was. Her wing was mostly better but not all the way healed."

"How did you find her?"

He walked along beside her, ragdoll-like, blond hair swinging about his elfin face. Green eyes like Colin's, but he didn't bear much resemblance to his father. Judging from the exquisite delicacy of Luke's features, Marisa had been a beautiful woman.

"Well, we used binoculars. We figured she couldn't have gone far, so we checked in all the nearby trees."

"Where was she?"

"Right on the tree outside the tree house. We looked all over the place, and that's where we found her."

Marisa, Colin had said, had been searching for an escaped bird when she was caught in a flash flood and drowned.

Lily and Luke went outside into the whine of mosquitoes.

"I beat Mosi at chess," he said. "I'm really good at chess. Sometimes I beat my dad."

"You're good at a lot of things."

"Did you know a boy died in the lake by my tree house there? He drowned. My dad told me."

The shade from the trees, and that mop of hair, hid his face. They walked back toward the cabin, both barefoot. Lily thought, *Colin's right. I won't go back to Santa Barbara to live. This is where I belong. These are my people. This is my world. I never want to leave.*

"The boy who drowned was my brother. He was two years older than you."

"Couldn't he swim?"

"He could swim. I don't know what happened." What had Colin told his son about Ryan's death? "I think he tried to take the canoe out by himself. He must have fallen in the water. I don't know why he drowned."

"My dad said his parents were really sad."

"That's true." *They still are.*

A bell rang—an old-fashioned dinner bell.

"Dinner's ready," Luke said. "That's how he calls me—when I don't help make dinner, that is. I help lots, especially after we go fishing."

"Do you like fishing?" Silly question. Everyone in Minnesota liked fishing. That was the point of living there.

"Yeah. I like it when my dad and I get up real early in the morning and go fishing."

Lily wondered how old Luke had been when his mother died. Three? Four?

"Some night I want your dad to bring you to my parents' house to meet them." It was the only way. Because if they spent time with this child they could neither dislike nor resent him.

"I don't think he gets along with them," said Luke. "Once your mom and my dad got in a big screaming fight."

This was the first Lily had heard of it, but she wasn't surprised.

"What about?"

"Well, your mom was yelling mostly. She said why couldn't we live somewhere else, and this place smells because of all the birds."

A valid observation, Lily agreed, but it wasn't as if her parents could smell the Aerie from their house.

Inside the house, Colin was putting plates on the table. He'd set the table with place mats in earthy colors, mismatched silverware and dish towels for napkins. Lily felt at home. Her own apartment in Santa Barbara was simple. Her things *did* match. Glasses she loved, heavy light-green glasses, and cotton sheets from Spain. Luxuries that would make her mother sneer. But Colin's style suited him and the cabin.

"The pizza smells incredible," she said.

He gave her a quick grin from beneath those bushy eyebrows. His hair still had plenty of wave, which was what she remembered from when they were teenagers together.

Mosi, whistling, glanced between the two of them. "I promised Luke I'd read to him after dinner."

"And I'm going to read to Lily," Luke said. He looked up at her. "Can you sleep over?"

"Yeah, can you?" echoed Colin.

Lily bit back a smile. Both invitations touched her.

Luke must get lonely. Did he have friends? *Someone needs to make sure he has kids to play with—friends his own age.*

How strange that Socrates had brought her back to Colin Gardner—and to Luke, who was motherless.

Could I be a stepmother?

She could be this child's stepmother. She could love him as her own, and in some way she already did.

Colin sat across from her at the table, Luke beside her, Mosi across from Luke. She had the feeling that the vet was an honorary family member.

She asked Colin, "How are you going to do home-school later on? Could you teach trig? Or chemistry?"

"He'll probably want to go to school when he gets older."

Luke shook his head. "No. I want you to teach me, Dad. I always want to be homeschooled."

Colin smiled and slid another piece of pizza onto Lily's plate.

WHILE MOSI AND Luke went into Luke's room to read, Lily filled the sink with warm water and started on the dishes.

Colin, drying beside her, said, "He'll be out cold about two pages into the chapter they're reading."

Lily understood, felt, knew.

She couldn't look at him.

Mosi emerged from the bedroom. "The sleep of the just. I'm taking off."

"Glad you came." Colin stepped away from the sink briefly to embrace Mosi. "Thanks for everything."

Lily and Mosi said good-night, too, and then she and Colin were alone, with Luke asleep in his own bedroom.

Colin's arms circled her, enclosed her, his mouth against hers, wanting like hers, exploring like hers. His eyes asked. His eyes knew her answer. Entwined, they stumbled, hugging, never stopping, to his bedroom and to the soft depth of the flannel-covered bed.

AFTERWARD, AFTER THEY'D MADE LOVE, they played a game of chess on the bed.

"Your parents will never accept me," Colin said. "Or Luke."

"They will. Eventually. It might take some time to sort out. That's all."

"If you had to choose, what—who—would you choose?"

Lily was her parents' last remaining child; much as her mother liked to pretend that Helen was the perfect daughter, she wasn't Marie's daughter at all. Lily was. "I don't think I'll have to choose."

"I'm glad I don't have to. I've never wanted to marry again because I knew I'd never love someone as much as I love my son. But I feel differently with you. You feel more like—part of the family. Part of me. Maybe part of him."

"I don't like the idea of people needing to choose between people they love." She imagined her mother demanding that she choose between the Morans and the Gardners. The scenario was so plausible that it sent a chill through her. "Love is bigger than that. If love is big enough that I'd be willing to risk sharing my life with a child who swings around in trees—a child as fragile as any human—" *as fragile as Ryan* "—then love is big enough that I'll never have to choose between my family of origin and you and Luke."

Colin didn't answer, but his eyes were so steady she knew they saw her mother more clearly than she, Lily, ever had.

CHAPTER FIVE

"WHERE HAVE YOU BEEN?"

It was two in the morning. Lily thought she'd been quiet entering the house, carrying treasures from Colin: a volume of his poetry entitled *Skywalker* and a photograph of Luke. The light over the stove was on, and she'd assumed her parents and Helen and Bert had gone to bed.

So her mother stepping out of the shadows at the foot of the staircase startled her. Marie wore a pair of loose cotton pants and a flannel shirt with the tails out, probably what she'd worn to bed. She looked as though she hadn't slept. Her gray hair was down, and her feet were bare and looked like an old person's feet, the nails yellowed. She reminded Lily of the raptors.

"I was at Colin's."

"I don't need to ask *what* you were doing there till two in the morning."

Good. Don't. "I hope I didn't wake you."

"Wake me? I haven't slept. Is this what's going to happen for the rest of the only visit you've made to Camp Boreal in twenty-five years? Going out to dinner with him and coming back at two in the morning or not at all? Helen and Bert wanted to spend time with you," she hissed, "but you didn't think about that."

The onslaught of words seemed endless. Her mother talking about her "visit" on top of a different picture painted by Colin. How would Marie react if Lily told her she was considering spending the rest of the summer at the lake, to finish her book, not at Camp Boreal but at the Aerie? Add her own doubts about being a suitable guardian for Luke—not doubts that she could do it but a sense of vigilance that overwhelmed her. She *could* be a good stepmother. When, in twenty-five years, had she ever glanced away from duty? No accident would befall Luke on her watch—if Colin let her rewrite the rules of the Aerie.

She and Colin barely knew each other, yet they seemed to have known each other forever. Lily had never felt so comfortable with another person.

But the biggest issue, the greatest barrier, to her happiness with Colin and Luke was her parents.

They'll never forgive us. Colin and her together.

"Whatever you do," her mother said, "don't bring him over here."

"I'm sorry for you."

Marie stared. "You don't have to be sorry for me. I just don't care to see the person who's responsible for Ry—it took a lot of nerve for him to move up here, as though we wanted him. He had to know we didn't."

"How could he know that when *you* continue to live here? Isn't the lake itself reminder enough? And does he remind you of Ryan's dying any more than you're reminded every morning when you wake up? I know you never forget, and you shouldn't. You can't. I know you can't." It was too late at night. *I shouldn't be saying these things.*

"Well, it's easy to see where your sympathies lie," her mother remarked dryly.

"With *you.* Not just because you lost your little boy, my brother, but because you're choosing not to forgive Colin, *and it wasn't even his fault.* It was mine. It was entirely mine."

"And I forgive *you,* Lily, and I forgive him. I just don't like him. And that's my prerogative. His poetry's terrible, and so are his photographs."

Neither Colin nor Luke had mentioned photographs, but one of the volumes in Luke's room had included some, and she'd seen others at Colin's house. He must sell those, too.

"It's just self-serving," Marie continued. "Supposedly he puts out those little books to benefit that place, but they probably cost more to publish than he makes from them. Tourists are the only ones who buy that stuff."

"I like them."

Her mother stared. "You're in love with him, aren't you? After using two wonderful men, promising to marry them and breaking the engagement and their hearts—*yes,* Drake called and told us how you've treated him. He'll still have you back. Now, you're going to do something absurd like marry Colin Gardner."

She'd said his name, but it didn't sound like progress. A twinge of hurt gathered in Lily's heart. "Wouldn't you like to have me closer?"

In the midst of her own bitterness, Marie saw her

daughter's face. She put a hand to her own. "Yes. Yes. Yes, I would. But why *him*, Lily? Why are you doing this to us?"

"I didn't mean it to happen, and I didn't expect it to. And maybe it'll come to nothing." But she knew the lie as she uttered it. Because she could still see Colin's open face, his pure eyes beneath bushy eyebrows. She remembered the easy comfort of lying beside him, and she'd seen winter nights ahead spent the same way. And snowshoeing and cross-country skiing and ice fishing and reading with Luke, teaching Luke math, shining light on the wonder of numbers, illuminating learning for him.

Her mother studied her face. Unexpectedly, she turned and held the end of the mast that served as the staircase railing.

Lily waited for her to speak.

"I suppose next thing you're going to ask if he can come tomorrow."

To scatter Ryan's ashes.

"No. I wasn't." It felt like a lie. Lily swallowed, then stepped forward and hugged her mother. "Mom, I wish Ryan hadn't died. I keep remembering things about him…. I'm so sorry, Mom. I failed. I'm never going to fail like that again."

"I know that. It's not a worry I have." Her glare was unutterably weary and bitter as an ax blade. "He'll never be part of our family, so don't even try. If you want to be involved with him, that's up to you, but I'll never accept him. If not for him, Ryan would still be alive."

There was a nasty truth in it, a selfish truth, but it

wasn't a selfishness Lily could deny her parents. Still, she pointed out, "If not for me, Ryan would be alive."

"I wish his aunt and uncle had never brought *him* here." Her mother went on as though she hadn't heard. "He was a troublemaker, kicked out of one school one year and another the next."

"Mom, he's forty-one years old."

"Character is formed early."

Lily hitched her purse over her shoulder and made a movement to start up the stairs.

"Of course, he may never marry again," Marie said. "She was the mother of his child, after all. On the other hand, he may be looking for a woman to raise his son."

"No, he'll just sell us both into slavery, Mom." Satisfied with the sarcasm of her parting words, Lily did mount the stairs.

"He'll never be welcome under this roof," followed her up.

When Lily reached her room, the room with the photograph of Ryan and her in the fall leaves, she shut the door and sank down on the bed in tree-shaded moonlight.

It came before her eyes so strongly it was almost as though it was happening again. Her mind, that seemed to have completely forgotten details, suddenly saw the house as it had been twenty-five years before, heard Ryan yelling, *I don't want to go.*

Go with your sister.

And Lily had said, *Mom, I told you last night that Colin asked me to go across the lake.*

And why can't you take your brother?

Because she thinks if I don't come, Colin will kiss her. But he won't. Ugly you are, Lily-puke-tian.

A brat you are, she'd snapped in reply.

Ryan, I forbid you to harass your sister and Colin. Just go along and behave nicely. Your father and I are going to the flea market.

Ryan did *not* say he would rather go with them. *Can't I stay here by myself?*

No, you may not. If you recall, you're not allowed because you took the canoe out by yourself last time. And Lily will tell us if you misbehave.

I'll deal with you myself, she hissed to Ryan behind her mother's back.

If he did that Yoda thing in front of Colin, she might just leave the little creep on the other side of the lake and go somewhere else with Colin.

But why did Ryan have to come at all? This was a date, or should have been! She'd told her parents.

And now Ryan was coming along....

LILY EMERGED from the past like someone arriving back in the present after a trip through a time machine. *He didn't even want to come. And he'd taken the canoe out by himself before and gotten in trouble for it.*

He didn't want to come, and I didn't want to take him, and I'd told my parents the night before. It was my mother who made me take him.

It didn't excuse her, Lily, for her negligence. Nothing would do that. She simply wondered if her mother remembered these details.

Yes, she must.

So how could she blame Colin?

Maybe to quiet the loudest voice of blame in her mind. That voice must be Marie's own. She must have been blaming herself for twenty-five years.

Colin blamed himself. Lily blamed herself.

Her mother must blame herself, too, *had to*. Because no mother would forget those words, forget any detail of the situation.

Which made her behavior all the more inexplicable and unjust, yet made Lily sorrier for her than ever. She felt terrible as a sister directly responsible for her brother's death. How must her mother feel as a mother even *indirectly* contributing to it?

But how hard of her mother, how brittle Marie was, that she never spoke aloud of her own guilt yet allowed Lily to bear hers.

Maybe she can't, Lily reasoned. *Maybe she just can't stand to say the words out loud.*

Or maybe, it occurred to her, her mother *had* forgotten that she was the one who'd made Ryan go with Lily and Colin. Maybe she'd blotted out the truth in favor of a version she preferred.

But what could knowing this change?

As she got ready for bed, she remembered Colin holding her close, holding her face in his hands, saying, *I don't want you to go.* Telling her to watch out for deer on the road. Telling her to be careful. Loving her with such sweet and urgent intensity. She'd seen him look in on Luke, who lay sprawled diagonally on the bed in his own room, blond mop of hair spread every which way, tiny elfin face turned upward in sleep.

For the first time in her life, she knew what it was to be in love and to be loved with the same strength in return. It had never been like this with Drake, with anyone.

Her mother had said plainly that her parents would never make Colin a part of the family. Lily believed her. Her father alone, perhaps—but he was a unit with Marie and followed her lead in such things.

Did it matter to her whether her parents ever accepted Colin and Luke? Would it matter to Colin or his son?

She fell asleep surprisingly fast and dreamed of him, dreamed she was having dinner at his house, dreamed he kissed her, dreamed he loved her.

THE PHONE RANG at one-thirty in the afternoon the following day. The plan was to scatter Ryan's ashes right at sunset. Lily couldn't remember if she'd told Colin when it was to happen. She definitely hadn't mentioned it the night before.

Her mother answered the phone. "Camp Boreal, Marie speaking."

Lily watched her mother's stern face for a moment, then turned away, determined not to react to whatever happened if it was Colin. Helen sat at the kitchen table where she'd been showing Marie the afghan she was crocheting to sell at a church Christmas bazaar.

The yarn was cheap, and Lily found herself saying, "You know, if you made it from wool or cotton, people would probably pay more for it."

"No. People want convenience: they want machine-washable, and no one wants to pay too much."

"But think of all the hours you're putting into it. It's *worth* a lot." *Why not choose materials that will make it look that way?*

"Lily, the phone is for you."

Yes, definitely Colin. Her mother gave her the frostiest of glances as she handed over the receiver. "You're right, Helen. Much better to economize."

"Lily, Luke's very sick. Mosi thinks it's meningitis—" Colin sounded as though he couldn't quite believe it "—and he's going to drive us to the hospital."

"He was fine last night."

"He woke up after you left. I thought it was a cold. I guess it's contagious, but Mosi says he could have picked it up on a trip to the library with me—or anywhere."

Fear shook Lily. Meningitis could kill children. But Colin must know that, too. They were doing the right thing, the only thing.

"He's going to be fine," Colin said quickly, reminding Lily that he'd said he believed Luke wouldn't be taken from him. But she could tell that now he *didn't* believe with such certainty. His voice sounded different, caught in unreality. "Would you mind coming over and feeding the birds and Winky? I don't have any volunteers today, and I don't know when I'll be back. I'll give you a call tonight to let you know what's happening. If I can leave him. I think I might be in a hospital room for a while."

"Okay. Yes. It says what they eat on those clipboards outside the mews?"

"Yes. Be careful. There are directions by the pressure cooker for the ones who need cooked food and also on the charts. Mosi will be back tomorrow, but just write down which ones you feed. If in doubt, don't feed."

"Okay. Kiss Luke for me. I'll pray for him, Colin." *Because I can't stand if something happens to him. God, don't let anything happen.* The unpredictable cruelty of life. "Where are you taking him?"

"Bemidji, to start with."

"Okay." *I love you both.* She didn't say it. She hung up and walked toward the stairs.

"Are you going somewhere?" her mother asked.

"Yes, to the Aerie." As her father and Bert walked into the house from outside, Lily encapsulated what had happened and what Colin had asked her to do.

"When will you get home?" her mother asked. "This is a very important day. This is the reason you came here from across the country."

"It's hours till sunset." Little Luke with his little elf face, the child she had loved from the minute she saw him. "I'll be back."

"I certainly hope so."

"I certainly hope Luke will be all right," said her father.

Lily met his eyes with a deep surge of gratitude, surprised not just by the sentiment but that either of her parents knew Luke's name. "Me, too. I love that little kid. You should see him climb trees."

"I have, actually. From the lake." He gave her a thoughtful look. "You seem a little rattled, Lily. Let me get the keys, and I'll drive you over. I've always wanted to see those birds."

Something ceramic banged down on the counter.

Lily didn't look. "Thank you, Dad. I'll just grab my handbag. My work shirt's in the car."

"Speaking of working," Marie said, "I haven't noticed you doing much work on that book you mentioned to your father."

I have to get out of here.

She hurried up the stairs but had not reached the top when she heard her mother say, "Is it too much to expect that on this *one day* you could stay here instead of driving her to *that man's* place? And looking at those birds with her?"

On the landing, she heard Marie's voice reach a shrill scream. *"Don't you care what happened to Ryan? Don't you care that we're putting him to rest today?"*

Lily couldn't hear her father's reply. That was usually the way of it. Her mother was loudest, angriest, most manipulative and meanest. As she gathered up her purse, she swept up her own car keys, just in case she reached the bottom of the stairs and found that her mother had talked her father out of driving her to the Aerie, which was entirely conceivable.

"I never expected *you* to betray me in this," Marie continued to her husband as Lily returned to the kitchen.

Bert, she saw, was examining some photos on the mantelpiece, clearly removing himself from the center of the family argument. In contrast, Helen sat at the table frowning and watching the debate between Marie and Patrick as though it was a tennis match, but one she'd been invited to referee.

Lily's father rubbed the back of his neck beneath his ponytail. "I don't know what to say."

"Of course, you don't! There's nothing to say," Marie replied. "We're scattering Ryan's ashes, and you want to go do favors for the man responsible for his death."

"*I* was responsible for his death." Lily could bear it no longer. "We've talked about this, and you know it's true." Could she say the rest? There could be no kindness in saying it. "I had a date with Colin, and he hadn't made a date to babysit. Ryan didn't even want to come with us."

Silence.

Her mother had not forgotten. Lily saw that. And saw another truth. "But it doesn't matter. You told me to take him, and it was my job to take care of him. It wasn't Colin's job. It wasn't Colin's fault at all. It was entirely mine. And you know it, Mom."

"Because you were *with him*. And you want to be with him again, maybe for the rest of your life."

"Surely there are many men in the world," chimed in Helen. "Especially in your life, Lily. You don't have to choose a man your mother dislikes, do you?"

The idea that her mother be allowed to choose the man she, Lily, should or should not love was so wildly dysfunctional that Lily could only stare at Helen in disbelief.

Patrick, however, replied, "Parents who expect to choose partners for their children expect too much. And too little."

For a moment, Lily actually wondered if her father would ask Helen to leave.

But it was Bert who said, "Helen, let's go out in the canoe and see if we can spot those loons again."

"We can do that later, after we know what's happening tonight," Helen told him.

"Well, I think I'll go." Bert went out the door to the porch without another word, and Lily saw him starting for the lake.

"I'd better go feed the raptors." Lily headed for the door herself, no longer expecting her father to accompany her.

"I'm ready," he said. "Marie, would you like to come?"

"Of course not! Lily, if you like Colin Gardner so much, why don't you just move over there?"

"Helen," Lily said, "would you please give the three of us some privacy?"

Helen gazed up at her defiantly. "I think I should stay and support your mother in this. I was there, Lily, remember? I know what happened."

"Actually, you weren't there. You were doing something else. I was Ryan's babysitter."

"I'll be all right, Helen. There's nothing to support." Marie turned on the kitchen tap to fill the sink with water and wash the few cups and saucers sitting on the counter. "Lily's an adult, and she'll do what she wants. There's nothing to talk about, either, but if she wants to talk, I can listen."

"I'll be outside on the swing," Helen told her, as though speaking to a person terribly fragile. "Call if you need me."

Lily had never in her life felt so close to striking another human being.

When the door shut behind her cousin, she turned to her parents. "I just want to say this. It was my fault. I will never forgive myself, never excuse myself. Colin is not the person he was at sixteen any more than I'm the fifteen-year-old I was. If you want me to choose between you and him, Mom, I will choose myself."

"The way you did that day?"

Lily paused. "I meant that there's no choosing between Colin and my family. I would never make that kind of choice. I can stay somewhere else, not at this house. Whether it's the Aerie is not the issue."

"Why does he have to inflict himself on our family and drive us apart? You're the only child I have!"

Lily had never seen her mother so irrational.

"This is the other thing I need to say, Mom. Hatred, bitterness—whatever—for what happened—it won't make anything better. I don't want to lay Ryan to rest in an atmosphere of animosity and sniping. I don't want to feel those things. I can mourn him, mourn what I did. But, Mom, if you keep blaming and hating, it'll just burn you up inside. How can you bear the pain of carrying all that rage?"

"I've done it for twenty-five years," Marie screamed. "Don't you dare try to tell me how I should feel about my son's death. I listened to all that crap when it happened, people saying 'God has His reasons,' and other nonsense. But I'm damned if I'll take it from my own daughter."

"That's not what Lily's saying."

Again, the anomaly, Patrick standing up to his wife. Lily knew he would pay—in less than two seconds.

"You be quiet! What have you ever done? Did you ever understand? Did you love Ryan like I did?"

"So much you wanted his company that day?" Lily said, then put her fingers to her lips, as though trying to place the words back in her mouth.

The slap came before she knew it. Hard and bright, memory of long-ago times, before Ryan had died. Because her mother had been known to hit. Her. Ryan. Their father.

Lily walked out of the house.

Helen turned her head, her face waxlike with its bowl haircut.

If I speak to her, I'll say something really bad.

I shouldn't have said that to my mom. No mother wants her children's company all the time. It doesn't mean she didn't love Ryan, didn't love him fiercely.

She had. Ryan was a genius, and Marie had shared musical interests with him. She had seemed much better able to deal with a son than a daughter. Ryan's fascination with *Star Wars* had been more understandable to her than Lily's wanting Guess jeans or Frye boots or so many other things that had mattered to her.

Boyfriends.

A date without her brother along.

Helen rose from the swing and passed her without a word, with a glance that seemed at once accusing and triumphant. *How could you do this to your parents? Fortunately, they have me to comfort them.*

Lily was glad to be behind the wheel of her own car, driving to the Aerie to do what Colin had asked. In the silence, alone, she could think about Luke, pray for his recovery, figure out if there was anything she could bring him and Colin at the hospital. Because she was going there after she fed the birds.

Ryan's ashes were important to her. His memory was important to her—and beloved. But her mother seemed not to want her. Rather, as she always had, Marie wanted some other daughter. A daughter like Helen. Above all, a daughter who would never love Colin Gardner.

Or his son.

SHE HAD JUST FED the eagles, getting the biggest birds over with first. She had carried a live rabbit to them in the small cage used to transport prey and released the rabbit into the mews, then shut the door when she heard tires on gravel outside.

Leaving the mews building, she stepped outside, expecting to see Mosi's pickup truck. Instead, she saw her father climbing out of the Land Cruiser.

Winky barked at him and ran to Lily, apparently to alert her to the visitor.

She hoped, stupidly, that perhaps her father had persuaded Marie to come along, but he hadn't. He was by himself.

"Oh, Dad. It was okay. You didn't have to come."

"I told you, I wanted to. Besides, I imagine there are parts of this operation where an extra pair of hands would be useful."

They didn't speak of her mother or of Ryan. They talked instead of the tiny Northern Saw-whet Owl, which could kill prey larger than itself. Lily had seen this one eat a shrew and told her father how particularly vicious shrews seemed. "Their teeth!" she exclaimed.

He agreed about the ferocity of shrews, and neither of them mentioned that other meaning of the word, label for a sharp-tongued, bad-tempered woman.

Lily introduced her father to Socrates and said that Mosi was taking the owl's X-rays to Minneapolis to see if one of the veterinarians there might be able to perform surgery on his wing. Her father assisted her in killing and cooking a chicken for the merlin. Feeding the raptors, including the juveniles, using the blind and hand puppets, took more than two hours.

When they were done and Lily was washing the pressure cooker in the clinic sink, she told her father, "Well, it's still a few hours till sundown. I don't know if Mom wants me there—"

"I'm sure she does."

"Dad, afterward, I'm planning to drive to Bemidji to see Colin. Under those circumstances, do you think Mom will want me there when you scatter the ashes?"

Her father pursed his lips.

She waited for him to answer.

"Lily, I know you think I've always let your mother be too much in charge in our family."

She said nothing. There was no being in charge of Marie, that was for certain. And her mother wasn't going to change. She'd been caustic and judgmental for as long as Lily could remember.

"I am in love with the woman. I always have been. She is difficult, but she's also brilliant. The soft part in her was for Ryan. I've never really found another."

"So you're saying she won't want me there to scatter Ryan's ashes if I also befriend Colin—even now, when his son is ill."

"No. In fact, I told her it was inappropriate to conduct this ceremony while you have other urgent demands on you. I told her we should do it while you're here and when you're able, and that we should extend an invitation to Colin."

"Did she slap you, too?"

He didn't answer.

"Why can't it be easier?" exclaimed Lily, sitting down on a bench made from a tree trunk. Winky jumped up beside her and sat down. "Ryan's being dead will never be *okay,* but why can't we be loving toward each other?"

"Lily, do you think it would've been better—the getting along part—had Ryan lived?"

Lily gazed up at him. He was right, of course. Why had she never seen that? Her mother had never been easy to live with and never would have been under any circumstances.

And regardless of whoever Lily married, her mother would criticize her—and probably her spouse—because that was what Marie did.

"You can't change your mother," Patrick said. "Don't try. But I came here today to urge you to do what is right for you. Make the choices that will make *you* happy. Your mother may come around in regard to Colin Gardner, and she may not. But that's no reason for you to turn away from someone or something you find important to your happiness."

His words filled her with peace. Of course. It was so simple. There was no need to acknowledge her mother's feud with Colin, let alone feed it with dramatic statements or actions. Wiser would be to go about her own life and…well…*ignore* Marie's sniping to the best of her ability.

"That said, I'm not crazy about your driving to Bemidji alone after dark. There are always deer on the road, and your car is very small. I wish you'd at least wait until daylight."

Lily heard the distinctive musical notes of her cell phone's ring. She walked to her car and reached inside the open window.

It was a Minnesota number. It would be Colin.

"Hello?"

"Lily. It's me."

"How is he?"

"It's meningitis. He's all right just now. He's sleeping, so I came out to call you."

"Do you need anything from home?"

He didn't answer at once. Then he said, "You'd drive down here?"

"Of course. Maybe not till tomorrow. I haven't thought that far."

"We're reading *The Lord of the Rings*. We're on *The Two Towers*. It's beside the bed."

His bed. The bed she'd shared with him.

"Okay. I'll bring it when I come."

When they said goodbye, Lily saw her father smiling up at the nearest tree house.

He said, "You know, Lily—I'm not sure if your

mother has realized the obvious advantage yet, but I'd love to have you nearer home. I miss you."

And, just like she had when she was a child, she rushed to him and embraced him.

He said, "Your mother and I both love you very much. Neither of us—and I know I speak for her—hold it against you that Ryan drowned while he was under your care. You're our daughter. You didn't murder him. You were a young person who made a mistake that I'm sure has caused you as much pain as it caused us. Different pain, but equivalent. And I can't remove your hurt any more than I can your mother's or my own. But we want you to be happy, Lily. We love you, and we want you to know every joy life can bring."

The tears sprang to her eyes, unexpected. A flood. The knowledge of what she had done—and thereby failed to do—had been battened inside her. Emotional knowledge.

She sobbed.

"There, there, Lily." Her father patted her back. "We all go on."

"Thank you," she said, not needing to say what the gratitude was for, unable to define it if he asked.

"Let's finish up whatever needs to be done here and go home to your mother," he said. "She needs you, too, Lily. She doesn't want to admit how much she loves you. I think she's afraid to realize it. Afraid of losing you, too."

As she drove home behind her parents' ancient Land Cruiser, Lily wondered if what her father had just said was true. Maybe, whether or not Colin Gardner was to be part of her life, she should come to Minnesota to live. The antipathy she felt for the place, she saw now, was not dislike of the midwest, its people, its cold winters, its mosquitoes in summer. It had simply been a tangible monument to the sickening error she had made at the age of fifteen, the error with such tragic consequences.

As she parked in the spot she'd been using near her parents' car and her father climbed out, he gave her a look that mingled humor and understanding and reminded her again that her mother would not change. She shouldn't expect miracles, in other words, even the miracle of civility.

Marie sat on the porch swing with Helen, Bert on the steps nearby. Marie and Bert were having cocktails.

"Gin and tonic?" Bert said to Patrick and Lily.

"Thank you," grunted Patrick and bent to kiss his wife, who tilted her head up.

Lily went to the swing and said, "Move over, Helen. I want to sit by my mother." And as her cousin laboriously slid over a few inches, murmuring something about the swing really not being big enough for three, Marie reached up and hugged Lily.

Lily said, "Mom, I was thinking. Maybe out there, we could each tell our favorite recollection of Ryan. You know, tie the canoes together? I mean, I don't know what you have planned, but…"

She expected her mother to say that of course Lily didn't know—of course she had never cared about scattering Ryan's ashes.

Her mother suddenly put her head back and laughed. "You know the one that keeps occurring to me? It was at Music Night. We'd all tuned our instruments and then we went outside to see that owl—"

A sudden break.

There had been an owl. Yes. Perched on the dock railing. So strange.

Years before Ryan's death.

Unexpectedly, Helen started laughing. "He *un*tuned the instruments."

They all laughed then.

Lily realized that her hand was in her mother's.

"Maybe, Lily—I don't know how long you're going to be here."

"In Minnesota? I think a long time, Mom. I do have a textbook to edit, and the publishers are hoping for another."

Her mother's eyes had gone from sharp to slightly vulnerable. "It would be wonderful to have you. I'm sorry, Lily. And your father's right. You have the freedom to see whoever you like. Whether Colin Gardner can ever be welcomed in this house—that's another question…."

"We'd better get out in the canoes," said Helen. "It's about time."

Patrick opened his mouth, but Lily said, "Right," and stood up.

With a rueful smile, but one that also commended Lily for not battling with a decision apparently made in their absence—to scatter the ashes that night—her father turned to Marie. "Shall I bring down Ryan's ashes?"

They were in her parents' bedroom, and the protectiveness with which they'd kept their youngest child near them touched her. The ashes were in a heavy iron urn, and they planned to sink it in the lake when they scattered the ashes.

Colin should be here. Colin was part of this.

But it hadn't mattered to Colin. He had said that her parents' needs should be met, and he was right. It didn't matter that her mother was unjust to him, either. And somehow, Lily thought he understood that, too. He was a scapegoat, and he was strong enough to play the part.

They took two canoes, she and her parents in one, Helen and Bert in the other, and paddled out to the middle of the lake. There were other people out, swimming from a dock on the opposite shore, fishing from an aluminum skiff.

As the sun turned the water orange and purple, the mosquitoes providing music, anecdotes about Ryan spilled out, disordered.

"Oh, God, Lily, do you remember," Marie said, "when you came home from that week of ballet camp and he told you Spinner had died?"

Their miniature poodle, who had been alive and well at the time of Ryan's tragic announcement.

The shared laughter brought new notes, more joyful than funereal, to the music of the sunset.

"I *believed* him, too!"

"He used to tell me all the time that I stank," said Helen. "Remember how he used to bring deodorant to me at the dinner table?"

Lily grinned. "You just made me feel *so* much better, Helen. I'd forgotten he ever picked on anyone but me."

As the sun fell lower, her father removed the lid from the urn and dropped the lid into the lake. Then he offered the urn to her mother, and Lily saw it was because he couldn't go on.

Marie shook her head and passed the urn to Lily.

She reached in, touching the ashes. Her parents could not touch these, could not make themselves. This was their child, her brother.

She dropped some on the surface of the water, then said, "Helen, could you please?"

Carefully, reaching over the water, she handed the urn to her cousin.

Helen matter-of-factly thrust one hand into the urn and lifted out some ashes. Scattering them, she said, "'Judge me by my *size*, do you...? And well you shouldn't. For my ally is the Force. And a powerful ally it is. Life creates it and makes it grow. Its energy surrounds us and binds us. Luminous beings we are, not this crude matter.'"

And Lily reached across the water again, this time to hold her cousin's hand.

CHAPTER SIX

"THEY'LL LOVE IT, Colin." It was the third weekend in August and the fourth time Colin had come with Lily to Camp Boreal. Luke, fully recovered from his illness, had been there more than a dozen times.

Marie liked Luke and was teaching him to play the piano. Rudeness to Colin she'd honed to an art. Instead of making Lily the target for ceaseless disapproval, she criticized Colin's hair, clothing, occupation, personality and family background—to his face, of course.

Colin had come upon the gift for Lily's parents while away with Luke, doing a raptor presentation at a summer camp near Omaha. It was a stone birdbath fountain with the figure of Yoda in the center. Engraved around the rim of the bath were the words: MAY THE FORCE BE WITH YOU.

It was in the back of Colin's pickup truck, under the camper shell. Luke sat between his father and Lily as they drove to Camp Boreal.

"I imagine," said Colin, "that at least one member of your family will find something not to like."

"We'll see."

"As a matter of fact, she might decide I'm mocking her grief."

That was not out of the realm of possibility.

"Luke, remember the plan?" he said.

"What plan?" asked Lily.

"You'll see."

Lily's mother came out on the porch to meet them as they started up the steps. "I wondered when you were coming. We didn't know whether to put the lasagna in. I just did, anyhow. I figured you could eat it cold if you were late."

"Mother, I'm never late," Lily pointed out, with an attempt at a smile.

"Those shoes look fancy. Are they new, or are they some of your things you moved from Santa Barbara?"

"From Santa Barbara." She had sublet her apartment there for the remainder of her lease and moved in with Colin and Luke in late July.

"What's that?" Marie's eyebrows drew together as she saw the birdbath Colin had brought from the truck. "Not some junk you picked up..."

It was particularly brassy, Lily thought, for either of her parents to talk about anyone else picking up *junk*.

But Marie came slowly down the steps. "Patrick. Patrick, come here! Colin, where did you find it? Oh, where shall we put it?"

She rushed down the porch to Colin, hugged him around the waist, and kissed his cheek against his short, sparse beard.

Lily's father walked to the edge of the porch, peered down at the birdbath, at Colin, at Luke, at his wife and finally at Lily. He gave his daughter a wink, and she grinned.

Marie said, "It's perfect, Colin. It's perfect. Does it work? Is it a fountain?"

"SO WHAT WAS LUKE'S PART in the plan?" Lily asked that evening as she and Colin sat on the end of her parents' dock, gazing across the lake to the place where tragedy had caught them twenty-five years before.

"He's doing it. He's inside minding his own business."

Lily pulled her legs up to her chest, crossing her bare ankles as the mosquitoes began to dine.

Colin looked at her, and she looked back. She couldn't see the color of his eyes in the twilight, but he had become familiar to her, her best friend, a friend like none she'd ever had.

He said, "Will you marry me?"

She had known, she realized. Men had proposed to her before, and she had known then, as well. "Yes."

"I had this made."

She had not expected a ring. She would've laid money that Colin would *not* have bought her an engagement ring, let alone had one made.

But he had. It was smooth and round, gold, and the design etched in it was like tree bark. Inside were set stones. An emerald, a diamond, a ruby.

It was the most beautiful ring she had ever seen, and it fit her.

"I love it," Lily whispered.

"I love *you*," he said.

They lingered on the end of the dock for a while, then wandered back toward the house.

"So—Luke knows?"

"Of course he knows. I asked him what he thought."

"What did he say?"

"He's excited, Lily. You've changed his life. Maybe even more than you've changed mine."

Her parents and Luke sat at the kitchen table playing Hearts. Luke looked up excitedly when Lily and Colin came in.

Lily said, "Colin and I are getting married."

"If you go through with it this time." Her mother tossed a heart onto the table.

Her father stood up and kissed her. He told Colin, "Congratulations," and shook his hand.

Lily showed them her ring.

Luke said, "I think it's pretty. I told Dad so. We went to the jeweler together."

Marie said, "See that you don't lose it."

Colin, Lily and Patrick all looked at each other, fighting laughter.

Luke said, "Yeah. It cost a lot."

"Too much, I'm sure. Ridiculous to spend so much money on jewelry. Luke, it's your turn," Marie muttered. "You two, there's a cake in the bread box. Why don't you serve it?"

Patrick took his seat at the table again.

Lily and Colin met each other's eyes and grinned. Marie would never change, Lily and Colin would always bear the weight of Ryan's death, but there was still joy in the world. Still laughter and love to be shared.

To Julie, a very much belated best wishes.

A VISIT FROM EILEEN

Janice Macdonald

Dear Reader,

Things happen for a reason. I hear people say that all the time, as I'm sure you do, too. You may have said the words yourself. They're often the response to difficult or painful situations. Although I want very much to believe that there is some sort of grand plan and it isn't just random chance that things happen the way they do, I must confess that sometimes I find the idea difficult to accept.

In my story, Eileen regrets her decision to leave Ireland and Kieran, the man she loves. "What if?" she keeps asking herself. What if she'd swallowed her pride? Stayed in Ireland? Married Kieran? And yet, as Kieran points out when they're reunited in Ireland twenty-five years later, if she'd stayed in Ireland he wouldn't have married the woman he did, had a daughter and now a granddaughter he dearly loves. But he, too, wonders: Was there a reason his wife died so young? Were he and Eileen ultimately meant to be together? Was there a reason for the twenty-five years she spent in America?

I imagine life as a vast and uncompleted jigsaw puzzle. From my vantage point, I can see only a few pieces and have no idea what the overall picture looks like. In my own life, I occasionally look back and wonder what if I'd taken this road instead of that. In some instances, I can see that not getting what I thought I wanted at the time was actually a great stroke of luck. But was it luck? Or destiny, perhaps?

I hope you enjoy "A Visit from Eileen." I love getting your e-mails and letters and try to answer every one of them. You can get in touch with me at www.janicemacdonald.com, or by writing to Janice Macdonald, PMB 101, 136 E. 8th Street, Port Angeles, WA 98362.

Best wishes,

Janice

CHAPTER ONE

Clonkill, County Galway, Ireland

KIERAN O'MALLEY STOOD on a stepladder in the bathroom of a house that belonged to the woman who, but for one of those quirks of fate, would almost certainly have been his mother-in-law. Carmel, her name was, although even when he was engaged to her daughter, Kieran had never progressed beyond Mrs. Doyle or Mrs. D. Spread across the floor below him were pages of newspaper set down to protect the robin's-egg-blue tiles, laid by him a week or so ago. The day after, in fact, Mrs. D got word that Eileen was finally coming home for a visit.

"Will you have a coffee, Kieran?" Mrs. Doyle called.

He didn't reply; it wasn't really a question. Experience had taught him that he wouldn't be allowed to keep painting without joining her in a coffee. A few more unanswered shouts and she'd bring the coffee up herself.

As far as Mrs. Doyle was concerned, Kieran often thought, he might as well be her son-in-law. "You're the son I never had," she was always telling him, a term of affection that came with a price. Mr. D had died years back, long before Eileen went off to America, and

Kieran had taken over the kind of tasks men did around the house. The phone would ring and it would be herself, "Ah Kieran, would you ever help an old lady out, then?" The front hedge needed trimming, the bricks down the garden path had worked loose and one of these days she was going to trip and break her neck. Or, Eileen's coming from America and the whole house needs a good spruce up, sure the spare bedroom hasn't been painted since she left and how long has that been?

Twenty-five years, that's how long it had been. Not that he was counting at all.

"Kieran," she called again. "Come down now and have a coffee and some jam roll."

In the kitchen, he took a chair at the table as Eileen's mother bustled around with cups and saucers. It was in this very room that Eileen had told him he was a no-good, faithless lout, the lowest of the low, and she'd had enough of him and this whole bloody country. Soon after that she went off to America. Los Angeles, and she hadn't been back since.

"Now then." After she'd handed him his coffee, Mrs. D sat in the chair opposite his and consulted a list written out on the back of an envelope. "First things first. Who will be meeting Eileen at the airport? I'll want to go of course—" Mrs. D didn't drive "—and I'd thought that after all these years Deirdre would want to go too, but no, everyone's already making too much of her sister's visit, Deirdre said to me last night. 'My sister's not bloody royalty.'" Mrs. D's face flushed. "Always has been jealous of her younger sister that one, wouldn't you think though at forty-eight she'd have grown out of it? *Forty-eight*." She shook her head and then, her brow furrowing, she eyed him. "If Deirdre's forty-eight…how old does that make you then, Kieran?"

"Forty-six." Kieran downed half his coffee, his thoughts already moving on to what he needed to do after he'd finished up Mrs. D's bathroom. It was the second week in December and Clonkill Lodge, the small hotel he owned and operated, was fully booked for the holidays. Between now and Christmas week when the guests would start arriving he'd so many things to do it made his head swim. He drained the rest of his coffee and stood to leave, but Mrs. D raised a finger to stop him.

"Just a minute, Kieran…I've something to show you." She reached for the brown handbag that, in all the years Kieran had known her, was always at her side, and drew it up on her lap. Head bowed, hands moving frantically, she'd soon accumulated a small pile of paper— receipts, shopping lists, envelopes—on the table in front of her. "Forty-six you say, well you don't look it and neither does Eileen. It's the last picture she sent me I'm looking for. I didn't show you already, did I? She looks lovely. She'd pass for thirty. Of course it was taken from a distance, now where…well, never mind. Have some jam roll."

"I'm fine thanks, Mrs. D." Kieran again stood to leave. "When is it Eileen gets here then?"

"The day after tomorrow, half past ten. I've a hair appointment at eight—Josie's opening the shop early, she's good like that. I thought I'd have a little color put in. Kieran, will you eat some jam roll? If you don't I'll eat it myself and I don't need—"

"I'd be happy to meet her," he said. He had the van he used to transport guests to and from the airport—

which would allow Mrs. D to come along—or there was his Triumph, which might be more in keeping with Eileen's style although it had seen better days and lately was inclined to be temperamental. He began to slowly back toward the door, although he knew Mrs. D well enough to suspect she'd yet to arrive at the real point of what she had to say to him.

"I'll be honest with you." Mrs. D's face had turned dreamy. "What I'd really like is to hire one of those big limousines to meet her at the airport. She'd get off the plane and there would be a chauffeur to open her door, with a glass of champagne in his hand—"

"Don't forget the red carpet," Kieran teased, familiar with Mrs. D's frequent flights of fancy. Twenty-five years later, he could still hear Eileen going on about her mother's proclivity for kicking everything up to the next level. "If I won a million pounds," Eileen used to complain, "my ma would be saying, 'Ah, it's a pity it wasn't two million, there's so much more you could do with that extra million.'"

"I hear they have limos with hot tubs in them," he said straight-faced. "That might be nice after her long flight."

Mrs. D eyed him dubiously. "Wouldn't that cost an awful lot though?"

"Not as much as one with a swimming pool."

"You can laugh, Kieran," Mrs. D said, on to him now, " but Eileen's used to the best."

"So I've heard." *A few thousand times.* Kieran winked at her and tried again to go back upstairs to finish painting.

"Now Kieran, one last thing," Mrs. D said, her tone

suggesting that she was finally getting to the point. "I don't know how to put this any other way than to just spit it out. Eileen has a gentleman friend."

"Donald Trump, is it?"

Mrs. D looked puzzled.

"The talk around town is that they just got engaged," he said. "And he's giving her a Learjet as a wedding present."

Mrs. D gave him a long look and then enlightenment dawned. She was not amused. "I wouldn't be saying this, Kieran, if I didn't think the world of you, but I don't want to see you get your heart broken."

Kieran scratched the back of his head. "I wouldn't worry about that, Mrs. D."

"Eileen won't be the same girl you knew when she left Ireland. She's a woman now, a very successful one. And she may, or may not, be bringing her gentleman friend."

"Maybe he'd like to go fishing," Kieran said. "I could arrange that. Would he be staying here, do you suppose? I could put him up at the lodge, if needs be."

"Yes, well…" Mrs. Doyle's thoughts seemed to have moved on. "I just wondered…well, you're not still carrying a torch for her, are you?"

"I had been," Kieran said. "But it was an awful nuisance clutched between my teeth."

"This is no laughing matter, Kieran."

Kieran walked across the kitchen, caught her face in his hands and kissed her forehead. "That was twenty-five years ago, Mrs. D. No one carries a torch for twenty-five years."

She peered into his eyes. "Are you sure about that, Kieran?"

"We've both moved on, Mrs. D." An understatement, if he'd ever heard one. Between stewing over his family and constant money problems about the lodge, the idea that, after all these years, he'd still have a crush on Eileen Doyle seemed a bit of a joke. He, himself, hadn't had a full night's sleep since his daughter announced that she and her husband were thinking of starting a new life for themselves and the baby in the States. *A new life.* Taking away his granddaughter even though he could hardly start the day without stopping in to see whether she'd grown another new tooth, brilliant child that she was, or whether she'd gurgle and coo in the way he knew was meant just for him. "Besides," he added, "I'd say Eileen's a little out of my league now."

"She is that," Mrs. D agreed. "Well, you've certainly set my mind at ease, Kieran."

With that, he returned to his painting—and found himself thinking about Eileen. Not that he'd suppose though that the Eileen he'd been reading about in the paper would have much in common with the Eileen he'd once kissed under a sky full of fireworks one long ago evening, or the Eileen who had promised to love him till salmon walked in the street or something like that. Poetry it was. He couldn't remember who wrote it, but back then they'd both known all the words.

He wondered if the Eileen about to make her much belated trip still remembered that line. This Eileen had a very important job as executive vice president of something or other and she was always jetting off to Hawaii or Mexico or rubbing shoulders with movie stars in posh restaurants and turning down marriage propos-

als from doctors and lawyers and millionaire business-
men with yachts as big as houses.

This Eileen had all the celebrity of a rock star about
her and she had no bigger fan than his daughter, Tara.
In a place as small as Clonkill, people were ravenous
for a bit of news and the village had been on the verge
of starvation until Eileen began sending letters home
about her brilliant new life. In fact without Eileen's
chronicles from America, he often thought, the local
paper would have little to fill the pages.

Tara, who had every one of Eileen's Letters from
America carefully pasted into a scrapbook, could talk
at length about the gown Eileen had worn to this fancy
affair, or the food she'd dined on at that. All harmless
enough, he supposed, but he was of a mind that his
daughter's interest in uprooting her family had its roots
in Eileen's glowing accounts from abroad.

He shifted the ladder and rearranged the newspapers,
his mind on all the bits and pieces he'd heard about Eileen over the years— either directly from her mother,
or indirectly from the news Mrs. D fed to the local paper.

"She's done very well for herself, Eileen has," Mrs.
D would say to anyone who'd listen. "Unlike her sister.
Very well indeed. I can't say I wouldn't like to have seen
her settle down and have children, but, to be honest
with you, I doubt she's ever met a man who was good
enough for her." And if it happened to be him she was
talking to, she'd pat his arm and say, "You're the excep-
tion of course, Kieran, but all of that was long ago. Before she knew what she wanted out of life."

Kieran stroked the brush across the wall, dipped it
back into the paint can and, deep in thought, sent a cas-

cade of eggshell white splattering to the floor beneath the ladder. He glanced down to make sure nothing had fallen on Mrs. D's pale blue tiles and there, as though he'd summoned it, was Eileen's picture. Smiling up at him with a blob of paint on her nose.

EILEEN DOYLE, in the full bloom of underachievement, sat with her elbows on the desk, absentmindedly chewing the nail on her right index finger as she stared blankly at the muted gray padded walls of her office cubicle and tried not to obsess about what her boss and the company president were talking about behind closed doors.

Eileen had a lot on her mind these days. First off, she was going to be fired—all the signs pointed to it. Yesterday Brandi, her girl boss hadn't even said good morning; this afternoon she'd snapped at Eileen for some trivial thing. The signs were there. And, as if that that alone weren't enough to obsess about, there was the trip home, lumbering down the track toward her like a runaway train. The closer it got the more she didn't want to go.

Her mother's last few letters had been full of the plans already underway for the visit, an itinerary fit for a visiting dignitary. "We all know what you're used to these days, Eilie," her mother had written, "but we're out to show you auld Ireland can put out the red carpet when the occasion calls for it. And, not to push, but you wouldn't be thinking of bringing your gentleman friend, would you? There'd be plenty of room and we'd all love to meet him. I was saying to Kieran that this is a man used to the best and Kieran said they could put him up at the guest house. It's quite nice with all the work Kieran's been doing on it. Only thing is Kieran needs to know soon on account of guests coming for the Christmas holidays. So let me know, Eilie."

Eileen had considered writing back to say she would have to cancel the trip due to major surgery that couldn't be postponed.

Gentleman friend. She hadn't slept well lately. Two o'clock this morning and she's standing in her nightgown microwaving a box of Stouffer's macaroni and cheese. In the wee hours, lonely and wishing to God you had someone to hold you, macaroni and cheese could seem a whole lot like love.

Spooning noodles into her mouth and telling herself that she could have, should have, swallowed her pride and married Kieran O'Malley twenty-five years ago even though she'd caught him kissing Libby Bartlett who used to be her very best friend.

Kieran had ended up marrying Libby right after Eileen left for America. Eileen's mother had included a clip from the newspaper that provided all the details: the pale pink silk of the bridesmaid dresses, the bouquets of matching rosebuds, the honeymoon in Majorca. All of it exactly what she'd planned for her own wedding to Kieran. Libby, of course, was quite familiar with the details since she was supposed to have been Eileen's maid-of-honor.

Kieran used to recite poetry to her, promising to love her until the ocean dried up, or something. And she would respond "I'll love you till the salmon swim in the street." Although she could never quite remember whether it was supposed to be sing or swim and she wasn't sure that Kieran had his bit right, either. It was the year they'd studied Auden in school. The same year she started suspecting something was going on with him and Libby.

For the longest time, she'd hated both of them. How could she not? His defection had not only hurt her terribly, it left her with doubts about her appeal to men. Discouraged her from even looking another man in the eye. The shame of it had reached across the ocean, kept her awake nights. Reduced, she was. Devalued. While they were blithely going on with their lives—a baby on the way, a new business and, of course, each other—she was living in a country that didn't feel at all like home, pinching pennies, going off to one dead-end job after another, going out with men who had as little interest in her as she did in them. Getting older. Drying up. It wasn't fair.

For years, she'd created scenarios of their demise. Hatred became familiar, comforting almost in its dependability. And then Libby had died and the shock was such that all the hate transformed into a gnawing guilt that somehow she, Eileen, had made it happen. As if all of her poisonous darts of anger and resentment had finally hit their mark. She'd written numerous letters to Kieran pouring out her guilt and remorse—never sent any of them. More years passed and, in time, the guilt faded too. Now, mostly, she just had a lot of unanswered questions.

Everything happens for a reason, her mother was always saying. Okay, but if that were true, if there was some grand design, what was the reason behind having her go off to America? Of having Kieran marry Libby instead of her? Of Libby dying so young? And the biggest puzzle of all. What, when you got right down to it, was the reason for Eileen Doyle in the first place?

A phone ringing in the next cubicle snapped her from her reverie, and back into the present moment. She was going to be fired. What else would her boss be talking to the company president about?

If she held her breath and inclined her head just so, she could sometimes catch snatches of conversation going on behind the doors of the big office. Her cubicle was just outside, so humiliatingly close to the group of clerical cubicles that people who didn't know she was an administrative assistant—and not just a secretary—were always poking their heads in to inquire as to the whereabouts of her boss, or to leave a message for her boss, or to ask whether her boss would be free next Tuesday or whatever. One time this arrogant jerk had actually asked if she'd get coffee. *The nerve*. She'd just pointed to her name plate on the cubicle wall and suggested he ask the clerical staff.

Ah jeez, life wasn't fair was it? What had she done to deserve this crock? No man, no children and a new boss young enough to be her daughter. Brandi, that was the girl's name. *Brandi*. And she looked exactly the way you'd expect a Brandi to look. Perky little Crayola-colored suits, perky little frosted blond do and a perky little voice. "Peachy," Brandi was always saying. "Peachy keen."

What was Brandi saying about her in there? Had Eileen heard her name mentioned? Eileen's too old, that's what Brandi was saying as the company president nodded agreement. She's not…hip. She's difficult to work with. She has this chip on her shoulder. She's not a team player. And I don't like her hair. Let's fire her.

The queasy bubble was growing into something larger. Eileen heard a chair move; maybe the meeting was over. She took her elbows off the desk and opened the Goals and Objectives file on her computer. Brandi was big on Goals and Objectives. Eileen's goal had been to have Brandi's job with the objective being to make enough money to move out of the crappy apartment she'd been renting for nearly ten years.

Suddenly, the door to Brandi's office opened and Eileen got very absorbed with the document on the screen. A moment later, Brandi stuck her head around Eileen's cubicle.

"I'm gone for the rest of the day, Eileen," she said. "My daughter has a ballet recital." Smiling, Brandi jiggled her red canvas briefcase, fat with important papers. "After that I'll be catching up on a little reading. I just wanted to say, have a nice vacation." She smiled. "Where is it you're going?"

Eileen returned the smile. "Hawaii," she replied without missing a beat. It sounded more exciting than going back home to Ireland and besides, if she'd said Ireland it was bound to lead to questions about how long it had been since she was last there and why it had been so long and she could hardly explain that to herself let alone her girl boss. "Honolulu," she added for good measure.

"Wow…" Brandi seemed momentarily at a loss for words. "I thought you were going… Well, cool. Good for you. Gonna have some fun, huh?"

"I'll try."

"D'you get a cute bikini?"

"Haven't got around to that yet," Eileen said. And I never will, she thought.

"Well, I'm sure you'll have a blast." Brandi waved her fingers. "Happy holidays."

Hours later, the phone rang Eileen from sleep.

"Eileen," her mother said as though she were calling from across the street, "I've had a good talk with Kieran about not getting his hopes up…"

"Huh?" Groggily, Eileen raised herself on one elbow. After all these years, her mother hadn't quite mastered the time difference between California and Ireland. "What about Kieran's hopes?"

"Well…you know, he was in love with you and—"

"For God's sake Mom."

"Don't swear, Eileen. I just wanted to say I think he's fine, I really do, so if you want to bring your gentleman friend, well I don't think you'd be ruffling any feathers."

CHAPTER TWO

"TRY TO TAKE THIS like a man, Kieran," Eileen's older sister Deirdre said when he walked into the kitchen of the lodge the day before Eileen's arrival, "but Madame may or may not be bringing a gentleman friend as part of her entourage. Should she do so, I've ordered a case of whiskey in the event you'll need to drown your sorrows and if that's not enough there's ammunition and guns—"

"I've already had a version of this talk with your mother," Kieran said, amused by Deirdre's sarcasm despite the black mood she'd been in ever since it was learned that Eileen would be coming home for a visit. It must be a woman thing, he decided, this idea of undying love. Nothing would make the lot of them happier than to have him come charging down River Street on a big white horse and whisk Eileen off into the sunset. Well, they'd want a decent wedding first, but then it would be nothing but grand passion till the cows came home.

"You've nothing to worry about," he added for reassurance, but Deirdre, pummeling the dough for the apple tarts as though it was Eileen's face beneath her fists, said nothing.

Eileen, everyone knew, had been destined for bigger things than an Irish village. Nobody, himself included, had really been surprised when she went off to America—despite her claim that he'd shamed her into leaving by carrying on with Libby. But while Eileen's success had been expected, Deirdre was a different story altogether.

Poor Deirdre, he'd find himself thinking although truth was she'd never invited sympathy. It was just the way she had about her. Large and raw-boned, Deirdre wore the strained look that made him think of someone who'd walked too long in uncomfortable shoes. While the sun had always seemed to shine on Eileen, Deirdre lumbered along, mouth turned down, brow knitted, under a perpetual cloud.

But Deirdre's dour look gave lie to her generosity and the softness of her heart. In the first few years after Libby died, she'd all but raised Tara and even today, he didn't know what he'd do without her. She'd been working for him for years—cooking, managing the books, a bit of everything. A while back she'd married Frank, the fellow who kept up the grounds of the lodge. The couple had no children, but Deirdre was as fond of his daughter, Tara, and now the baby, as though they were her own—and had no hesitation about letting him know what she thought of Tara's wanting to go off to America. Or of the hoopla over her sister's visit after all this time.

"I've no patience at all with such nonsense," she'd say, neatly summing up her feelings about both topics.

At the sink, Kieran scooped Deirdre's peelings into a plastic pail that would be emptied outside on the compost pile. Deirdre was quite the tyrant about composting, that and saving the corncrake, a little bird that built its nest on the bogs and was in danger of becoming extinct. Deirdre and her corncrakes.

"*Crex crex,*" he'd heard her cooing to the baby the other day and it was a fair imitation too. "*Crex crex.*" Next she'd be fitting the baby with Wellingtons and taking her off on a bird walk.

"And another thing, Kieran," she was saying now. "If I were you, I'd make very sure my sister doesn't fill your own daughter's head with foolish notions. This morning Tara said to me that she'd a fancy to live on the beach in Malibu and wasn't that where Eileen herself had a cottage?" She shook her head. "They'll be gone before you know what's happening, you mark my words."

Kieran looked at her. When the phone rang a moment later, he was grateful for the interruption.

"*Kieran.*"

Mrs. Doyle always sounded as though something terrible had just happened and, even though he knew her habit, he'd steel himself to hear the worse.

"What is it?"

"I was thinking that, to be on the safe side, you should keep a room reserved just in case Eileen brings her gentleman friend."

Kieran took a breath. "And what name should I put it under?" he asked. "Mr. Trump, will it be?"

"YOU WANT TO GO WITH ME to Ireland?" Eileen asked Mr. Schwartz, the old man who lived in the apartment across the hall from hers. "My mother thinks I'm bringing a gentleman friend. I don't want to disappoint her."

Mr. Schwartz paused from dishing slices of beef brisket onto a platter. "You gonna tell her you're after me for my money or my looks?" He speared another slice of beef, looked at her again and did a double take.

"What'd you do to your hair?"

"You like it?"

"It's a different color."

Eileen laughed. "You could say that." After work, on an impulse, she'd had her mousy brown frizz bleached and straightened so that now it fell in long smooth wheat-colored strands about her shoulders. She'd been letting her hair grow out, ever since the last blond bombshell picture she'd sent home to save money for the upcoming trip. After the hair, she'd maxed out one of her credit cards at some trendy little boutique in West Los Angeles where a pair of jeans had set her back roughly the amount of her weekly take-home check. She'd also bought a bunch of other things designed to show the folks back home that Eileen Doyle in the flesh was every bit as glamorous and successful as the Eileen Doyle portrayed in her letters from America.

Mr. Schwartz had turned his attention back to the brisket.

"What d'you think?" she asked.

"It's kinda dry around the edges, left it in too long."

"My hair. Does it look good?"

"What's wrong with the way it was?"

"Boring and mousy for starters."

He grunted. "So they didn't fire you after all?"

"Nope. False alarm."

"Told you that, didn't I? Think the worse and that's what you're gonna get. You want corn or green beans?"

"Whatever. But I didn't get fired though…. Remember, I thought Brandi was gunning for me?"

"She's gonna wait till you get back from vacation, that's all."

"Oh, jeez, thanks a lot. If that doesn't ruin—"

"I'm yankin' your chain, kid. Quit taking life so seriously." He opened a can of corn, peered into the contents and glanced over at her. "This stuff's got those bits of red—"

"Pimentos. That's cool." She watched him empty the corn into a blue enameled pan. Another one of her purchases had been a microwave oven—a Christmas present for him although she had her doubts he'd ever use it. Deeply suspicious of what he dismissed as lazy people's gadgets, he'd only started using the toaster she bought him for his birthday and that was mostly because his back had given out, making it hard for him to stoop to use the oven grill. "Hey," she said, "this time next week, I'll be in Ireland."

"I know it. Even got a bottle," he said gruffly. "Thought we'd raise a glass to your journey."

"Ah…" Smiling and simultaneously on the brink of tears, Eileen wanted to throw her arms around him except that the gesture would have embarrassed both of them. But it felt so good and familiar to be sitting in his windowless little kitchen, her refuge from the rest of the world. Mr. Schwartz, the only person she felt safe enough around to be completely herself. Whoever that was.

Twenty-five years she'd lived in L.A. and, as pitiful as it sounded, Mr. Schwartz was pretty much her only friend. My Friday-night date, she called him. They'd developed this routine that had been going on for more than five years now, ever since he moved into the building. Every week when she did her grocery shopping, she'd buy a brisket for Mr. Schwartz and apples or bananas for his turtle, Gulchy, who slept in a cushioned dog basket under the old man's kitchen table. David his first name was, although she'd never called him that. They'd share the brisket as they watched old movies on TV. The brisket was the basis of an ongoing argument over whether it was better as Mr. Schwartz prepared it, or as corned beef—the only way to eat it, Eileen maintained.

She told him everything. He knew about her dead-end jobs, her dead-end relationships. He knew she was bummed about not getting the promotion at work, that she'd just about given up on even getting married, much less having kids, and he knew that her one big regret was that she hadn't swallowed her pride and married Kieran O'Malley, even though she had caught him kissing Libby Bartlett. She'd even told Mr. Schwartz about the way her letters home had somehow taken on this weird life of their own.

When she first arrived in the States, the letters she'd sent back to Ireland had been meant to reassure everyone that she was doing fine, that although she missed the family, she'd made the right decision. And then a funny thing began to happen. The more she'd reassure them she was fine, the more desperately lonely and unsure she'd find herself. And invariably, just as she'd be on the verge of confessing the truth, a letter would arrive from her mother to say how proud everyone was of her and how brave she'd been to come to America all by herself and how no one but Eileen had that kind of courage and determination. With tears splashing all over the letters, she'd tell herself there was no way she could let them down now.

So a year went by and then two. There was talk of Eileen coming back home for a visit, or of one of them coming to see her. Her initial reaction to both prospects had been panic; she couldn't let anyone see how pathetic her life really was, but neither did she have the money for a return ticket.

It was out of this panic that the fictional high-powered executive Eileen was born. Eileen with the impossibly demanding schedules, constantly flying here and there—never anywhere near Ireland, unfortunately—with little time to breathe, let alone entertain visitors.

When her mother wrote to say she'd forwarded Eileen's letters to the local paper where they were being published under the heading, Eileen's News From America, Eileen abandoned any idea of coming clean and began to think of the whole thing as a kind of game. She'd find gossip column items about the lives of the rich and famous and weave celebrity names and exotic locales into her letters. She'd describe a meal she'd eaten in this ritzy restaurant or that, the details gleaned from a newspaper review that had caught her eye, or flip through a fashion magazine for the outfit she wore on last night's date with Mr. Right.

Year followed year and she'd make vague promises that one of these days she was going to *make* the time to come back. Still no one really pressed her. "As much as we miss you and would love to see you, everyone in Clonkill knows the kind of life you have and we understand how busy you are," her mother would write. "And we're all so proud of you, Eileen. P.S. You didn't tell us about the dress you wore to the Oscars. We want a full description next time. The reason I ask is I could have sworn that was you I saw on TV standing next to Julia Roberts. Your back was to the camera, but you were in silver, am I right?"

This sort of thing might have gone on forever, but then her mother had a mild stroke and Eileen's sister, Deirdre, wrote to remind Eileen that their mother wasn't getting any younger and it would mean the world to have Eileen home for Christmas…no matter how busy Eileen might be. Deirdre, with whom she'd never been close, had made it clear that it was their mother who would benefit most from the visit.

Naturally, Eileen had taken that dilemma to Mr. Schwartz.

"What's the worse thing that could happen if you go home?" he'd asked.

"They'll find out I've been lying all this time," she'd replied.

"So they shoot you?"

"Maybe they should."

"If they shoot you for anything," the old man had said, "it should be that it's twenty-five years since you've been back. What d'you think that says about you?"

"I don't know what it says to *them*…all I know is I didn't have the money."

He'd given her a disgusted look. "If you can't come up with anything better than that," he'd replied, "*I* should shoot you. Anyone who's got too much pride to ask for help when they need it…"

"Yeah, yeah, yeah." She knew all about his views on pride. "Pride, schmide," he'd say. "Pride's like a big, fat, s.o.b. trying to squeeze through a narrow door. It takes up so much damn room, there's no place for anything else to get through. Go already."

His voice, telling her to eat up before everything got cold, brought her out of her reverie. Seated across the table from her, he was carefully pouring sparkling wine into two tumblers.

"So." He handed her a glass. "What d'you want to drink to?"

She studied the froth of pink bubbles in her glass. "Kieran O'Malley," she said before she could stop herself. "And second chances."

He clinked his glass against hers. "You got it, kid."

SO NOW HERE SHE WAS strapped into her seat in the main cabin of an Aer Lingus flight bound for Shannon, peering through the window and seeing nothing but her still unfamiliar reflection with its curtain of pale blond hair staring back at her.

She turned from the window to admire, once again, the understated chic of her traveling outfit—denim jeans and jacket. But not just any old jeans and jacket. These were sophisticated and well-cut, which they should be for what they'd cost her. And there was more of the same crammed into her newly purchased designer suitcases—which she'd actually jumped up and down on so they wouldn't scream NEW too loudly and make it seem she was trying to impress anyone.

Kieran was to meet her at the airport, her mother had called to inform her.

According to her mother, everyone in the village had been falling all over themselves for the right to transport Eileen from the airport, but Kieran had been the most persistent. Even allowing that her mother had a certain talent for embroidering the truth (and had evidently handed it down), Eileen couldn't help but feel a little buzz of excitement.

Could it be, was it too much to hope, that after twenty-five years, marriage, a daughter and now a granddaughter, Kieran still felt something for her? Some ember that time and life hadn't managed to extinguish? The thought sent a small thrill through her. "You want something bad enough," Mr. Schwartz was always telling her, "it's gonna happen. You just gotta be patient."

Okay, fine, but how do you tell where patience becomes delusion? They'd both been twenty-one, now they were more than twice that age. The young Eileen and Kieran who had vowed to love one another till salmon swam in the street would not be the middle-aged version that would meet up again at Shannon. People change. Maybe he'd grown garrulous, the way she remembered his father, or glum and resigned like his mother had been. *Maybe he had hairy ears now, like his granddad.*

"Breakfast?" A flight attendant with red curls and startlingly pale skin handed her a tray. If I looked like that, Eileen found herself thinking as she ripped open a package of salt and sprinkled it onto a dish of scrambled eggs, Kieran would be smitten. She was always doing that, fixating on other more attractive women, envisioning their perfect lives, their perfect relationships. Women who never woke up baggy-eyed with fright-wig hair. Thin women who didn't polish off everything on their breakfast trays, even plastic-wrapped muffins with fake blueberries that tasted like grit.

She flicked a muffin crumb from the front of her jacket, downed the glass of orange juice. Glancing through the window, she saw a gray diaphanous curtain stretched below, shredded in part to reveal low white clouds casting dark shadows on green hills and fields. My God. She stared, transfixed by the brilliant, verdant greenness and felt the sting of tears in her nose. *I'm home.*

She gave up her tray to another attendant (long black braid, slim hips, perfect life) and grabbed her cosmetic bag from the travel bag under the seat.

The Occupied sign in both toilets glowed red. Her hands clasped around the cosmetic bag, Eileen stood and waited. How would Kieran greet her after all this time? Would he run to her with open arms and a huge smile on his face like some corny commercial? Kiss her passionately? She opened her mirrored compact, squinted at her reflection. Her lipstick had flaked, ditto her mascara.

"Ma'am." The red-haired flight attendant tapped her on the shoulder. "You're blocking the entryway."

Ma'am.

Eileen flipped back a strand of wheat-colored hair that suddenly seemed ridiculous, as ridiculous as the designer jeans that were cutting like a knife into the flesh at her waist. *As though she were pretending to be something she wasn't.*

Well? Her face hot, she returned to her seat.

I don't want to do this, she thought. I don't want to see Kieran. I don't want to pretend to be something I'm not. I want to pull the blanket down over my head and shut out the world. I want to go home.

She *was* home.

CHAPTER THREE

"YOU'RE NERVOUS, Daddy," Kieran's daughter, Tara, observed. It was the day of Eileen's arrival, an hour before he had to leave for Shannon, and she was following him from room to room, distracting him as he tried to remember where it was he'd put his keys when he came back from getting his jacket from the cleaners.

"Nervous?" He frowned at her. At twenty-six Tara bore a startling resemblance to her mother at the same age. On occasion though, something—the way the light hit her face, or a certain angle of her head—would so intensify the resemblance that it would bring him up short. This was one of those times. She'd just come in from outside, the shoulders of her red anorak wet from the snow, her hair glistening, her face pink from the cold. The keys temporarily forgotten, he just stared at her.

"Daddy." Laughing now, she reached on tiptoe to kiss his cheek. "You look demented."

He rallied, moved to the office and lifted a stack of papers to see if the keys were underneath. They weren't. Swearing, he set the papers down again. Too close to the edge, they fell and scattered across the floor. "Damn it." Retrieving them, he banged his head on the edge of the desk. From the lounge where Tara had put the baby to sleep in a carrier bed, he heard a loud wail. "I know," he muttered, "I feel the very same way."

The weather wasn't helping either. He'd woken early that morning to a blanket of wet snow. The day before had been perfect. He couldn't quite decide why it mattered that Eileen have nice weather—any more than it would matter for any of the guests who stayed in the lodge—but it did somehow. He'd wanted her to see that California wasn't the only place with winter sunshine, daft really but there it was.

"It would be so much better if you'd let me go with you," Tara said, picking up the theme she'd first introduced when she'd rung him that morning. "That way you won't have to think of things to say to her."

"I'll have no trouble thinking of things to say to her." He strode into the kitchen. Tara, after quieting the baby, followed on his heels. "You're all a lot more excited about this visit than I am," he grumbled. Although he was beginning to realize that wasn't entirely true. And then recalling Deirdre's comments the day before, he asked, "And what would you have to talk to Eileen about anyway? Her house in Malibu?"

Her face turned even pinker. "I'm just being practical. We're going to go one of these days, Daddy, you'd better get used to the idea."

"You've talked Joe into it?"

"I didn't have to *talk* him into it," she shot back. "There's nothing for us here."

"What about Dublin?" He'd temporarily forgotten his search for the keys. "I thought that was something you were considering."

"Dublin." She made a face. "I don't want to go to Dublin. It's the States for us. California."

This wasn't the time to talk about it, he decided. He resumed his search for the keys, pulling out cabinet drawers, even checking the fridge just in case. Nothing. He headed for the door, but Tara stood in the entrance blocking his way.

"Daddy." Her eyes were intent on his face. "Will you just let me say one thing?"

"Not if it's about—"

"Do you know the term synchronicity?"

"Is it something you eat with chips?"

"Daddy."

"No, I don't know the term."

"It means things happen for a reason."

"Tara."

"Listen to me, Daddy. Joe and I have been talking about going to America for a long time now, but nothing really fell into place. We just decided that the time wasn't right. But then—" her eyes widened with the importance of what she was about to say "—this woman, Eileen, this big successful woman, comes home for a visit—"

"Do you know the term coincidence?"

"There is no such thing as coincidence, Daddy," she said in the same patient tone she'd tell a small child there was no dragon under the bed. "Everything happens for a reason. It's all part of a plan. You don't know it, maybe Eileen herself doesn't know it, but she's coming here now, at this time, because we're meant to go to America."

As Kieran opened his mouth to speak, Deirdre appeared in the doorway behind Tara, a pile of folded sheets in her arms, her face thunderous.

"I've never heard such a load of cod in my entire life," she said. "If I didn't know better, I'd think some sort of virus had infected the lot of you, making you all light in the head. I've a good mind to take a holiday myself, get away until this whole visit is over. And Kieran," she dangled the keys in front of him, "you left them on the car bonnet, nice and handy should someone want to make off with it."

With all that, he arrived at the airport twenty minutes before the flight was due. Inside the terminal building, he stood before a flickering monitor while people with dazed and vacant looks milled about him.

He hadn't been nervous about meeting up with Eileen again, or at least he hadn't thought so, and it wasn't that he was nervous now. A bit rattled was more like it, if for no other reason than the prospect of Tara and the baby leaving. And that look in Tara's eyes when she'd been going on about whatever it was she'd called it— that had shaken him a bit, too. His inclination had been, still was, to scoff at that sort of thing. New-age psychobabble was what he thought of it, but lately—maybe it was age, he didn't know—he'd found himself having thoughts along the same lines. The way you could plot and plan your life and then, out of the blue, something happens to change everything. Like Libby dying, or thinking that they had all the time in the world to have more children. You just never knew and that was the truth of it.

And what if there was something to all that? What if it wasn't just chance that Eileen was coming home at this time? What if someone up there had it all worked out and Eileen herself was, at this very moment, some sort of instrument of change flying into all of their lives?

He shook the thought away. A load of cod as Deirdre would say. He glanced at his watch, saw he still had fifteen minutes before her flight arrived, and walked over to a café and ordered a coffee. He'd have loved a pint, but meeting Eileen with beer on his breath didn't seem like a good idea. While he drank the coffee, he found himself wondering about Eileen and her gentleman friend. As he helped her into the car that had definitely seen better days, would she be comparing him to this American joker? Thinking to herself she'd made the right choice twenty-five years ago?

Eileen, when he knew her, had been small and pretty. Agile, as quick on her feet as she'd been with a quip. She'd had the most beautiful forehead—seemed like a funny thing to single out, but it was true. Smooth and pale, her hair springing back from it as though it had a life of its own, and long sweeping brows that never seemed penciled or plucked the hell away the way most girls wore them.

He spooned sugar into his coffee, noticing as he did, that the right cuff of his shirt was frayed. Ah well.

EILEEN STOOD in the Arrivals concourse where it had been arranged she would meet up with Kieran. The details had been communicated by her mother who, Eileen realized now, had neglected to say exactly where in Arrivals she was to wait.

With her stack of brand-new luggage at her feet, her purse looped over her shoulder, she searched the faces of the milling crowd. Would she even recognize him? She yanked at the seat of her jeans. Despite what they'd cost her, they rode up just as uncomfortably as the kind she usually wore. More than anything, she wanted to undo the top button, but she couldn't because the jacket didn't come down far enough. Her feet had swollen, her eyes were itching, her hair had gone frizzy and she wanted to find a restroom but she was scared she might miss Kieran, although that might actually be better than letting him see her like this.

She felt dazed and unreal. I'm back in Ireland, she kept telling herself.

She listened to the accents of a couple of girls standing nearby. "Mind you," one of them was saying, "it could have been worse." The other agreed, "It could indeed." I used to sound like that, she thought. A tall guy with blond hair was walking toward her. She licked her lips, pushed back her hair. As he got closer, she saw that he was probably in his twenties. The same age Kieran had been when she last saw him.

She started looking at the faces of older men. Would he be bald? Gray? A paunchy man in a brown windbreaker glanced her way. She met his eye just long enough to know it wasn't Kieran. The crowd began to thin.

On the plane she'd had this image of Kieran with roses in his arms, waiting to greet her as she set foot on Irish soil once again. It kept reappearing, an annoying pop-up ad on the computer screen of her mind. She would have had time, after all, to fix herself up. Maybe he'd had an accident. Maybe he'd forgotten altogether. If he didn't show in five minutes, she'd call her mother. She pulled a piece of gum out of her jean jacket, started to peel off the paper.

"Eileen?"

Oh, my God.

She shoved the unwrapped gum back in her pocket, turned around and there he was smiling widely at her. Kieran. Looking a little uncertain, like maybe he wasn't sure whether to hug her or shake her hand.

"Howdy, ma'am," he finally drawled in a terrible parody of a Texas accent. "Name's Kieran O'Malley, but *mah* friends all call me Blue. On account of the eyes."

She laughed, pulling him close in a big bear hug. Smiling into his shoulder, her chin buried in the tweed of his jacket. Kieran. She pulled away to drink in the details of his face. A few lines around the eyes, the usual stuff, a little more weight about him, but it was Kieran, no doubt about that. All the strangeness she'd feared vanished in an instant.

"God, it's good to see you," she said impulsively. "I've been eyeing all these men because I'd no idea what you would look like after all this time."

"Have you?" He was still smiling. "D'you see anything that struck your fancy?"

She shrugged. Not until you walked up, she thought.

"Sorry I wasn't there when you got off the plane," he said. "I'd allowed plenty of time, enough to have a coffee, but then I got lost in thoughts…"

His voice trailed off and as people circled around them, they stood there motionless, cataloguing the changes. He looked…like Kieran. An older version than the one she remembered the day she flung her engagement ring across the room at him. His hair still thick but threaded with gray now. A tweed jacket, open-necked shirt.

I rejected this. She shook away the thought.

"This is so incredibly strange," she heard herself babbling. "I get onto a plane in L.A., fly for God knows how long, get off in Ireland and here you are."

"It's called modern travel, I believe," he said.

She smacked his arm. "Wise guy."

They were both grinning like idiots still, relief it seemed that the first hurdle had been passed. Take away the changes the years had wrought and they were the same old Kieran and Eileen.

"You sound like a Yank," he said.

"I guess I am."

"You guess? I'd think after twenty-five years there wouldn't be much doubt."

"You'd think so," she agreed. "But…I don't know. Even after I became a citizen, I still had this feeling of not quite belonging. In the States I'll always be Irish, here I'm a Yank. It's weird."

"You look…very different," he said. "If I hadn't seen the pictures over the years, I'm not sure I'd have recognized you."

Vanity reared its head. Different in what way, she wanted to ask. Older? Better? Instead she glanced down at the luggage at her feet. "Well…shall we? Are you parked nearby, or should I take off these boots that are absolutely killing me?"

He laughed, grabbed two of the heaviest suitcases and headed toward the exit. "It's a bit of a walk…the closest spot I could find though. You can wait, if you'd like and I'll bring the car around."

"That's okay," she said, "I'll walk."

"You might want to take off the boots," he said with a glance at her feet. "They look like weapons of medieval torture. Smart though, I'll say that. My daughter will be wanting to borrow them."

"Your daughter," she said. "Wow, that sounds so strange. She's how old now?"

"Twenty-six." He glanced at her. "Older than you were when you left and now she's a mind to do the same thing."

"Go to the States?"

"Right. She has a husband in the *gardai* and a four-month-old baby and she thinks they could all do a lot better in America than they can here." Another glance at her. "California, they're thinking."

She shook her head. Something in his voice told her he wasn't very happy about it. "That would be tough on you, I should think."

He laughed, a short bitter bark. "You could say that, but there'll be time enough to discuss it. If I don't bring the matter up, Tara will. She's convinced it's the reason you're here."

"Huh?"

"Ach, it's a load of mystical nonsense. Pay no attention to me, I shouldn't have mentioned it before we're even out of the airport."

But you did, she thought. Which says a whole lot about how important it must be. They walked along in silence for a few minutes, out of the terminal and into a cool misty morning. I'm home, she told herself. Back in Ireland again.

CHAPTER FOUR

"HAD THE CENTER of the city—William to Quay Street—been pedestrianized when you left?" Kieran asked Eileen as he maneuvered the car into the throng of traffic around Galway.

"No." She shook her head. "I don't think so."

"Well, now if I want to go into, Salthill, say, I have to plan my route before I even start driving. Traffic's heavier than it's ever been and it can only get worse."

Eileen, looking through the window, was shaking her head in disbelief. "I can't believe it all. Everything looks so different...and what's that, that big building over there? I don't remember that...and that." Turned in her seat, she was pointing through the window. "Where's that little shop, what was the name of it?" Now she was turning again, back to face him once more. "This is so strange, Kieran. I mean I know things don't stay the same but..."

He laughed. It had been like that the entire way, Eileen exclaiming about this or that, shaking her head, wowing to beat the band. And he'd enjoyed every minute of it. If Tara, and—okay he might as well admit it, himself too—had worried about what he and Eileen would find to talk about, they could've both spared themselves. As soon as they'd set eyes on each other again, it seemed to him—and he thought to Eileen, too—it might have been twenty-five minutes, not years since they'd parted.

"Did you notice?" he asked. "How long it took us to get this far? From Shannon into Galway, I mean?"

Eileen frowned, glanced at her watch. "Not really. Why?"

"Even ten years ago, when there were fewer cars, I'd allow about eighty minutes. Today, it took…" he pushed up his sleeve to check his watch "…two hours and twenty-five minutes."

"As bad as L.A.," she said. "Complaining about the traffic is part of life there. Nothing ever happens though except they build even more freeways and houses farther and farther away. People spend three hours every day on the freeway and think nothing of it."

"Tell that to Tara," he said before he could stop himself. It was good being with Eileen again, just talking casually and he never intended to bring up the whole matter of his daughter again but Tara was never far from his thoughts. "Sorry," he said. "She's just on my mind."

"If there's anything I can do…? Set her straight about what it's really like?"

He shrugged. "Maybe. We'll see. She's eager to meet you."

Eileen smiled, a bit wistful suddenly.

"What will you do while you're here, Eilie?"

"I know my mother's probably got something planned for every day. I'd like to take some long walks, do a lot of thinking."

"Well…if you find yourself in need of some company…"

She turned to look at him. "I'd like that."

"After all, you'll need someone to show you around Clonkill."

"*Clonkill?* What's there to show?"

"Ah well, there's been big changes. The news agents is now a Tandoori takeaway and remember Cleggans bar? It's a gentleman's club now, if you please. Not that I'd have any firsthand experience of it, of course."

Eileen laughed and then, encouraged, he started laying it on thick, talking about all the changes, some real, some created for her entertainment. The housing developments where fields used to be, the airport and a shopping mall built over the bogs, the bowling alley and the cinema.

"And now for the biggest surprise of all." He turned into a lane on the edge of the village and pulled up outside a small cottage with a sagging roof and a few listless chickens in the yard. A farmer standing by a donkey with a badly sagging back gave them a passing glance.

"Your mammy's new house," Kieran said.

Eileen, her back to him, appeared frozen.

"And there's your mammy herself," he said as an old woman dressed in black appeared at the door wiping her hands on an apron.

Eileen whipped around to look at him and he burst out laughing. In a minute, she was laughing too, tears running down her face. Over her shoulder, he could see the old woman watching them. He gave her a little wave.

Five minutes later, they were at Mrs. D's.

A banner over the door said Welcome Home Eileen.

As he pulled up, the front door was thrown wide open and half the population of Ireland, led by Mrs. D, came spilling out, arms outstretched. He reached over, squeezed Eileen's shoulder. A moment later, she was out of the car and lost to the mob.

He carried Eileen's suitcases inside the house and up the stairs to her bedroom, came down again and found her, still in the front garden, being hugged and kissed and looking more than a bit dazed. He tried to imagine her reaction if he hadn't been able to talk Mrs. D out of hiring a brass band.

"Sure you haven't changed a bit," he heard someone lying.

"Where are your suitcases?" Mrs. D wanted to know. "You brought the dress you wore to the Oscars, I hope."

"…and here's your Uncle Fred's boy, Conor." Someone had pushed a gangly teenager at her.

"Sure the whole town wanted to come out to meet you," Mrs. D was saying now. "I didn't like turning anyone away, but then I thought, no I'd like some time alone with my daughter before everyone else gets their hands on her. Now I'll show you where you'll be sleeping."

"Have you a house on the beach, Eileen?" someone was asking.

By some sort of miracle, Kieran managed to catch her eye. "Bye," he mouthed. Then he winked and left her to it.

"DEIRDRE?" Eileen's mother looked about, her expression absent as though Deirdre were a pair of eyeglasses she'd just set down. "Wasn't she here earlier? Sure, there was such a crowd, I couldn't tell. Now Eilie, what can I get you? A glass of sherry?"

"I'm fine, Mammy." All the presents she'd brought

for everyone, expensive and elaborately gift-wrapped, had been distributed—except for Deirdre's and Kieran's. When she'd shopped for Kieran's she'd only been able to guess how things would be with them and she'd bought him a sweater—the neutral sort of thing you could give to a brother, or a best friend. After their ride from Shannon, a certain promise in the way they'd laughed and talked together, she was sorry she hadn't chosen something more…meaningful, although red boxers with hearts would've probably been jumping the gun.

Her gift to Deirdre had been turquoise jewelry— bracelets, earrings and a necklace she'd bought during a weekend trip to San Diego. At the time, she'd realized she knew nothing at all about her sister, not even her dress size, thus the jewelry. And although there had been God knows how many people there to welcome her home, she was fairly certain Deirdre hadn't been among them.

There was probably some logical explanation, she decided. At the moment, sitting on the edge of the bed watching her mother sort through the clothes in the open suitcases, she felt too frazzled and overwhelmed with everything to give it more than a passing thought. Her mother, exclaiming over a rose-colored cashmere sweater, was clearly happy to have her back. The contents of her suitcases were also scoring big.

"I can tell this one was expensive." Her mother had the sweater by the shoulders. "Deirdre will tell you it's all the marketing you pay for, but I'd know the cost of this from a mile off."

Eileen stifled a yawn. Instinctively she glanced at her watch, still set on California time, but couldn't work her brain around the significance of the time difference. Should she be feeling tired? Wide awake? Her face felt stretched from all the laughing and smiling, her eyes hollow. I'm home, she kept telling herself, but somehow the idea wouldn't sink in.

"How does it feel to be home?" people had been asking her ever since she arrived. "Great," she'd reply. "Fantastic." In truth, she didn't know how it felt. After all these years, maybe this couldn't really be called home. But then Los Angeles never felt like home, either. "I'm going home," she'd told Mr. Schwartz and he'd understood right off that she meant Ireland.

"Will you wear this for Kieran's party Saturday?" Her mother was holding up a little black cocktail dress.

A little black cocktail dress for a December evening in Clonkill.

Embarrassed, Eileen stretched out across the bed and closed her eyes. *Kieran* was having a party? She opened them again. "What's the party for?"

"Well, you, of course. Dierdre says he's been planning it for weeks."

"Oh." She smiled and sat up. Kieran was having a party for her.

"Now I wouldn't bother you with this," her mother was saying, "but you were asking about Deirdre and you'll find it out for yourself soon enough. See she took it hard when you told her she couldn't come to visit. Mind you, I was disappointed too, but the difference between us, Deirdre and myself that is, is that I understand the demands your life places on you. Anyway, I was thinking, maybe you could help her smarten up a bit for the party. I think it would do an awful lot to mend fences."

DEIRDRE DROPPED BY the next morning. When Eileen wrapped her arms around her, she could feel her sister's stiff resistance. After a few formalities, they seemed to run out of things to say to each other. They were sitting around the table and Deirdre casually set a newspaper down over the clutter of breakfast things. Half listening to her mother talking about the bus trip to Dublin she'd planned for the three of them later that week, Eileen realized that the picture on the front page was of Deirdre. She reached for it, aware that Deirdre was watching her.

"It's nothing," Deirdre said. "An appointment to the bog preservation committee. Nowhere as grand as the sort of things you do."

Eileen shook her head. "No, this is interesting. I didn't even know the bogs needed preservation."

"They didn't when you left," Deirdre said. "Now they're chipping away at them. They want to build an airport on—"

"Oh right, Kieran mentioned that in the car yesterday."

"How did he seem to you?" Deirdre asked in a flat voice as though the question held no particular interest.

"He looked good," Eileen said truthfully, although she felt her face color. "I didn't know what to expect, but…" She picked up the newspaper again. "So Deirdre, talk to me about this—"

"Ah no, Eilie." Her mother groaned. "Not bogs at this time of the morning. Bogs are bogs, they don't change very much in millions of years so after twenty-five years you'll not see anything different. Now listen, Deirdre, Eileen's bought some lovely presents for everyone. I've opened mine, wait till you see it, I think I'll wear it for

Kieran's party. Go upstairs and bring Deirdre's down," she commanded Eileen.

Eileen, who would have preferred to wait until she and Deirdre had established, reestablished, some sort of sisterly bond, started to protest but her mother had that dogged look on her face that said no one would have a moment's peace until the present was unwrapped.

"Am I to open it now?" Deirdre asked with no other comment when Eileen handed her the box.

"Sure, go ahead." The turquoise jewelry was all wrong, she could see that now. Embarrassed already, she watched Deirdre's stumpy, purple fingers work the wrapping paper.

"Ooh, what is it?" Carmel wondered aloud as Deirdre lifted the square of cotton over the necklace. "Oh, it's lovely." She'd grabbed the necklace and was holding it in front of Deirdre's black knit cardigan. "Oh, look at that will you? See how the color brightens her eyes, Eileen."

Deirdre waved her mother away and set the necklace back in the box. "Thank you, Eileen," she said stiffly. "Very nice." She rose and carried her teacup to the sink. "I should push on, I've a lot to do today. Kieran's got guests booked and though his daughter is meant to help out, between the baby and this notion about leaving for America..." She glanced at Eileen. "I gather Kieran intends to talk to you about—"

"He did," Eileen said. "Almost before we were out of the airport."

"Aye, well he's worried sick about it, the girl's as headstrong as they come. She can twist the boy she's married to around her little finger, as she can Kieran."

She drew on the gray cloth coat that had been draped

over the back of her chair. Head down, she appeared to be studying her feet. "Ah...welcome home, Eileen. It's nice to have you back and...uh, Friday, I'm leading a bog walk for some schoolchildren. If you're interested, you'd be welcome to join in."

"Thanks," Eileen said, touched. "C'mere." She hugged her sister again and this time Deirdre wasn't as stiff. "Thank you," she said again. "I'd like that."

CHAPTER FIVE

"WHO'S A LOVELY BABY THEN?" Kieran asked his granddaughter. "Who's the most beautiful baby in the whole world? Yes, it's you little Stella," he told her. "And you know why? It's because you have a very handsome grandda."

"Will you listen to him?" Tara said to no one in particular as she piped meringue over a tray of lemon tarts. "His old flame blows back into town and he suddenly sees himself in a whole new light."

"It's a pity for you darling," Kieran told the baby, "that you have such a foolish woman for a mother. Are you sure you'd not want to come and live with me? I'll feed you ice cream every night and chocolate biscuits on Sundays."

Tara, shaking her head at the folly of besotted grandfathers, went on with her work. He'd requested the tarts for Eileen's party the following night. Much to Deirdre's annoyance, he kept coming up with more kinds of food that he wanted to serve, more of this, more of that. Yesterday, Deirdre had thrown up her hands and again threatened to leave town until all the foolishness over Eileen's visit had blown over.

"I should've known better when I told her to come

in the first place," Deirdre had grumbled. "I was thinking it would do my mother good to see the girl again. Little did I know it would create this uproar."

As for himself, he'd hardly stopped thinking about Eileen since he'd dropped her off at her mother's. Even now, grabbing a few minutes of cuddle time with the baby, his mind kept turning to Eileen. Now and then though, the baby's flailing foot would kick at his heart, or he'd find himself caught up again in the pink perfection of her ears, but, he had to say it, Eileen was giving Stella a bit of competition.

"So, Daddy, what was it like seeing her again after all these years?" Tara, ever the incurable romantic, as her mother had been, wanted to know. "Did you kiss her?"

"I did not," he said. "And I'll remind you that she has a gentleman friend back in America. According to Mrs. D that is."

"Did you not ask her yourself?"

The baby had gone to sleep in his arms and he shifted her into a more comfortable position, making sure her head was supported as his daughter Tara had instructed. *His daughter instructing him.* As though *he* hadn't once held *her* just as he was now holding this child.

"Da. Did you not ask her yourself?"

"I did. 'Not being one to beat around the bush,' I said to her, 'is it or is it not true that you have a gentleman friend back in the States and, if it's not true, there's a new motel on the Galway Road, American style so you'll be quite comfortable.'"

"Daddy." Tara, pretending to be scandalized, covered her ears. "Don't tell me things like that. And in front of the baby, too."

"No, I didn't ask her," he said. "That's your answer."

"But you like her?" Her back to the counter now, the piping bag in one hand, she was watching him, amused but clearly intrigued. Her father, who fell asleep over a book before ten each night, behaving…well, not quite himself. "She's attractive, you said?"

"She's easy to be with," he replied. "That and we laughed a lot together, just as we used to. I liked that."

Tara slowly shook her head. "You're gone, Da."

THE DAY OF EILEEN'S PARTY, Kieran stood at the door of the dining room surveying two long sideboards laden with platters of thinly sliced roast beef and an assortment of cheeses. In the kitchen, the refrigerator was full of more food—Irish, he'd insisted although he had nothing against the curries and other foreign dishes the new cook had been trying to introduce, much to Deirdre's disapproval, into the dinner menus.

Still, Irish food had changed a great deal in the years since Eileen left and it wouldn't hurt her a bit to know that while she dined in Beverly Hills restaurants, it wasn't all taties and cabbage back in Ireland.

Ask him why it mattered that Eileen be given a taste of the best of Irish and he'd be hard put to explain, but he'd ordered Limerick ham, prawns from Dublin Bay, Galway oysters…telling himself all the while that it was really just national pride.

Deirdre clearly disapproved.

"You've gone a bit overboard, haven't you?" she'd inquired when she read the bill from the fish market. "Lobster?"

He'd shrugged.

"Maybe it's not my place to say it Kieran, but if you're doing this to impress Eileen—"

"You're right," he'd cut her off. "It's not your place."

Now he glanced at his watch and drew in a breath. The day was slipping away and he still had a lot to do before this evening. Fortunately, there were just five guests staying at the lodge and he'd invited them all to the party.

Out in the back garden, he opened a gate at the far end and walked out into the field where Deirdre's husband had stacked a towering pile of wood for the bonfire later that night. This, too, had provoked comment from Deirdre.

"For God's sake, Kieran. You've a band set to play in the lounge for dancing. D'you really think anyone will want to traipse out into the cold night to stand around a fire?"

"Maybe not," Kieran said. He didn't particularly care. It was one of those softheaded romantic ideas, he supposed, but he'd once kissed Eileen in the light of a bonfire and it seemed fitting that there be one at her welcome home party. Remembering, of course, he thought after he'd trudged back into the lodge, that she had a gentleman friend back in the States.

He mentally checked off the things that still needed to be done and found Tara and Deirdre in the kitchen making barmbrack. He kissed the baby, who was gurgling happily in a portable swing, and rubbed his hands, cold from the outdoors. "Right then," he said, "I'm off into town."

Tara gave him a sly grin. "The way I cut your hair isn't good enough, Daddy?"

He scratched the back of his head. "What're you saying?"

"Someone called from the new hair salon wanting to know if you could come in at ten instead of half past since they've had a cancellation."

Kieran, down on his haunches, shaking a rattle at Stella, glanced up to see both women watching him. Deirdre with a face that could curdle milk, Tara with a mile-wide grin.

"Ah stop it," he said. "I needed a change is all."

"Don't forget your Armani suit, Kieran," Deirdre called after him. "Wouldn't want Eileen to see you looking like an Irish lodge-keeper."

Wait till they find out about the fireworks show, he thought as he got into the car to drive into town.

"TWENTY-FIVE YEARS," one of Eileen's plump aunties was marveling. "Sure it seems like only yesterday that you and Kieran were courting and your mother was over the moon at the thought of him marrying into the family and now he's a grandfather and look at you. Now will you tell us about Julia Roberts? She has an awful big mouth on her I don't care what anyone says. I was just saying to your mother—"

"Never mind about that…" Another aunty tugged at Eileen's arm. "Did you bring photos of your house on the beach, Eileen? The reason I'm asking is we're thinking of a visit to the States next year and—"

"Twenty-five years," a man with a bulbous red nose and watering blue eyes, possibly her Uncle Pat, said. "And you've not wanted to come back in all that time?"

"Just so you know," the first aunt whispered in Eileen's ear, "every time I look over at Kieran he's looking at you."

Eileen, juggling a plate of food and a bottle of beer, stood in the smoky, jam-packed main lounge of Kieran's guest house, a vast room with a timber ceiling, a bright wood fire crackling in the grate and the rugs and furniture pushed back for the dancing later. In every chair and couch people were eating with plates on their laps, while more people stood or leaned against the walls laughing and talking and shooting surreptitious looks or nods at the guest of honor, then smiling if she happened to look their way.

It felt weird and not entirely comfortable being the center of all this attention and Eileen had to stop herself from speculating on the conversations going on around her. "God, but she looks old, doesn't she?" Or, "If you want my opinion, Kieran did himself a favor by marrying Libby."

Still she'd worn one of the new outfits, a midnight blue *Sex And The City* number with a neckline down to there and a skirt that floated sexily around her calves. And there wasn't much time for brooding with her mother grabbing her by the arm and taking her off to meet this aunty or that cousin. "Here's your Uncle Pat" or "Say hello to your cousin Margaret," or, bringing her up before a spike-haired girl with sooty eyes, "And this is Grainne, who you'll not remember since she wasn't even a gleam in her parents' eyes when you went off to America."

Although she kept trying to catch a glimpse of Kieran, it wasn't easy. There had to be at least a dozen aunties and untold cousins and second cousins and second cousins once removed and she felt as though she'd been introduced to every one of them. Her glass was carried off periodically and refilled and between hugs and beery kisses and stuffing her mouth with the food people kept giving her and shaking hands moist from clutching pints, she was also trying to put names with faces.

Who was the one who'd just whispered that Kieran was looking at her from across the room? *I'd say he's still sweet on you.* Was it Una or Finola? And could that one with the tight gray perm and ample bum, moving like a couple of flour sacks under a pink pleated skirt, really be Aunty Rose who, when Eileen had left for the States, had probably been about the age she herself was now and yet, even then had seemed old.

Ah, there was Kieran across the room, talking to a girl who looked exactly like Libby. His daughter, obviously. Watching the two of them, she had a weird flashback to the day when she'd just caught him kissing Libby. For a moment, she found herself hating this girl with her bouncing black curls. She quickly shook it off.

"Kieran's done well for himself, hasn't he?" someone beside her was saying. Nodding, she found herself lost in how her life would've been if he'd married her, not Libby, and it was their daughter and grandchild everyone was cooing over now. But she had no time to think for long because now she was being told about a brother who'd gone off to America years ago.

"Grand Rapids," the woman said. "Last name's Flaherty. You wouldn't have heard of him, I suppose?"

"Eilie." Her mother had her by the arm again. "You're looking a little peaky. Give me your drink and go and put on some lipstick."

"Leave her, Carmel," the other woman ordered. "Now Eileen, is it Beverly Hills where you live? The reason I'm asking is…"

"You look peaky, all the same," her mother said. "Does she look peaky to you, Margaret?"

"That's a lovely dress, Eileen," someone said.

"Expensive." Eileen's mother fingered the material. "All of Eileen's clothes are expensive, of course. She can afford the best."

AROUND ELEVEN, Kieran began steering everybody outside. Clutching bottles and glasses, the noisy throng followed him down the back passageway and into the dark night, torches on either side of the pathway illuminating their way. A couple of the musicians, local lads he'd hired, brought up the rear.

He'd imagined taking Eileen's hand, leading her down to the field himself, but at the last moment his nerve had given out. He'd no desire to look like a fool at all, much less in front of all her friends and family, so he held back, consigning himself the role of stage manager. Much as he'd have preferred leading man.

"Ah, this is lovely, Kieran." Mrs. D pushed up beside him to whisper in his ear. "You've outdone yourself, you really have."

The weather was out of his control though. The wind had picked up and was whipping at his jacket. Women were clutching their hair, pulling their coats around them, shivering ostentatiously at the whimsy of him dragging them outside into the cold night air, even though he'd thought to provide a cauldron of hot cider liberally spiced with Jameson which, from the way some of them were walking, they'd already availed themselves of. In front of him now was the towering pile of wood. The musicians, as he'd arranged earlier, had moved to the front of the line and were playing "Galway Bay."

The moon—he'd ordered a full one—shone down on the lot of them, highlighting the backdrop of bare trees. The few wisps of gray clouds that blew across the moon's face, like bits of torn gauze, were a nice touch, he thought. Waving at everyone to stay back, he ran across the field, touched a match and a dozen or so small fireworks he'd set in the ground earlier fused and rose, exploding like a burst of chrysanthemums. The crowds began to applaud.

On cue, the musicians broke into "The Cliffs of Doneen," a piece he'd chosen especially for Eileen.

"You may travel far far from your own native land," a lad from the village sang softly. "Far away o'er the mountains, far away o'er the foam. But of all the fine places that I've ever been, sure there's none can compare with the cliffs of Doneen…"

Kieran glanced back at the crowd. Amid all the upturned faces, lit by the colored lights, he finally spotted Eileen's, tears pouring down her cheeks.

With a quick prayer that the *gardai* would turn a blind eye, he struck a match to light the bonfire, then sprinted back to where she stood—momentarily, and miraculously, alone—watching the flames leap into the night. In an instant she was in his arms sobbing into his shoulder.

"Ah, come on now," he whispered, suddenly unsure of himself. The tears he'd expected, but not the violent sobs that were shaking her body. He hugged her closer, patted her back. "I was just trying to show you what you've been missing all these years."

"You have, trust me," she said, the words muffled because her mouth was still half buried in his shoulder. "Oh, Kieran." She pulled away to look at him, sniffing, eyes damp. "God, I wasn't prepared for that."

Kieran went on holding her, aware that none of this was going unnoticed. As the fire sent crackling flames leaping ever higher, the eyes that weren't following the embers as they rose in the air like a second fireworks display, were fixed on the sight of Eileen Doyle back in his arms after all these years. Everyone wondering no doubt what her fancy gentleman friend would have to say about all of this.

Other than a passing thought that perhaps he should round up a bucket of water just to be on the safe side— for the fire that would be—Kieran could hardly have cared less about what any of them thought. The party had gone off very, very well and at this moment, with Eileen, smiling now through the tears, he was a happy man.

"Welcome home, Eilie," he said.

CHAPTER SIX

"YEAH, SURE YOU LOOK like a million dollars," Mr. Schwartz said to Eileen in her dream. "And everyone thinks you're a big deal and the boyfriend's back and it's all hunky dory. But you're a fraud, kid. A fraud. Fraud. *Fraud.*"

"Okay!" Eileen shouted, waking herself up. "I get it."

Her eyes were swollen and burning as if she'd been crying all night and the song the kid had sung at the party was still playing over and over in her brain. *You can travel far far, from your own native home... Welcome home, Eilie,* she heard Kieran say. *"But there's none can compare..."* The song again. God. She wiped her nose with the back of her arm. She had the shaky feeling that whatever she set her eyes on, listened to, thought about, anything at all, would have her bawling uncontrollably.

Oh what a tangled web we weave...

Shut up. She pulled the pillow over her head.

You can travel far, far...

Shut up. She tossed the pillow to the floor, went down the hall to the bathroom, which looked nothing like the one she remembered. "Ah, well it needed a little spruce-up," her mother had said while she'd been giving Eileen a tour that first day. "Kieran did the work himself. He's good like that."

Judging by all the other changes and modifications she'd noticed in the house, Kieran must have been quite busy over the years. Just quietly helping out her mother. No big deal, no expectations of anything, just there to give a hand when needed. And Deirdre, plain solid Deirdre, working away to preserve the bogs and birds. And you, Eileen? Twenty-five years of building a stupid, phony facade. You must be so proud.

At the sink, careful to avoid her reflection in the chrome-framed mirror, Eileen removed toothbrush and toothpaste from her silver toiletry bag. When she'd set the bag out on the little shelf arrangement over the toilet, even that had prompted her mother to whisper, "Oooh, expensive," in the kind of reverential tone you'd hear in church.

Eileen faced her mirrored self, looked away. She squirted toothpaste onto the brush and scrubbed her teeth. Back in the bedroom, she sat on the edge of the bed. She wanted to call Mr. Schwartz for advice. She practiced the conversation in her head.

"This isn't going quite the way I thought it would. I thought I could just put on this act, play the part and not really feel anything. But being back is, well, I didn't know I was going to feel like this, like a part of me is back where it was always supposed to be. In one way it feels so right…"

"So what's the problem?" Mr. Schwartz would say.

"Well, *duh*. I'm not really who people think I am. I'm not this rich, successful woman, I'm just me, Eileen, and I want to tell them that."

"So tell them."

Eileen started crying. Mr. Schwartz wasn't helping, not like this. She lay down again, pulled the covers up to her face and studied the dolls. Her mother had dolls all over the house—china dolls in crinoline skirts with elaborate hats and curls, dumpy cloth dolls with yarn hair. Inexplicably, one wore a little name badge that said, "Hello, I'm Deanna." There were dolls that stood several feet high, a set of tiny dolls that lived in mismatched teacups on the mantelpiece in the parlor, Barbie dolls in crocheted dresses. On the shelf opposite the bed a gray-haired granny doll seemed to be looking directly at her—disapprovingly.

"Go to hell," Eileen said.

"Eilie." It was her mother's voice outside the door. "Cup of tea?"

"Thanks." Eileen sat up, wiped her eyes and swung her legs over the side of the bed. "I'll be right down."

"Stay where you are. I've brought a tray. I thought we'd have a cozy little breakfast up here, just the two of us. There now." She set the tray down across Eileen's knees. "A full Irish breakfast. Looks lovely, doesn't it?"

"It does," Eileen agreed. Fried eggs with yolks the color of oranges, thick rashers of bacon, slice of brown bread. *Full Irish breakfast for a half-Irish fraud.* She watched as her mother settled herself in the armchair next to the bed and poured the tea.

"To having you home again, Eilie." Her mother clinked her teacup against Eileen's.

"To being here," Eileen said and started to cry. "I'm sorry." She sniffed. "I'll be all right, it's just everything's kind of overwhelming…last night—"

"Kieran did a lovely job, didn't he? I was surprised myself, what with the fireworks and the food! Deirdre said it must have cost him a fortune. To her way of thinking he'd gone a bit overboard, but I said to her, that's Kieran's business." She paused to sprinkle pepper over her eggs. "I told Kieran…" she said in a hushed voice as though he might be on the other side of the door "…and I'm just saying this so…well anyway, I told him not to get his hopes up."

"Mom." Eileen set her fork down. "Kieran's a grown man. I don't think he needs you telling him…anyway, what if I…what if—"

"What if you what?"

"What if I still…if Kieran and I…"

"You're not saying that you and Kieran—"

"I'm not saying anything, Mammy." God she was starting to cry again. "I don't know, I mean everything's fine…great, it's just that, well, it feels so good to be back."

"It's lovely to have you back."

"But, you know, I just think sometimes, what if I just came back for good?"

"What?"

"Just came back," she said in a small voice.

"You can't be serious," her mother said, clearly horrified. "Why would you throw up everything you've worked all these years for, just to—"

"Maybe it's not that big of a deal. Maybe I don't care."

"But Eilie—" her mother leaned closer "—what about your gentleman friend?"

"Maybe he's no big deal, either."

"Ah, come on." She peered into Eileen's cup, poured some more tea. "It's the jet lag is all. 'Twas the same with Mrs. Donovan's son when he came back from Canada. He'd hardly walked through the front door, she said, before he was saying that's it, he never wanted to leave Ireland again. But, sure enough by the end of two weeks, he was ready to leave and I don't think he's been back since."

She started to clear away the dishes. "Now, speaking of Mrs. Donovan, she's laid up with a bad back and I promised I'd look in on her this morning. Would you want to go with me? Or maybe you'd like to stay here and rest a bit."

"I might go for a walk," Eileen said. "Leave the dishes, I'll do them."

"Wouldn't hear of it." Her mother eased herself out of the chair, picked up the tray. "What you could do while you're here, Eilie, if you wouldn't mind, is help Deirdre smarten up a bit. I think it would do an awful lot for her self-esteem."

Eileen waited until she heard her mother leave the house, then pulled on jeans—another designer pair she viewed with the same loathing she suddenly felt for everything else in her ridiculous and expensive luggage that she'd be paying off for the rest of her life—added a sweater and the jeans jacket, pulled on the boots, ran a brush through her hair and headed out.

Immediately, the cold zeroed straight to her bones. By the time she reached the bottom of her mother's street, her teeth were chattering uncontrollably. *Serves you right. That's what you get for showing off.* About to turn the corner, she stopped, ran back to the house, grabbed one of the sturdy coats her mother had hanging on the hallstand—this one black cloth with a little fur collar, rabbit probably—yanked off the boots that Kieran said his daughter would admire and stuffed her feet into a pair of her mother's faux leather ankle boots with little ruffs of gray curly wool. When she looked down at herself, despite her fragile mood, she wanted to laugh. All she needed was a headscarf and a shopping basket over one arm.

The hell with it. She opened the front door again, stood in the entrance looking out at the street, then ran back into the kitchen, found a plastic shopping bag and dropped the fancy boots inside.

THE CONNEMARA REGION of Ireland was known for wild sweeping landscapes of towering mountain peaks, bogs and lakes. It was not known for its warm sunny weather, particularly in mid December. As Kieran tried to explain this to a couple of guests who'd arrived early that morning and were now complaining that the horseback ride along the beach he'd just suggested would be fine, except it was too cold and damp, he felt a surge of irritation. Go to Spain then, he wanted to say.

By the time he'd got them sorted out, sending them off to Galway for an afternoon of gallery hopping—not how he'd choose to spend his afternoon, but he'd seen the woman's eyes light up when he'd brought out the brochure—Tara, who was filling in for Deirdre who was off on a save-the-corncrake mission, clattered down the uncarpeted wooden stairs to tell him one of the bedroom ceilings was leaking.

"Leaking." He was standing at the lectern that held the guest register. Propping his face in his hands, elbows on the wooden ledge, he stared at her. "A big leak?"

"I didn't measure it, Daddy." She had an edge in her

voice because she really didn't want to be there, yet he clearly needed some help. "But enough that you'd better have a look at it. Haven't we a full house tomorrow?"

"We have." He started for the stairs, then stopped. "The afternoon tea?"

She saluted. "Under control. Six, no, seven old birds chomping down on cucumber sandwiches. Scones warming in the oven."

"Good," he said. "Thank you."

"Right."

A few minutes later, he'd rounded up a large soup pot from the kitchen, and was carrying it upstairs to place under the drip until he could get someone in to take care of it, when Tara burst into the room.

"Daddy. *She's* here."

"She?" As if he didn't know.

"Eileen. Just ordered the cream tea."

"Oh." The pot still in his hand, Kieran gawked at her.

Tara started laughing. "You should see your face, Da. Go." She took the pot from him. "Close your mouth first though and run a comb through your hair."

He did both, but as he clambered down the stairs, his heart thumping to beat the band, he kept in mind the gentleman friend.

In the lobby, a couple of guests—middle-aged Americans back from a shopping spree—provided him with an additional moment or so to work on his composure while they trotted out, for his approval, their purchases of Irish linen tea cloths, Aran sweaters and shamrock-patterned tea things. All the while he had half an eye on Eileen, visible through the open door of the small library that, every afternoon, became the tearoom.

"Very nice…ah yes, very warm," he said as he dutifully felt the wool of the sweater, wondering how many Aran sweaters he'd fingered, so to speak, over the years. If Eileen hadn't been there, he'd have given the guests a bit of history about how each sweater was knitted in a different, distinguishing way so that if the fisherman who wore it was unfortunate enough to drown, the sweater would be his identity.

He would have told them, but he saw Eileen glance at her watch so he made his excuses and walked into the tearoom. Without a word, he sat at the table right in front of her.

Her face, he was pleased to see, lit up immediately. She even blushed a bit. Now what did that say about the state of things?

"Hi, Kieran."

"Hi to you, too."

And that pretty much exhausted their conversation. All they seemed able to do was sit there and grin. She looked nice—in her blond new Eileen sort of way. A black coat with a little collar that looked so familiar, after he'd looked at it for a while he could have sworn he'd seen it on Mrs. D.

"Good scones," she finally said, breaking their smile-a-thon. "Want a taste?"

"No. Thanks though. I've tasted plenty of them, over the years." An innocuous, inconsequential thing to say if he'd ever heard one. He found himself wondering what her gentleman friend did for a living. And what did he talk to Eileen about? Theatre? Art? Amusing little wines with pretentious noses?

"So are you busy?" she asked.

"Right now?" He laughed. "I look it, don't I?" He leaned closer, lowered his voice. "It's an act though. Just trying to convey the impression of a man of leisure. We've a full house from now till after Christmas," he said back in his normal voice. "And unfortunately we're also short-staffed. One of the maids is off having a baby and a chef just gave in his notice and..." He put the brake on his mouth before he went on about the leaking ceiling and the fence that needed to be mended around the horse pasture. "There, now you have it. The trials and tribulations of an Irish lodge-owner."

Eileen looked thoughtful. "You enjoy it though?"

He tried to look thoughtful, too. "I do," he said. "On the whole."

So much for that, they fell into silence again.

"That was a lovely party you gave, Kieran," she said after a while.

"I'm glad you enjoyed it." He studied her plate for a bit—scone crumbs on pink china—trying to work out how to get past the fits and starts of small talk which he could see sputtering along until one or both of them, but most likely Eileen, got bored enough to leave. The thing was though, every sentence that came into his brain was along the lines of: "And this gentleman friend of yours..."

Eileen was still talking about the party. "The fireworks and the music...it was incredible. Do you do that sort of thing very often, have parties like that I mean?"

"Only when I'm trying to impress women from America."

She smiled.

"D'you go to a lot of parties, then?" he asked, ever so casually. "I'd imagine you would, in your line of work that is." Then a thought struck him and he looked at her. "I say that as though I know what your line of work is. In fact I have no idea."

"Oh…" Now she was studying the plate and her face had turned scarlet. "It's kind of difficult to explain." She laughed, awkwardly though. "Actually, it's not all that interesting. I mean it sounds it, but it's not, if you know what I mean."

"I don't," he said, "know what you mean."

"Kieran." She paused. "Can we talk about something else?"

He shrugged, a bit mystified. She seemed on the verge of tears. "We can talk about whatever you want to talk about. Bog preservation. Corncrakes, although that's really Deirdre's specialty…hold on." He nodded to Tara who had just appeared in the doorway, clearly eager to come over. "My daughter." He looked at Eileen. "She's been dying to meet you, but you were surrounded at the party and she didn't want to barge in. You don't mind if I ask her to join us?"

"Of course not," she said, but kind of uneasily as though maybe something was giving her trouble.

With a nod from him, Tara was over and beaming at Eileen with the look of a dazzled fan meeting a big film star. Kieran watched his daughter, pink-cheeked, the curly black hair around her shoulders. She wore turquoise earrings he hadn't seen before and a light green shawl tied in some way that he imagined was all the fashion these days—knotted at one shoulder and slipping off the other. She hadn't been wearing it earlier and he thought she'd probably pulled it over the plain black dress she wore just to impress Eileen.

"I've really been looking forward to meeting you," she said as she slipped into the chair across from Eileen, "but I've yet to catch you by yourself. Can I get you some more scones? Some barmbrak?" Leaning forward, she lifted the lid of the teapot. "More tea?"

"No, thanks," Eileen said. "I'm fine."

Across the table, Kieran briefly met his daughter's eye. He knew exactly what was coming next.

"Eileen," Tara said, her voice low and intense now, "I want so much to move to the States...."

CHAPTER SEVEN

IF EILEEN HAD HELD any doubt that love could survive twenty-five years of separation, that it could, despite little or no nurturing, continue to send up fresh green shoots of incredible tenderness, Kieran's obvious pain as his daughter spoke was all she needed to convince her.

He looked baffled and sad and terribly weary and it killed her to watch him. She wished she could get up and walk around to where he sat, hold him. "It's okay," she would say, soothing him. "It's okay. Everything will be fine."

A brief but intense flame of hatred for this girl disconcerted her. Looking at her from across the table, she couldn't help but be reminded of Libby, the woman who had stolen Kieran away. And now Libby's daughter was so casually inflicting pain on him. Describing in a fast, urgent voice the acting course she intended to take, the schools she'd heard of that offered day-care nurseries where she could leave the baby and then of course her husband would have to find a job.

Something about the turquoise earrings the girl wore looked familiar. As she listened and nodded, Eileen tried to recall where she might've seen a similar pair. And then it came to her. They were the earrings she'd given to Deirdre who, Eileen could only surmise, had passed them on to Tara. With difficulty, Eileen brought her attention back to the moment, aware as she did that Kieran was watching her.

"The thing is," she finally interrupted after another five minutes or so of the girl's nonstop monologue, "it's not so easy to just pick up and leave everything—your home, your friends. The people who love you." At this, she heard her voice crack. She drank some tea. "You really have no idea—"

"I have Joe and the baby," Tara said. "It's not as though I'll be alone. But, Eileen, what I wanted to ask you about is—"

"Listen to Eileen, will you?" Kieran spoke sharply to his daughter. "Hear her out before you jump in."

"It's more than just the loneliness," Eileen explained. "You find yourself desperate for things you'd never imagine you'd even think about. Butter in America doesn't taste quite the same as the butter we have here, the bread tasted all wrong to me, too. A bit sweet, so I couldn't make a cheese sandwich, say…and that's if I could find decent cheese, which most of the time I couldn't. I know that sounds like a little thing, but, the little things begin to pile up."

She stopped, caught up in her memories but sensing that, while Kieran was listening intently, this wasn't what his daughter—head bowed, playing with the fringes of her shawl—wanted to hear.

"Tara." Kieran nodded toward the doorway where an elderly woman seemed undecided whether to go or stay. "See if she wants tea, will you?"

Tara frowned. "It's almost past serving time," she grumbled in a low voice, but rose, readjusted her shawl and with a long-suffering sigh went off to talk to the woman.

Eileen met Kieran's glance. "Not a happy camper, huh?"

"She's dead set on going and that's all there is to it. Nothing you tell her that doesn't fit her notion of the way things will be is going to sink in."

"It's got to be tough for you."

"Ah…" He made a sweeping gesture with his hand.

She thought of the way he'd so quickly brought up the issue, before they'd even left the airport. "I wish I could help in some way," she said feeling ineffectual. What did she know about a parent's pain?

"You warned her that it wouldn't be as easy as she thinks, but you can see for yourself, she has her mind set. And the trouble is, she's looking at you and seeing that, despite everything, you've made a go of things. Well, more than that, you're a success story, so of course she's thinking she can do it, too."

Eileen's breath caught. A moment that could change everything came and went. Another moment passed. She reached for her purse on the floor by her feet. "Well, I think the plans for tonight are dinner out. I should get going."

Kieran stood. "I'll walk you home."

"Great." Tara and everything else forgotten, her heart began to beat ridiculously fast and then, smiling up at him, she caught a glimpse of something so soft and tender it almost took her breath away.

It's still there for him, too.

The rain had started—or never stopped. Misty mornings had a way of turning into rainy afternoons, or vice versa, and the prospect of rain seemed always just over the mountains. In drought-ridden California, rain was another of those things she'd missed desperately, welcoming every meager drop that fell on the dusty palms that lined her street. Now as they walked down the gravel road that led away from the lodge to join with the main road into town, Eileen lifted her face to the soft wet air, absorbing it like a thirsty plant.

Eileen and Kieran taking a walk together.

Inside the folds of her mother's coat, her body felt warm with promise.

"What's his name then?" Kieran asked, out of the blue.

"Whose name?"

"The gentleman friend. Your mother never told me his name."

Eileen dug her hands deep into the pockets of the coat, looked at her feet in their absurd little boots. In her peripheral vision, she caught Kieran's sideways glance. "Fauntleroy." The name had just popped into her head.

"Fauntleroy." A moment later, he asked, "That would be his last name?"

"It would," she said. "Little Lord is his first name. First and second actually."

"He's a famous person and you're not able to tell me?"

She grinned. "Yeah, that's it. He's married to a famous actress. If word got out that I was the other woman, she'd kill me." And then she said, "Kieran, there is no gentleman friend."

"So what your mother's been saying…?"

She sighed. God, she wanted to drop this whole stupid story, to just be Eileen. "My mom kept writing me all these damn letters, worrying about did I have someone? Wasn't it time I settled down with one person instead of going from one man to another? On and on, blah, blah, blah. Finally I just invented the gentleman friend to shut her up."

"Could you not have told her it was none of her business?"

"Hah!" She shot him a look. "Have you ever tried saying anything like that to my mom?"

He laughed. "You've a point there."

They'd reached the Strand now, big bay-windowed houses along the seafront where the well-off had once lived. People like Dr. Connaughton, who used to run the local hospital and had delivered half the people in town, a solicitor from London who only came to Clonkill on fishing holidays. As a girl, she'd thought them the grandest places anyone could possibly have. Now they looked forlorn, aging dowagers staring out at the unchanging sea.

"So," she challenged Kieran. "Share and share alike. I told you about my gentleman friend, or lack of. What about you?"

"Do I have someone? Is that what you're asking?"

"Yes."

"No."

They kept walking, past St. Augustine's Abbey with its high walls topped by bits of broken glass, which she and Libby had once tried to scale. On down the steep narrow road that wound under the mossy stone bridge and around to the harbor.

The sea was out, fishing boats like stranded beasts rested on their sides in the mud. A dog, chasing a seagull, barked at the distant edge of the water. The sun was setting, streaking everything with bronze highlights, vivid in the gathering gloom.

"I was seeing a woman in Galway for a while," Kieran said. "But…there's really been no one important…since Libby."

"I'm sorry about Libby, Kieran. I should've said it long before now, but…I wrote you so many letters. Somehow I could never get the words just right."

He said something she didn't catch, and put his arm around her shoulder. The effect was electrifying. The solid weight of him, his physical closeness, the side of his body—hips, thighs—brushing hers. All that the gesture implied. They walked a few more steps, then stopped. Wordlessly, he pulled her to him and kissed her. She wanted to crawl inside him. His lips pressing harder, harder, her mouth opening to his. Teeth, tongue. His hands clutching her hair now, backing her against the railing.

Afterward, she stared at him, dazed. He looked as stunned as she felt. A physical and emotional ambush that had left his mouth swollen, his eyes feverish and distracted. Tears clogged her throat, stung her nose. Kieran. Oh, Kieran. She took his face in her hands and kissed him on the lips, a soft, soft, gentle kiss that spoke of everything she didn't know how to say.

"I'VE NO IDEA what's wrong with everyone," Deirdre said huffily after Kieran had snapped at her for the second time in an hour over a minor transgression, the last being that peas were on the dinner menu for the third night in a row and would it be asking too much to have a little variety once in a while. "What with Tara slamming out of the place."

"When was that?" Kieran roused himself from the gloom that had descended after dropping Eileen off at her mother's, a gloom more pronounced because of the euphoria he'd felt just a short while before. *This is how it will be when she goes back to the States*. He glanced at his watch. Dinner would be served in half an hour and she was needed to wait tables.

"Whatever it was Eileen said to her—"

"Eileen's not to blame," he said. "It's time Tara grew up a bit. She seems to forget she has a child now." He stopped, his head too full of Eileen at the moment to tackle anything else. "Deirdre," he said. "Sit down."

She did. Arms folded across her chest, she waited.

"I'm about to make an awful fool of myself."

"Eileen?"

"I wasn't prepared for it," he said. "I laughed when your mother warned me…how did she put it? Something about not getting my hopes up. I may even have made a joke of it."

Deirdre folded her arms across her chest. "They say there's no fool like an old fool."

Kieran laughed. "Ah *jays,* thanks Deirdre. That's all I needed to hear."

"Well catch yourself, Kieran. She's a woman you knew as a girl, that's all there is to it. Now she's back with her bleached hair and fancy clothes and maybe that appeals to you, sure there's no accounting for taste."

"That's not fair," he said rushing to Eileen's defense. "You're making her sound like a tart. She's a good-looking woman."

"And what is it you have in common with her? What do you say to each other?"

He shrugged, trying to recall. "Nothing much, I suppose. It's just…nice to spend time with her."

"Well I'd say make the most of it then, before she goes back to America the week after next."

"TARA'S ON THE PHONE for you," Eileen's mother called from the kitchen, where the only phone in the house sat on a lace doily on top of a little table. *"Eileen!"*

"I heard you, Mom." She'd been lying on the couch in the front room, flipping through magazines and seeing Kieran's face on every page. Now she wondered why his daughter was calling. Maybe the girl had seen her father having his face kissed off and was seeking an explanation.

In the kitchen, her mother was using the moment to describe to Tara all the gifts Eileen had brought from America. "…lovely cashmere twin set. Pale blue, not just any old blue, a bit of mauve in it, you only see the color in more expensive things. Of course everything Eileen has is—"

Eileen grabbed the phone. "Sorry," she said, the apology meant both for her mother and Tara. "Hi. What's up?"

"You left your boots at the lodge today," Tara said. "I thought you might be looking for them."

Eileen frowned. "My boots?"

"In a bag under the table where you'd been sitting. My da recognized them, said they were yours."

"Oh, oh, oh," Eileen said, enlightenment dawning. *My brain's addled from kissing your father.* "Actually I was going to ask if you'd like them. Your dad had said something about them being the style?"

Tara's breath was audible. "Oh, Eileen, they're gorgeous. But I couldn't take them from you—"

"Sure you could. Do they fit okay?"

"Only as though they were made just for me." She laughed. "I had to try them on, of course. They're exactly the style I saw this actress on a chat show wearing. Eileen, really, I don't know what to say. I've never had anything so expensive. Are you sure? Really?"

"Really." A complex swell of emotion washed over her; the feel-good pleasure of making someone happy mixing uneasily with shame over this ongoing charade and the fear that she'd inadvertently strengthened Tara's determination to leave Ireland for a place where she, too, could afford Italian leather boots.

"Thank you, thank you, thank you," Tara said. "I'm never going to take them off." She paused. "Eileen, do you mind if I ask you something?"

Immediately wary, Eileen began thinking of excuses to get off the phone. "Uh…"

"It's about my father."

"Go ahead."

"Well, I know you were…sweethearts, I suppose you'd say, before he married my mother and…" She laughed. "From the way he's been behaving since you arrived, I've a suspicion that, well you know, that it wouldn't take much to get things going again."

"Hmm," Eileen said, noncommittally, curious to see where this would lead. "And?"

"And, well this will strike you as a bit far-fetched, I'm sure." Again she laughed. "But it's the way my mind works. I was thinking to myself, now what if Eileen feels the same way about Daddy and—this is the bit I'm getting to—what if we all went to America? That way Daddy would see Stella grow up and I'd be there and you, too. You know the funny thing is now I've said it, it seems like the only thing to do. I was trying to explain this to Daddy just the other day. It's called synchronicity. "That's why Eileen's here," I said.

CHAPTER EIGHT

"OH YOU CAN FIND all sorts of things in the bogs, " Deirdre was telling the cluster of schoolchildren who sat in the small amphitheater of the bogland interpretive center. "Even a body or two."

"Eww," the kids squealed in unison.

"And here's something to tell your mammies," she suggested. " In the old, old days, before my time even…" she paused for a laugh "…people would put their butter in the bogs to preserve it, the same way you'd use a fridge today."

"Ew," the kids squealed again.

In the back row, Eileen smiled—at the children's response as well as for Deirdre, who was clearly in her element. A pity, she found herself echoing her mother's oft-repeated lament, that Deirdre had never had children of her own. A few minutes later, after the room had been darkened for a slide presentation, she closed her eyes, letting her thoughts wander. It seemed no time at all that she and Kieran and Libby, then the age of these children, had gone off on bog field trips. There'd been no amphitheater then, but she could still recall the eerie, solitary sense of standing with the fog falling all around them, the cold wind in their faces.

Absorbed at the time, she'd jumped ten feet when Kieran had crept up behind to touch the back of her neck with a piece of rotting wood. He'd also known some pretty spooky bog stories of headless men and skeletons. She'd have to ask if he still remembered them.

Kieran. Had his daughter shared her mass emigration plan with him, she wondered. He'd rung that morning early to see if she'd like to join him. He was taking a group of guests for a horseback ride along the beach. She'd declined. For one reason, she didn't know how to ride a horse—a detail she'd chosen not to share. So much fabrication and dissembling already, what was one small omission? She'd also promised to visit Deirdre at the center. Deirdre's volunteer work with various preservations groups was clearly an important and admirable focus of her life. Since expensive gifts were not the way to Deirdre's heart, Eileen had decided the least she could do was show a little interest in her sister's work.

"I DIDN'T REALIZE the bogs were so endangered," she told Deirdre later as they ate cucumber-and-tomato salads and buttered brown bread in the center's cheerful little café. "I guess they just seem like something that has always been and always will be."

"Nothing lasts forever," Deirdre said cryptically.

"Yeah, I guess." Eileen drank a sip of strong tea from a sturdy white mug, which did in fact have the look of something that could last forever. Deirdre was right though, things changed. Some for the good, some not so good. And some things, herself for instance, only appeared to have changed. Superficially at that. She'd tried to call Mr. Schwartz that morning and, for the third time, there'd been no answer. Not wanting him to go to the expense of an overseas call, which he well might, she hadn't left a number. Now she felt a vague unease. If he didn't answer the next time, she'd leave a number and tell him to call collect.

"Not exactly great dining, is it?" Deirdre nodded at Eileen's untouched plate. "Sorry, but I'm not the fancy restaurant type."

Eileen picked up her fork. "This is fine, Deirdre, really."

"Mammy has applied for a credit card," Deirdre said.

"What?"

"A credit card. Never had one before in her life, but this morning she tells me she's applied for one."

"Why?" Eileen gaped at her sister, mystified. "I don't understand. What does she need to buy that—"

"It's to impress you," Deirdre said flatly. "She'd kill me if she knew I was telling you this, but it's something you need to know. She's got it into her head to book a fancy hotel in Dublin. Three hundred Euros a night, if you please, but nothing's too good for our Eileen."

Jolted by a quick surge of anger, at herself for not just denying the whole stupid pretense, but also at Deirdre's flat, accusatory tone, Eileen set her fork down. "I didn't ask her to do anything like that," she said. "It's of no interest to me to go to Dublin. Where did she even get that idea?"

"Oh, catch yourself, Eileen." Deirdre's lips pressed tight with rage, opened and closed again. "Where d'you think she got that idea? You swanning around with all your designer clothes and handing out expensive gifts as though they were penny toys." Red splotches colored her cheeks now. Her hand holding the teacup shook.

"All right, you're a big deal in America, but did it ever occur to you for just one minute to tone it down a bit when you came back to Ireland? Did you give any thought at all to how people would see you? Giving away boots to a starry-eyed girl, boots that cost more money than she's probably seen in a lifetime. Leading on a decent man like Kieran. No regard for any feelings other than your own. D'you ever think about anything, Eileen? Really think, I mean? *Ach...* I'm too disgusted." She pushed her chair back from the table, fished in her handbag and threw down a few bills. "There. My treat. I'm one who has no need at all for your charity."

WHEN KIERAN STOPPED in at Mrs. D's to see Eileen, the older woman was on the phone, the receiver cradled between her head and shoulder as she painstakingly copied down information.

"I'm sorry, I didn't quite catch that," she said. "Shorts, is it? No? Shartz... Wasn't that what I just said? Mr. Shartz and he's a friend of my daughter's? Now is this Mr. Shartz I'm talking to? He's what? Just a minute, I'll have you talk to my...son." One hand over the mouthpiece, she appealed to Kieran. "I can't make head or tails of what he's saying. I thought he said he was a Mr. Shartz, but now he's saying Mr. Shartz is dead."

Kieran took the phone. A man with an American accent identified himself as Frank Schwartz—he spelled the last name—told him that his father, who apparently was a friend of Eileen's, had died of a sudden heart attack.

"The old guy was always talking about her," Frank Schwartz said. "He thought the world of her. She lived in the next apartment, took real good care of him. Even did his shopping for him. I live on the East Coast so I wasn't able to see him too often, but thank God he had Eileen. Brought him a beef brisket every week. It was a thing they had going, I guess. He passed away the day after she left. Eileen had left a message for him, said she'd been trying to call him, so I thought I'd better let her know."

"Right," Kieran said. "I'm sure she'd appreciate that." He motioned to Mrs. D for the pen she'd been using, jotted down the number the man gave him, offered his condolences and said goodbye.

"Well…" Mrs. D, hands on her hips, was all agog. A plump little bird, beak open for the smallest scrap of enlightenment. "What was that all about?"

"A friend of Eileen's passed away, it seems."

"Ooh." Mrs. D's hand flew to her mouth. "The gentleman friend, d'you think?"

Kieran said nothing. It didn't seem his role to set Mrs. D straight. Nor did he want another warning from Mrs. D about getting his hopes up, which any talk of a gentleman friend would almost certainly lead to. He accepted a coffee, listened as he drank it to ten minutes or so of speculation about what this Mr. Schwartz might be to Eileen, then left.

Eileen had said very little about her life in America, he mused as he walked back to the lodge, but he'd used his imagination to build a picture of what he thought it must be. The idea of her routinely buying beef brisket for an elderly neighbor didn't fit in anywhere, and yet the funny thing was it didn't surprise him, either.

AFTER DEIRDRE STORMED OUT of the bogland interpretative center, Eileen remained at the table to finish her tea and salad. For more than an hour she sat there quietly staring through the cafeteria's picture window out to the bogs, which lay like a dark, slightly undulating blanket for as far as she could see.

Everything about her visit had gone horribly wrong. The fictional Eileen she'd dreamed up to compensate for her own dismal life had succeeded in creating this huge gulf between her and all the people who mattered most to her. God, how could she have been so stupid?

The damn turquoise jewelry for Deirdre that Tara now wore. All the other expensive gifts she'd lavished on people. A cashmere sweater she was saving for just the right moment to give to Kieran. Meaningless. The only gift they needed from her, the only gift she could afford to give them, was the one she least wanted to part with.

She found Tara in the lodge kitchen, sitting by the high chair absorbed in feeding the baby orange stuff from a jar. "Hiya," Tara called cheerily when she saw Eileen in the doorway. "We haven't quite got the hang of this, have we love?" she said, looking back at the gurgling baby.

Eileen pulled a chair up to the table and sat. Tara, she noticed, was wearing the boots, the legs of her jeans neatly tucked in. For a moment, she heard herself offering all the other designer stuff in the suitcases—hell, the suitcases themselves, she didn't care. Ironic wasn't it, that when Kieran kissed her she'd been wearing her mother's old coat.

"Deirdre's around somewhere," Tara said as she scraped a trail of sloshover from the baby's chin. Ducking her head toward Eileen as though about to share a confidence, she whispered, "She slammed in here about twenty minutes ago in a terrible mood. I think it's the change. Daddy's off on some errand or other. They'll both be back soon though to get dinner underway."

Eileen nodded absently. She'd caught a whiff of meat roasting in the oven, registered the pan of peeled potatoes simmering on the stove, all of it background to the activity of her brain as she planned how she would do this. Kieran and her mother, she'd tell each of them alone. Her mother because reality would come as the most crushing blow, and Kieran...just because.

Deirdre appeared at the doorway in that instant, saw Eileen and turned to leave. Eileen called her back. When her sister didn't reappear, Eileen got up, and tracked her down in the dining room, slamming down silverware.

"I need to talk to you," Eileen said.

"I've nothing to say to you that hasn't been said," Deirdre snapped.

"Well, I've plenty that hasn't been said." Eileen took her by the arm and brought her, stiff and resisting, back to the kitchen. "Sit," she ordered.

Tara, standing over the high chair now, wiping splatters of orange off the baby's face, looked up and, evidently catching the tension, sat down again, waiting, her eyes fixed on Eileen, as though a movie were about to begin.

"Okay," Eileen said. "There's no easy way to say this, so I'm just going to plunge right in. There is no high-powered, successful Eileen, she was a figment of my imagination—and a little of my mother's, too. At first, I just wanted everyone to know I was okay. Then,

I don't know, the story took on a life of its own. None of it's true though."

She stopped for a moment. Both women were watching her, transfixed. Only the baby, banging her spoon on the plastic tray, broke the silence in the room.

"Deirdre." She addressed her sister. "You called me the successful one. Let me tell you what I see when I look at you. You're a responsible, giving woman who people know they can always depend on. You didn't have children of your own—biological children that is—but you practically raised Tara and no grandmother could love a baby more than you love Stella. And the volunteer work you do is truly impressive. I admire you, Deirdre, if that means anything at all."

Deirdre said nothing, but her face had softened a little.

"And Tara. You want to go to America. You want to leave the people you love, to uproot your little family, break your father's heart and go off to a country you think will offer you more than you have right here. Well, let me tell you something. You already have everything you need and I'm not just talking about Ireland. It's in here, Tara." She stabbed at her chest. "Everything you need to make you happy and fulfilled is right inside you. You can chase the dream of happiness forever, but it will always elude you until you realize it's not something external. Those boots will never make you happy, Tara, because outside stuff can't do it. Only you can make you happy."

KIERAN WAS STILL THINKING about Eileen and her mystery neighbor and how she'd take the news of his death when he walked into the lodge and heard her voice from the kitchen, loud enough to recognize but not to make out what she was saying. Smiling in anticipation of seeing her, simultaneously registering the smell of dinner already cooking—thank God for Deirdre—he started for the kitchen.

The tableau he saw inside burned into his brain. Tara sat at one end of the big center table, Stella asleep on her shoulder. Next to her, Deirdre, arms folded across her chest, the way he always thought of her. Both were listening so intently to Eileen, seated in a chair at one end, that neither seemed aware of him standing there. If Eileen, with her back to him, had any clue that she now had another listener, she gave no sign of it.

"...and I could take you to meet Irish people in America, Tara, who will tell you they never should've come to the States in the first place and if they could just get back to Ireland, they'd be happy."

"You know what though?" Elbows on the table, she was peering into Tara's face. "They wouldn't be happy back in Ireland, either, because they're looking for something outside of themselves to make them happy, so they're never going to find what it is they need."

Tara, frowning now as she patted the back of the sleeping baby, shook her head. "I understand what you're saying, Eileen, but there are practical realities to consider. We could make so much more money in the States."

"For what?" Eileen demanded. "A bigger car? Better clothes?" She shook her head. "Stuff. In the end, it means nothing."

"As I recall, no one had to twist your arm to make you leave," Dierdre said. "It was you who wanted it."

"I know that Deirdre, but I've spent the past twenty-five years regretting what I did. I want," she addressed Tara, "what you have now. A home, a family, a man who loves me."

In the doorway, Kieran stood rooted to the spot. Around the table, the women had fallen into silence as if retreating into themselves.

Tara glanced up then and saw him. Eileen, following Tara's gaze, turned her head, saw him too and rose from the table.

"Well," she said to the other women. "There you have it. Eileen's Not So Grand Adventure."

Kieran caught her arm as she tried to move past him.

"No, Kieran." Head down, she pulled away. "I don't know how much of it you caught, probably enough though. I'd intended to tell you when we were alone but—"

"Come on." His arm around her, he glanced over his shoulder to see Deirdre checking the roast in the oven. She closed the door, straightened and made a shooing gesture with her fingers. In his office off the hallway, he sat Eileen on the small leather couch, where in quiet moments he'd sometimes have a quick snooze. Excusing himself, he poured a couple of sherries from the decanter in the lounge and returned to her. "Drink it down, you'll feel better."

She took the glass from him. "How much did you hear?"

"When I came in, you were—"

"Well let me cut to the chase." She took a sip of the sherry. "It's a very American habit that, getting right to the point. Well, here it is. I'm a big phony. A fraud."

"How's that?"

A flicker of irritation crossed her face. "Oh, jeez, Kieran. Do you want me to spell it out for you?"

"You haven't an important glamorous job, is that what you mean?"

"That's part of it."

"And the gentleman friend, you've already told me, doesn't exist, so what else is there?"

"I'm just not…not what everyone thinks I am."

"Eileen." He set his glass down and took her hand. "You gave a good talk out there to Tara and Deirdre, all that advice about the stuff inside being what's important, but my guess is you're not entirely convinced yourself."

Eileen leaned her head back against the couch, closed her eyes. "It all seemed like such a big deal and now it's out and…I don't know, I just feel kind of pitiful."

"The only pitiful thing is that you were too proud or—"

"Proud." She smiled. "Like I had so much to be proud of. Pride, *schmide,* Mr. Schwartz is always saying."

"Eileen." Kieran swallowed. "There was a call today. Mr. Schwartz died. The day after you left. His son called to tell you."

CHAPTER NINE

DAYS PASSED before Eileen could even accept the news and more still before she could think about Mr. Schwartz without crying uncontrollably. Even after she'd called his son, heard him go on at length about what she'd meant to the old man, she just couldn't get beyond the idea that he was dead. The idea of going back to L.A., of unlocking her door and not finding a note under it, or a grocery coupon for brisket. Or knocking on his door and hearing the shuffle of his feet. Even thinking about the turtle, asleep in its dog basket reduced her to tears. The week before she was supposed to leave, she'd called Brandi the girl boss to say she'd be taking another two weeks off. Brandi hadn't been pleased, but Eileen didn't care. At the end of the first week, she'd called Brandi to say she wouldn't be coming back. She'd been looking for a job when she'd found that one. There'd be others.

Her mother had taken to walking around mumbling to herself. The Oscar parties, the jetting off to Mexico and Hawaii. All those lovely clothes. And the gentleman friend? Maybe it was just a lover's tiff that would all blow over in time, she wondered aloud.

Tara hadn't entirely given up the idea of America, but

she'd conceded that perhaps now, with the baby so young, was not the time and that Eileen's visit, coming when it did, may have been meant to convey that. So, in that sense, the synchronicity was right on target. And although Deirdre hadn't initiated any sisterly, heart-to-heart talks, the other day she'd been wearing the turquoise brooch on the collar of her good wool jacket.

Eileen took long, long walks across the boglands, along the beach, through miles and miles of Irish countryside. Walks meant to straighten out the years of jumble and confusion accumulated in her head. Often Kieran walked with her.

"What happened with us?" she asked one day.

"Your version or mine?"

She grinned. "Let's hear yours first."

"You were as intent on going to America as Tara has been," he said. "I knew that, as well as the fact I'd no interest in going there myself. As much as I loved you, and I did, I'd started to get a bit tired of hearing about it. We were fighting all the time. Libby was calm and perfectly happy with Ireland. One day I kissed her and the rest as they say is history."

"My version is that I wouldn't have gone to America in the first place if I hadn't caught you kissing Libby."

He laughed. "And I wouldn't have been kissing Libby if you hadn't made my life miserable about going to America."

"And round and round and round," she said. "Did you love her?"

"Of course." They walked along in silence for a bit and then he said. "It's funny the way things turn out. The times when I found myself wishing that things had turned out differently with us, but I'd look at Tara and now Stella and...well, I couldn't even imagine my life without them."

"D'you think there's some grand plan?" she asked. "Everything just happens the way it's going to, no matter how you plot and plan and fight against things?"

"I think it's highly possible."

"I'm thinking of not going back to America," she said.

"I think that's a very good idea."

She smiled. "Yeah?"

"Of course, you'll need money to pay off your fancy things, so I thought maybe you'd like to work with me in the lodge."

"With you, or for you?"

"Well, I suppose I could hire you on as a chambermaid, but I thought you might like to be the landlady. Mrs. O'Malley has a nice sound to it, don't you think?"

"Is that a proposal?"

"It is."

"Your streak of romanticism is overwhelming."

He put his arm around her. "Shall I get down on one knee?"

"No. I'm happy with plain and unadorned. Just as long as I know it's real."

"I've always loved you. I don't mean to say I didn't love Libby, I did. But I never stopped loving you. I realized it the minute I saw you at the airport. Blond hair and all. I think we were always meant to be...we just took a roundabout way."

"Mr. Schwartz's son rang me this morning." She swallowed. "He, the father, left me some money. There's quite a lot. I wanted to make sure you weren't marrying me because of it."

He looked at her. "Is that a fact? About the money, I mean."

"Yeah." She bit her lip because she could feel the tears starting again. "I didn't mean to sound flippant about it, you marrying me because of it. I just…all these years and I had no idea. I'd pay for his groceries because I thought he was struggling, tell him it was a present. I never expected anything out of it, of course. I just did it because I wanted to. Now this whole money thing. I feel, I don't know, that I don't deserve it."

"You made him happy, Eilie," Kieran said. "That's exactly what his son told me. 'She made him happy.' What more can any one of us do for another than that?"

He took her hand then and they tramped along, through verdant grass and icy spots where snow still lingered beneath tree branches, the sun on their faces, the wind at their backs.

"What was that thing we used to say to each other?" he asked. "About salmon walking in the streets?"

She laughed. "Your version, or mine? We never did agree on who had it right."

"I did of course."

"You don't even remember. It isn't salmon *walking* in the street."

"What is it then?"

"Okay, listen. 'I'll love you till the salmon sing in the street.'" A moment passed. "Or is it swim?"

"Let's come up with our own version," Kieran said. "'I'll love you till…what? Cows jump over chimney pots—"

"And pigs sleep on satin sheets."

"Perfect."

"Think so?"

"Absolutely." She grabbed his arm, pulled it around her shoulders, leaning into his side. "I think we've finally got it right."

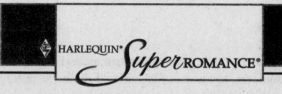

HARLEQUIN *Super*ROMANCE®

THE WINTER ROAD

**Some say life has passed Emily Moore by.
They're wrong.
She is just waiting for her moment....**

Her moment arrives when she discovers her friend
Daniel is missing and a stranger—supposedly Daniel's
nephew—is living in his house. Emily has no reason not
to believe him, but odd things are starting to occur.
There are break-ins along Creek Road and no news from
Daniel. Then there's the fact that his "nephew" seems
more interested in Emily than in the family history
he's supposed to be researching.

**Welcome to Three Creeks,
an ordinary little Prairie town where
extraordinary things are about to happen.**

**In
THE WINTER ROAD**
(Harlequin Superromance #1304),
Caron Todd creates evocative and compelling characters
who could be your over-the-fence neighbors.
You'll really want to get to know them.

Available October 2005.

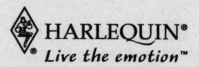

HARLEQUIN®
® *Live the emotion*™

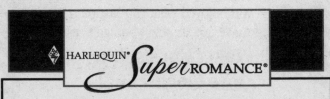

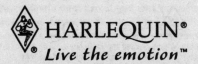

If you enjoyed what you just read,
then we've got an offer you can't resist!

Take 2 bestselling love stories FREE!

Plus get a FREE surprise gift!

HARLEQUIN®

AMERICAN *Romance*®

40 & Fabulous

Dianne Castell

presents three very funny books about
three women who have grown up together in
Whistler's Bend, Montana. These friends are
turning forty and are struggling to deal with it.
But who said you can't be forty and fabulous?

A FABULOUS HUSBAND
(#1088, October 2005)

Dr. BJ Fairmont wants a baby, but being forty and
single, her hopes for adoption are fading fast. Until
Colonel Flynn MacIntire proposes that she nurse him
back to active duty in exchange for a marriage
certificate, that is. Is the town's fabulous bachelor
really the answer to her prayers?

Also look for:

A FABULOUS WIFE
(#1077, August 2005)

A FABULOUS WEDDING
(#1095, December 2005)

Available wherever Harlequin books are sold.

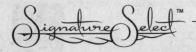

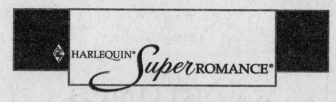

COMING NEXT MONTH

#1302 BACK IN TEXAS • Roxanne Rustand
Home to Loveless County

Kristin Cantrell had leaped at the chance to return to her childhood home to be part of their innovative Home Free program—accepting subsidized land in exchange for the service she can offer the dying town. She didn't expect her reputation to be tarnished by a crime her deceased father had supposedly committed. She also didn't expect to see Ryan Gallagher again, even though his father, the senator, practically owned the Texas Hill Country. Now she had to prove not only her father's innocence, but also her own.

#1303 NOT WITHOUT HER SON • Kay David
The Operatives

Julia Vandamme's nightmare began after she said, "I do." Her only comfort is her sweet little boy, and she has stayed in her marriage just for him. Jonathon Cruz is her one chance for escape, but before she and her son can know freedom, Julia and Cruz are forced to do the unthinkable.

#1304 THE WINTER ROAD • Caron Todd

For Emily Moore, leaving Three Creeks has never been an option, but she doesn't mind. She's had a good life, a full life. Besides, someone has to look after her mother. But everything changes when a dark and mysterious stranger starts living in town.

#1305 RULES OF ENGAGEMENT • Bonnie K. Winn
Hometown U.S.A.

When Tess's soldier brother is killed in action, she starts to question everything. Then she ends up with the missing laptop computer of Cole Harrington, CEO of Harrington Industries—recently returned from a year's deployment overseas. Falling in love has never been so easy...or so hard.

#1306 MARRIAGE BY NECESSITY • Marisa Carroll

The last person Nate Fowler expected to see at his doorstep was his ex-wife—with a child, no less, and a proposal of remarriage. But when Sarah explains that she has to have a life-threatening operation, and there's no one to care for little Matty but her, Nate agrees to go along with her plan. Against his better judgment. After all, what happens if Sarah survives?

#1307 MONTANA SECRETS • Kay Stockham
Going Back

As a physical therapist, Grace Korbit has had some tough cases, but returning to her hometown to care for Seth Rowland will be the most difficult of all. Seth isn't pleased to see Grace, either, considering she left him without an explanation ten years ago. What Seth doesn't know is that Grace had a really good reason for leaving....

HSRCNM0905